T✦KEN VAMPIRE

FROM INTERNATIONAL AWARD WINNING AUTHOR
KIA CARRINGTON-RUSSELL

CRYSTAL
• PUBLISHING •

DEDICATION

A huge thank you to my readers for their support and a giant hug to my intimate book family- an amazing group of women who live in separate locations around the world, and have helped me through the process of releasing this book. Leading up to the editing process and publication of this book, I was dealing with a lot of personal issues. Without them, I would have been entirely lost. Thank you to Julia Summers, Lydia Gaona, Jennifer Kritz, Sarah Hardwick, Kaila Eileen Turingan-Ramos, Sydney Leffler Hopke, Sharon Richmond, Vanessa Charles and Amanda Hammond.

A huge thank you to my family and friends, for supporting me during this time. And mostly a huge thank you to the characters and different world of my book, which was able to consume me and take me somewhere else. I was well guided by the strength that Esmore carries, and the urge to fight off the same darkness, that we can all be taken in by. I am ready for my new journey and to find out who I am. Thank you to everyone x

BLOOD LUST

Darkness;
it consumes us all.
Uncertainty;
it defines our own inner strength.
Struggle;
the ability to overcome the temptation.
Vengeance;
a fake inner peace and reassurance.
Death;
a new beginning.
My world;
completely destroyed, unbound and renewed
I don't know this place, but I can smell the one thing
above all else.
Blood.

CHAPTER I

WHAT HIT ME first was the damp and muggy air as I tried to breathe. My body pressed against the cold stone floor. My heart pounded, and my stomach lurched from being teleported. My sight took a moment to readjust to the darkness that surrounded us. I sat in the dark; the stone flooring beneath us cooled my fingers when I brushed them along it. Goosebumps pricked my skin. I was used to being underground in the Hunter Guild, but this was far deeper into the network of tunnels than I had ever been. Tythian had teleported Chase and me, his hands still rested on our shoulders now as we all struggled to regain our composure. Only seconds before, we were watching the hellish scene of the Guild burning to the ground. My fellow hunters who'd turned on me were screaming in the distance. I didn't know how many survived. I couldn't even feel guilty for not caring. My emotions remained stagnant, like they always did.

Chase and I clung to one another for support as we tried to get our bearings. We were both exhausted. My mouth was parched as I inhaled the scent of blood, imagining its warmth filling my mouth. I knew it would restore the energy that was stolen from us during the ordeal with James and Campture. Relief rushed through me as Chase's fingers trailed over my cheek, grabbing my attention. It was only at his touch, or my mother's, that I could truly feel and it was overwhelming. One thing screamed out at me, and that was the fact that everyone I loved was now safe. I looked to Chase with simple relief; my Chase, my familiar, whom I would die for. He brushed my cheek with a smile, a wicked glow in his eyes. *I need to drink some blood*, I confessed to him telepathically.

His smile widened. *I know Esmore, I'll find us something*, he replied.

The vampire lifestyle was not one I could get used to anytime soon. My body screamed for blood, but the other thing that was heightened, despite my exhaustion, was the torture of not being able to ravish Chase then and there. We had both almost died today. I had my chest blown out and yet, I'd survived. I watched the man I love be tortured. All I wanted to do now was to shred the clothes from his body and devour him, to claim his as my own again. Another smile spread across Chase's lips. He knew it, he could sense it from me.

"Are you both going to just sit there all day?" Tythian interrupted with his hands behind his back as he looked at us impatiently.

We were interrupted by a sound. I heard Dillian's voice in the distance followed by a scream. It was enough to startle me out of my stupor, and I immediately ran into a narrow dark hall. When I turned the corner, I came to a rocky circular room lit by candlelight. The wooden chairs and tables were spread about. Above was a small chandelier with candles. I quickly scanned the room, assessing the occupants.

My mother and biological father, Cesar, watched me from the corner, alongside two unfamiliar male vampires. One had black hair and blue eyes. He eyed me coolly as he leaned back in his chair so far that the front legs balanced in mid-air. The male beside him watched on with a childish smile. He beamed as if toys were being presented in front of him. His hair was long and blond. He wore no shirt, but there was a large wooden cross adorning his chest as a necklace. His eyes were the same color as the wood, which contrasted nicely against the light tan of his skin. His body was covered in various black tattoos.

To my right, huddled in the corner, a larger male vampire stood over Dillian, baring his fangs. Dillian stood in front of Julia protectively. The hood had fallen from her head, revealing her sheer terror as she cowered behind Dillian.

"Just one taste, eh, boy?" the vampire mocked. He was Dillian's height, if not taller. His black hair was cut short, and his green eyes shone like a snake's.

Neither Dillian nor Julia had weapons to protect themselves. Dillian could hardly stand after being so severely beaten. I took only four steps forward at my most heightened speed, but the vampire seemed to have vanished. Instantly behind me, his rough hands brushed over my plaited golden hair.

"Mm, you smell yummy," he said. Before I realized it, I'd turned and grabbed the vampire by the throat, lifting him from the ground. Growls swept past us, but the loudest was my own. I could sense Chase behind me. I kept my eyes on the vampire savagely.

"They are mine!" I said, remembering how Chase had to objectify me in such a way within the Council. "And if you ever touch me again, I will break your spine into small shards and feed it to you."

I dropped him to the ground, and he slithered toward the other men angrily. Chase walked around the vampire with his hands in his pockets and a smirk on his face. It was both he and Cesar who had growled. *Shards of spine, really?* He spoke to me within my mind. I felt the touch of a smirk on my face as well. My aggressive instincts shattered when Chase looked at me in such a way. Chase obviously realized I didn't need him to protect me.

"Be good to your sister, the lot of you!" Cesar bellowed, kicking his boot into the vampire who had threatened Dillian. Dillian was still on guard as he hugged Julia protectively.

"Their what?" I hissed. The thought of being connected to these vampires in such a way sickened me. My mother also looked around, somewhat shocked.

"Oh, so you're the little sister we've heard so much about," the blond-haired male with the wooden cross on his chest said while standing and stretching his hand out to shake mine. "Call me, Yolo."

Yolo obviously sensed my disdain because he pointed his outstretched hand at Chase. Chase looked down at his hand, his hands still in his pockets. He raised an eyebrow at the gesture and looked at him tiredly. "Yolo. *Seriously?*"

"Hey man, when I turned vamp I could choose whichever name I desired. I was a new me, thanks to Cesar. So, Yolo, right. You Only Live Once." He said it with a cheesy grin, but the smile faltered somewhat when he realized Chase wasn't going to shake his hand. He withdrew it hastily.

I looked back at Tythian, who still stood in the doorway. His expression mirrored my contempt. I turned to Yolo and couldn't help but glance in confusion at the cross that rested against his many tattoos.

He smiled again as if my gaze alone was all he needed to initiate conversation. "My parents were Catholic, you see. So I keep to that. I love my mom and dad, even after their passing. I never had the chance to see them again after I got turned. It took over one hundred years to be able to contain my thirst, so Cesar didn't let me near any humans or civilization."

"One hundred years?" I choked, thinking of my own burning desires. I was struggling to keep myself from indulging in the necks of Dillian and Julia right now. If it weren't for my exhaustion and determination not to get any closer, I shuddered to think what might happen.

"Connor took the longest." He pointed to the dark-haired male who had been balancing on his chair. He seemed timid, and he looked at Tythian for reassurance. It forced me to question if he was mute. "Connor was found in 1936, during Hitler's reign. He had the blue eyes but not the blond hair," Tythian said as he walked over to him. He spoke affectionately of Connor. Despite being an introverted man, I could see the respect he held for Tythian. "His family was murdered. Connor was left for dead, except Cesar turned him. Connor never forgave any human after that. He got a little twisted and saw the vampires as a more heroic race and the humans as parasites and beasts. It took a while to dilute that hatred."

I looked to Connor as he leaned shyly forward, assessing us. His blue eyes were piercing and held so much sadness. He continued to stare even when our eyes met.

"And that's Balzar!" Cesar bellowed with a monstrous laugh, pointing at the vampire who had threatened Dillian. "My daughter is only eighteen years of age, and you are over one hundred and fifty, yet you still get your rear-end handed to you!"

"Yeah, would someone like to explain that?" He tsked under his breath. "She doesn't even smell like a vampire." I looked at my mother, who seemed just as uncertain as the others. At first I thought she might've been familiar with them or this location, but her tense body language indicated otherwise.

"Well, when a daddy vampire and mommy hunter love each other very much," Cesar continued, rustling his hand through Balzar's short hair. "They create a vampire-hunter baby girl who is stronger in everything because of that. The end."

"You suck!" Yolo laughed and pointed at Balzar. Balzar grunted under his breath at the insult before pouncing on Yolo. Both of them ran down a hall childishly.

"And you also forgot to mention that she carries the Descendant gift within her which is perhaps the biggest cause for concern," Tythian said, now standing with his hands strapped across his chest in an unscathed dress shirt, despite the ordeal we'd been through.

"Why have you brought us here?" I asked, not wanting to waste my time with stupid introductions any longer.

"Because you are safe here, and you can build your energy back up. You'll need it," Cesar said, resting a hand on my mother's lower back.

"In the next few months, a war will begin. And this time we, our own coven, will not step aside and let the humans or Council rule," Tythian began.

"You're a coven?" I narrowed my eyes on them in judgment. They were at times no better than the sabers. Yolo and Balzar returned after hearing my raised voice.

"Not all covens are bad, Esmore." Tythian brushed me off.

"We've just chosen to live more freely from the start," Connor's rough voice interjected, surprising me. So, he wasn't mute.

"Cesar turned all four of us, so we were indebted and bound to be a part of his coven. But we would have stayed even if we had the choice to leave. We are family here. And there are many other covens around the world we're aligned with that think the same way. Of course, not all agree or care," Yolo said, shrugging his shoulders.

"So why attack the Council?" I asked.

"It's not just the Council, my beautiful daughter," Cesar bluntly stated. "The humans too have been gathering power. We cannot live in a world where there is another war, and the Council takes further control and power. They demand one ruler. If all are combined under one Council, it could be a free-for-all hunt on the covens. We hit them from the side before they gather that power, which is why I had Tythian infiltrate Fier's Council. They've been gathering numbers for a while now, and his father, Arab's displeasure with covens has been known since the day they tried to rally us all against the humans."

"You met Arab?" Chase asked.

"I did," Cesar confirmed smugly. "And I met your mother as well. Who was far nicer than you, might I add, pipsqueak."

Chase growled under his breath, enraging Cesar. When Cesar's demeanor changed, both Yolo and Connor growled in support.

"Stop with the macho dance," my mother interjected. "Cesar, tell her about the humans."

"I ..." His attitude dissolved at the request of my mother. "The humans have been hiding. You hunters lost contact with them, but the government of the humans has been functioning. They're trying to create a new form of hunters. Stronger ones to overcome their predecessors and by extension, the Council."

"I don't know why they don't let it go. I mean, the world has already turned to shit. It won't be like the good old days of the early 2000s," Yolo said, stretching back on his chair.

"How do you know this? Do you have proof?" I asked.

"Yes," Tythian interjected in a quiet yet angry tone. His jaw was quivering, and his hands were still across his chest. "Whitney was one of their victims. When I found her, she was left for dead." I shivered at his words, and I felt Chase straighten beside me.

"But Whitney had been dying from cancer. You saved her from a pack of sabers when her father was killed," I said, repeating Whitney's story. Chase's fingers brushed past mine, but I refused to accept his hand. I could sense the guilt rolling off him.

Tythian exchanged a look with him before continuing. "It's what we made her believe," he said under his breath.

"I don't understand," I said. Slowly it clicked together. I stared at Chase accusingly. "You tricked her mind?"

"Only because Tythian asked me to. Esmore, with enough suggestive thoughts people can forget their darkest nightmares. I spared her that pain. It was Tythian's familiar, and his call." Chase tensed. He was trying to smile, and I could sense that his mind was thinking of something funny to say like he always did to dispel serious situations. I felt the rumble of darkness within me tap lightly in my stomach, like butterflies trying to escape. Only Chase could create this feeling within me, and I hated it. But I was too weak for rage to sweep through. I hated how close I stood to him. I was able to feel the betrayal, lies, and pain he had caused.

"I asked Chase to do so," Tythian confirmed. "I found my love—my sweet, beautiful Whitney—abandoned beside her dead father at dusk. It is true sabers attacked her, which I didn't lie about, and that her father died at their hands. But where they had come from was a secure place for humans ... where technology remains highly advanced. They are trying to create stronger beings. According to our research, the injection killed most; and in Whitney's case, the disease spread through her for many years. I was feeding her my blood every night without her knowing. I could have never turned her into a vampire because of the parasite disease, even if I tried. However, after so many years of my blood rejuvenating her, it stopped working."

"It was her brother who injected them both," Yolo spoke up now, allowing Tythian to slip into a subdued silence. Now I knew if he had the choice he wouldn't have respected Whitney's wishes. He would have turned her anyway. But if that were to happen to Chase, I would have done the same. I could not judge, yet I felt sick by the lie.

"How do you know all this?" I retorted.

"Yolo, here is a part of that human group," Cesar interrupted. "He was the only one who could infiltrate them."

"How?" I demanded. How had the Guild been so left in the dark about this kind of intel, with so little inclination?

Yolo stood up tall. I could see a lightly quivering mist surrounding him. Within seconds a human woman with long blonde hair in a tight skirt, shirt, and high heels approached me with a velvet voice. "Because I am Jenn Cadolwadt: engineer and specialist at the Human Activist and Regaining Existence Movement," she said, holding out a hand for me to shake. Yolo even smelled like a human woman with a strong smell of flowers.

"He can bypass all the scans. He comes up as human," Connor spoke from the corner of the room.

"Why a woman?" Dillian asked from behind me. It had been the first time he'd spoken amongst this mess.

The woman gave a sheepish smile in response. One that made my whole body cringe. "Well, mostly because of these," Yolo said, grabbing hold of his bountiful chest. "It is a pretty nice rack, if I do say so myself."

My stomach turned. "I think I'm going to be sick."

"She needs blood," Chase growled, ending the conversation. "She's lost too much."

"Of course, sorry for having not noticed sooner," Cesar bellowed, evidently irritated that Chase had noticed it before him. "Connor, if you would be so kind as to show those two to their room, and Tythian, can you show the two other hunters their room?"

"No!" I said savagely, looking at Balzar. "They stay in the same room as us." I would protect them no matter what.

After much hesitation, Cesar agreed. "Very well, but you only have a day's rest until you are to come out and meet the rest of my coven." He dispelled us within moments, and the others went their separate ways as Tythian escorted us silently through the rocky and cool halls.

CHAPTER 2

THE ROCKY STONE walls felt as if they were closing in around me. The subtle hint of stagnant air forced me to assume we were well underground and somewhere well hidden. There was a lingering smell of blood in the air. Old blood that made my appetite stir, but repulsed at the thought of it not being fresh. More than likely, they'd been hiding here for a while now. I was used to underground tunnels, but the eeriness here of both being followed and watched, reminded me to keep on guard and prepare to slaughter a houseful of vampires if required. Feel, an understated and meaningless word to me, a symptom and only reflex.

I looked to one of the walls trying to control my thirst. As Tythian led us further into the dark tunnels, all I could hear was a tiny droplet of water constantly dripping close by. I could smell the sweat that followed me on Dillian's and Julia's necks. I sensed Chase try to grab my hand beside me, but I couldn't help but pull it closer to myself as I walked.

My sensitive hearing focused on the saliva that mixed around in Julia's parched mouth, her tongue's scratchiness desperately trying to add moisture. Her small whimpering breaths which exerted heavily seeming more like a pant enticed me. Julia was so fragile. Chase tugged on my hand, snapping me out of my daze. For a moment I'd forgotten we were walking. I looked at Chase with such hatred, it wasn't directed at him, but only the disgust I felt for myself. Julia, I thought her weak, and I realized that my hands were bunched with such temptation to grab her by the throat and dive deep into her, to quench my thirst. I had been fixating on her weak traits as easy prey.

Chase raised his eyebrows at me as he forced his thoughts into my own, even when I tried to block him. *Stop frowning and pouting it ruins your features.*

I looked away again, catching an interested side glance from Tythian.

"Do you think me a monster, little vampire?" Tythian asked. If I hadn't known him in any other way, I would have thought he was almost teasing me. "Or are you simply pinpointing your hatred of yourself onto others at the moment. Let me guess, the thirst has really gotten to you now, and you now realize that having your edible friends in the same room as you, wasn't a clever idea."

"I'm fine," I hissed under my breath. There were many names and accusations I wanted to throw his way, but as my walk staggered, I couldn't find the energy to fight. I could hardly walk, though I feigned stability. Our distaste for one another was evident, and the tension that rose with that made the remainder of the walk a silent one.

I listened out to inspect if anyone else were in the tunnels nearby, but my hearing faltered or they were all so quiet. Tythian stopped in front of a tilted door, which around the edges, the wood began to chip away. Beneath the closed door, the shadow of candlelight flickered. He grabbed the handle and revealed the room to us as he spoke.

"You may stay in this room, do keep it down, I'm sure with delectable meals you won't want to alarm the other vampires here. Although Cesar has given them warning, which is punishable by death, nothing can be guaranteed." Tythian evenly looked at Dillian. "My apologies."

"Do you have a supply of blood?" Chase asked. I knew he asked on my behalf, but he looked no better than me.

"You may have noticed, this isn't a classy motel. But yes, there is a bottle of cold blood in there. It's only recently been put there. You'll have to excuse the accommodation however, there is only one bed." With no more to say, Tythian dismissed himself and continued walking into the tunnels with adamant purpose. I had the urge to follow him; to discover and understand the coven that we were now stuck in, but Chase grabbed my hand. I looked down at it, a shot of betrayal sweeping in. I was still so pained to learn of Whitney's true illness.

"Esmore? I need to get Julia away from this place," Dillian interrupted. I pulled my hand away from Chase and looked down the hall and behind them, to make sure no one was within hearing distance. I ushered them all in, closing the door behind us. There was an uncomfortable bed that looked as if it could only fit two at most. One table and two chairs beside it with a bottle of blood as Tythian had guaranteed. How the thought of it made me thirst.

"I'll get you out of here. All of us, I want nothing to do with a coven." Shivers ran up my arms at my inability to run further into the tunnels and kill every one of them. That was my purpose, I tried to remind myself, or that's what I once did.

"Are you sure, Esmore, but now you are a…" Julia hid her face in response to my daggered glare.

"A vampire? I can assure you I am not." My eyes instantly fixated on her neck and I regretted it as Dillian spooned Julia further into his arms, in a sense of warning toward me.

"For now, we just need to rest, and we can sort this out tomorrow. We've all had a long day," Chase reassured us all. I looked down at my shirt which still revealed part of my breast. I had been shot in the heart. That should have been my death. With all my might and resisting the urges to attack him, which I truly battled with, I placed my hand on Dillian's shoulder. The thought of tenderness and frailness compared to the strength I could unleash on him terrified me. My dear friend, Dillian, who now instinctively I marked like a predator. I took one large gulp and looked him dead in the eyes.

"I will protect you both, no matter what. Rest easy. You know I'll never be your enemy," I said with an even tone. I resisted the torture of the crisp feeling of my fangs ready to pierce through my gums. I was wavering on my ability to handle our proximity. I dropped my hand and walked toward the table, to put distance between me and what my body screamed at as a meal. Chase followed me with his gaze. I looked down at the blood, disgusted at myself. I didn't crave that cold red tainted gore in a bottle. I wanted it hot, fresh, and that repulsed me. I wouldn't act or be a vampire, I insisted to myself.

Grabbing the bottle, I offered it to Chase. "Hurry up and drink it," I said with a slightly exhausted stumble as I walked toward him.

"Esmore, you have to drink," he chastised.

"I will not be told what I must and mustn't do. I will not be this monster." I paused, recalling the same mimicked word that Tythian spoke. *Monster.*

"I understand your desperate thirst, you are weak," Chase said, trying to reach out to me.

"You either drink this now, or I smash it. I will neither be weak in my physical state nor my temptation of this." After much resistance, Chase grabbed the bottle and drank it, he knew I wasn't one to be forced into things, no matter how crazy the temptation might've been driving me. I couldn't become what I hated most, especially in front of Dillian.

"Esmore, I have an apple if you would like one." Julia's voice spoke from the darkness as only little light was emanated from the candle on the table. Obviously, the small backpack she had under hooded attire was pre-packed with food. The sobbing Julia I had found in her room and thought to have rescued from the Guild; might have already been planning her escape and rescue of Dillian, before my intervention. She rummaged through her bag before presenting it to me. I could see the slight pulse in her wrist as she offered it to me.

"Please, throw it to me," I said nonchalantly, not daring to go any closer. I was pushing a certain part of me that was too greatly tempted. Snatching the apple out of the air, I tore the empty bottle from Chase's hand and smashed it over the table, so I was left with the remains of the shattered glass as a weapon. The shattering of pieces forced Dillian to jump. I'd never seen him so rattled, especially because of me. What did I look like for him to be so alert? What was it that he now saw?

"I'll watch over the door, you all get rest," I instructed to Dillian and Julia, ignoring the expression Chase gave me.

You are so bossy, Chase interjected into my thoughts. *Yet, it turns me on.* I could sense the purr in his tone. I gave him an effective look. He always fooled around, no matter how serious the issue at hand. Already understanding my thoughts, he replied. *Esmore, we escaped death today, and yes we have a lot of problems at hand now, but just for today, please show me one smile, which I never thought I would see again.*

You lied to me about Whitney's conditioning. I am struggling to think of our next plan because I am so damn thirsty. But I can't be a monster anymore, a creature that defies death and normality. I am a Huntress, in a coven full of vampires, and yet I am hiding in the shadows uncertain of whether to kill them or not. I am not okay. Most certainly not okay with you lying to me.

He blew air from his cheeks dramatically. Dillian exchanged an odd glare between the two of us as he perched on the edge of the bed and watched over Julia as she sat in the corner eating a pear.

Chase grabbed my attention once again as I sat on the wooden chair against the door. *An apple will not sustain you. You may be able to eat both human food and drink blood as a vampire, but let me assure you that the one and only thing that will sustain you now is quenching your thirst. No matter how arrogant you are to this Esmore, you are a new vampire. You can't control it without being taught.*

Again I felt that tender mixture of darkness and love for Chase torture me. Why could I only feel love or appreciation with Chase or my mother? Why were my emotions, or what little emotions I had, so heightened? I wanted to kill him and kiss him all at once.

I took a savage bite into my apple and looked to the dirty rocky walls, with the broken glass bottle still in hand. I thought in the distance and pain of memory; of two prominent white wings protruding from my back. I knew what that was, that surge of strength and dominance, it was the Descendant. And as my chest was blown into tiny pieces, and I felt my world and life dip into unnatural darkness of what should have been death, I knew what that color of black which tainted my right wing now was. I had been affected by darkness. As if my hunter self was my purity, and now with my vampirism a very real and daring part of me, I had been tainted. I starred at the broken bottle which was still colored with remnants of blood. What have I become?

CHAPTER 3

MY VISION CONTINUOUSLY faded in and out, my mouth becoming dryer as the hours ticked by. Julia had fallen asleep, but Dillian still watched me from afar, silently. They weren't safe here, and I had to find a place where I could take and protect them. I also had to find a way to manage my burning sensation to label them as food.

Chase often flicked a stone in my direction or scraped his chair along the ground heavily. I snapped him an evil glare, it was the response he anticipated as he gave me a very sensual grin. Would he never stop playing around?

I wanted to be mad with him, so mad I could hardly think. But my body ached for his lingering touch, the sweet taste of his blood to fill me and consume me into an erotic haze. Having him merely a meter away was too tempting.

After hours of awkward silence, there were only a few steps outside the door to distract us from this rising tension. Dillian was the first to break the silence and spoke.

"Why don't you get that teleporting vampire, Tythian, to take us to the human camp near the Guild? We can live amongst the humans for a while until we figure something else out," he said, tucking back a part of his long black hair and then continuing to stroke Julia's brunette locks.

"We don't know if they were attacked when Fier led the sabers to the Guild. They might've continued through and found their camp. They might all be wiped out," I responded, thinking of the massacre that might've occurred if the sabers had found them. Their camp was situated days away from our own, and there was no guarantee Fier didn't know of their location as well.

"But maybe they didn't. We don't know until we inspect it," Dillian counteracted.

"Even if the human camp is safe, what's to say that your fellow Guild members who wanted you both dead, haven't thought of the same thing?" Chase pointed out the obvious as he swung on the back of his chair.

We sat there for a moment in silence.

"Esmore, you know we're not safe here, please let us at least check it out," Dillian pleaded. "Have Tythian take us close to the Guild. From there, we'll walk so we're not followed to the human camp."

Chase whistled, drawing attention to himself. "After everything that Guild put you through, you still want to make sure the human camp is safe." Dillian frowned at Chase's statement, insulted.

"I spent my entire life contributing to the survival of that human camp. I won't simply lead a vampire who is a part of a coven to that very location."

"We can do that, Dillian, but please think of what Campture and James did to you…" Dillian cut me off with a bewildered smile.

"I know too well what they did to me, and they would do it all again. But I have no purpose, we have no purpose, if not for sustaining the human camps." I stared at Dillian for a moment and then Chase to see if it were plausible that Tythian would help us. Already knowing my thoughts, Chase sighed.

"You can try Tythian, but there's no guarantee. He's not a train." Chase looked between Dillian's and my bewildered expression as I tried to scan my memory and education of the human world, and what he referred to as a 'train.'

"Never mind," Chase continued. "Tythian's teleportation exhausts him, he needs a lot of blood to restore him every time. Esmore, am I the only one here recalling that right now, Tythian hates our guts, and for whatever reason brought you two toward some kind of bargain, that you won't tell me about, he will expect something more out of this. Tythian does not waste his time nor energy for free. He'll want something in return."

Dillian wavered an interested glance my way as Chase waved his hands dramatically about the bargain between Tythian and me. It was our agreement that I would help him bait and kill Fier, Chase's step-father of sorts.

"Then I'll talk and barter with Tythian. Are you able to call him here?" I asked Chase, feeling too exhausted myself to try and reach his mind. Chase gave me a cheesy grin.

"Well, darling, if I do something for you, so he can do something for you, what will you do for me?" Chase tapped one of his fingers on the table in anticipation.

"Has he always been like this?" Dillian asked, looking between us in bewilderment.

"Trust me when I say, you should be thankful you didn't have to live with it in the Council," I said, rolling my eyes. Dillian would have only ever seen Chase's serious side, whenever that might come out to play.

"My agreement is, I will contact Tythian right now and call him to this room. But afterward, you have to drink from a human."

"Absolutely not," I snapped.

"Then there is no way I can contact him. It pains me to see my familiar in such a way. I just can't escape these theatrics and my uncertain mind." Chase gasped suddenly, and snapped straight into his chair seriously. "What if you turn into some mutant vampire because you won't eat?"

"Wouldn't I already be considered a mutant vampire?" I said testily under my breath. "Chase this is serious, I need to protect Dillian and Julia above all else."

After a long moment, Chase looked to Dillian and then the resting Julia. "Fine. Tythian is on his way now."

The light patter of two sets of feet motioned toward the door that I guarded. I was alerted by the second set of footsteps. I opened the door to greet Tythian and the stranger. Chase was behind me, both his hands resting on my arms as his hot breath stroked down the back of my neck. I could feel his strength behind me, supporting me, in comparison to my weakened state.

I opened the door and looked down the left of the narrow corridor. Out of the dark crept the figures of Tythian and Yolo. Yolo waved with an upbeat bounce to his steps.

"Sissy," he said childishly.

"Please mature within the instant," Tythian directed as he approached me. He looked taller than usual, or perhaps it was the difference I felt in our power because of my weakened state. Yolo looked Chase up and down, disapprovingly.

"Remind me why Cesar has allowed him to stay?" Yolo asked Tythian.

"Why wouldn't he, he's my familiar," I spat, defending Chase quickly.

"That my little sis, would be the only reason why he is here," Yolo said, arching a very feline smile. But his eyes still stalked Chase's every movement and narrowed on his lingering fingers that held me protectively.

"Let's talk in private little vampire," Tythian said.

"I'm not leaving him anywhere near my companions," I said, gesturing to Yolo. Yolo smiled and began toying with the large wooden cross on his bare chest, evaluating me.

"Let me assure you that out of all the vampires here, I am the least of your concern. I'm here to guard them, while you and Tythian talk in private. My gift of being able to transition into a human body, also gives me the ability to greatly suppress my thirst. Let me assure you that this was a gift that many fought to acquire. I don't sink my fangs into hunters unless I really want to. And with Cesar's one gift policy for his sons, well, it would appear I'm all filled up," he purred. Chase's hands tightened on my arms, awakening me to his touch once again.

"I can protect them, Esmore," he purred, and stroked part of my unbound braid.

"You were the one who summoned me, little vampire," Tythian said with great impatience. He began walking away. With a moment of hesitation, I followed him. I watched behind me as Chase and Yolo walked back into the room. Tythian grabbed my arm. I was surrounded by darkness as the nauseous feeling of being teleported elsewhere took hold of me. My eyes adjusted from the darkness of the tunnels, to the resurfacing on land. We were now standing under a pale moon, that fought against the darkness of consuming clouds. Dead leaves swayed in the light breeze of night. The cracked ground beneath me swept coolness up my legs. The mist swirled around our sudden appearance, slowly settled, and consumed up to our ankles.

"Where are we?" I demanded. I was not settled that I was now so far away from Dillian and Julia. I couldn't protect them from here.

"We can now talk in private. Don't waste my time, what do you want?" Tythian questioned. He crossed his arms and stared at me intensely, with the expression that I was always a sore sight.

"I need you to take us back to the Guild. I need to make sure Dillian and Julia are somewhere else, safe."

"Are you daft? Don't you recall that your old Guild had been over swept by sabers?" Tythian studied me for a moment. "Unless of course that isn't the destination you have in mind. Being a Hunter Guild, you surely would have a human camp nearby. How utterly predictable."

"Can you do it or not?" I put bluntly.

"Firstly, let me be the one to explain to you the predicament you find yourself in. You're worrying and bargaining about your hunter friends, but have you considered where your familiar might be on the scale?"

"Chase is fine," I said, not understanding his hidden question.

"Chase is not fine by your side within the coven. I took you there in the mere moment because we were safe there against the explosions and sabers. But let me assure you, that under those tunnels, he is not safe."

"Why wouldn't he be?" I understood that I was missing something of great importance, and felt that it was something of vampire logic that I didn't quite understand.

"Chase has told you himself once, I am sure, about his mother and the vampire who was leader to his coven. The very vampire Chase killed. The smell lingers on Chase. To become a coven leader, you must kill the current one. Other vampires can smell Chase's stench from a mile away. His smell is different from that of our coven's, whether Chase took the leadership role or not, he is a threat in our coven. He is by far, considered an enemy. The fact that his stench still lingers confirms the issue that his coven is still alive, which means he has vampires at his disposal. Granted, in Chase's situation, they are hunting to kill him; but this is coven law. Cesar has allowed him into the tunnels for protection, for a short time, but others will lash out and try to kill him. Chase won't leave your side, which is what endangers him. He has indefinitely risked his own life, as any familiar would."

I stood there for a moment, enjoying the cool sweeping wind over my face. Chase hadn't mentioned any of this to me, how was I to know?

"Well then, if you can teleport Dillian, Julia, Chase, my mother, and I away, he will no longer be at risk."

"Whether your mother wants to go or not, is not of your choosing. I can, however, teleport you to your Guild, but I have my conditions."

"What are they," I hurried, already conscious of the time we'd spent away.

"Firstly, you are to come back to me, you are obliged to help me kill Fier. This is already a promise made between us. Secondly, for this next favor you ask of me, I want you to kill a vampire within the coven for me."

I looked at him for a moment before I felt the creeping of a smile dance across the corner of my mouth. He wanted me to kill one of the vampires within that coven? I never thought that would be his request.

"Why do you want this vampire killed?" I asked, not needing any real reason to want and be able to kill it. *It,* that vampire being what I am. I let the confusion subside. I was good at killing vampires.

"He's one of the older vampires within the coven. He challenges Cesar a lot. Cesar simply won't kill him. But I think it's time for him to go. Myself, and Cesar's fellow three sons have agreed. You, Esmore, will be the one to do the dirty work."

"I feel like there is something you're leaving out." I felt the hint of a lingering ambition amongst it.

"Does it really matter? That is your option, you either take my agreement or not. His name is Thomas. He has black hair and is short. He is fast with no apparent gift. Be wary though, he's old and strong. He might be a struggle for you, in your current weakened state."

"Careful, your tone might indicate that you actually care for my wellbeing. When do you want me to do it?" I asked.

"At the meeting where you'll be introduced to the rest of the coven, which I believe will start in any minute. You are not a part of this coven, so be careful. We get very protective of our own."

"You want me to do it in front of a room full of coven members?"

"It's all politics, little vampire, and sometimes a spectacle has to be made. But don't worry, I'm certain you'll be safe as Cesar's only blood and born child. You are more protected than any one of us. Shall we?" Tythian offered his hand out to me, in a gesture to teleport back. With that simple agreement and discussion, our bargain had been made.

CHAPTER 4

T HE OLD DUST lingered over my nose as it swamped Tythian's and my sudden appearance in front of the door. I hunched over slightly and gasped at the heavy feeling in my stomach. Tythian smiled, aware that I hadn't yet become accustomed to his gift. We were no longer in the fresh air beneath the shadowed moon and cloudy night. I opened the door and inhaled the familiar scent of Dillian, Julia, and Chase. Both Chase and Yolo looked up surprised, and as if they'd been caught doing something they shouldn't.

There was some form of game positioned between them. Chase held a piece in the air, before placing it down slowly. Still looking at me as if he weren't doing anything wrong, he stated, "Checkmate," to Yolo.

"Are you seriously playing a game right now?" I asked. Dillian exhaled exhausted. He seemed to be more comfortable now than when I had left.

"They started playing almost as soon as you vanished," Dillian said. He rubbed his head, tiredly. "They've been using vampire speed the whole time, this is their twelfth game."

"Yolo here, lost twelve times," Chase said with an accomplished smile.

"Please, you totally cheated," Yolo declared.

"Yolo, truly? Have you not organized Cesar's familiar before the meeting?" Tythian asked. He had a lot to say, more so then the Tythian I knew, who had only watched and said very little when Whitney was around, or should I say, when she was alive. Perhaps it was as Chase had said—Whitney had calmed Tythian, and made him into a better vampire. But now that hope of salvation was gone.

"Cesar is bringing her, himself. Connor will be with me as well, to watch over them," Yolo dismissed. With impeccable timing, my mother's faint footsteps approached. My mother, Cesar, Balzar, and Connor, crept from the shadows of the hallway. They all stood beside Tythian now, outside the door. Balzar looked at the wall, unimpressed by our gathering. Connor reminded me much of Tythian as he silently watched and emitted a certain power about him.

"Ahh, my daughter," Cesar said in his rough accent. "You don't play very nice do you, and by the looks of you, you still haven't drunk anything. I give you credit for having the restraint of not eating your friends. In your state, it must feel like you haven't eaten for weeks." I gulped hard at his happy go lucky nature. I did feel like I was starving, but would never admit it. My cruel gaze must have indicated so. "Such a blazing gaze, I wouldn't expect anything but, from my own child."

"I'm not your child," I hissed and crossed my arms.

"Well now, what would you say if I had a treat for you, perhaps a certain two weapons you are certainly fond of, ey?" Cesar said with a teasing smile. I looked at Mom in caution, before approaching.

"You have my Barnett crossbow and sword?" I asked.

"Perhaps. It comes in handy when one of your sons can teleport anywhere, doesn't it? But before we get to the presents, you have to come meet the coven. But only you, Tythian, and Balzar are welcome. Your mother, familiar, and friends will be protected by Connor and Yolo."

"I'm not leaving her side," Chase said. He had crept up from behind and stood by my side, protectively. *I know you can handle yourself, but this is unfamiliar ground, and you are weak.* Chase said telepathically.

I was on unfamiliar ground the day we met. But as my bargain with Tythian involves this meeting, I must go alone. You know I can handle myself. I patted his hand lightly. *I don't trust the other two, so protect my mother, Dillian, and Julia. I doubt I can relay the whole meeting with you and updates of what is happening during it all.* That was because, although I didn't want to admit it to anyone, I felt weak and that walking alone, was anguishing. So this is what it felt like to be a vampire who had not fed for days or weeks. We had starved so many vampires in torture techniques, within the Guild. I now understood why so many had turned delirious and into a saber, after only a month. But I wasn't so weak, I knew discipline. I considered myself still as Huntress, not vampire.

"Let's get this over with," I said. My mother watched me wearily as we crossed paths, and she entered the room. It felt as if we were both looking at the ghost of one another, of our former glory. We weren't sure who we were looking at anymore. So much had changed in that time, that I thought her dead. I never believed it, but this discovery and everything else weren't what I had anticipated upon our reunion.

"That's the spirit," Cesar cheerily said. "C'mon." Silently, Tythian and Balzar took separate sides to me while being led by Cesar. I remained silent, unsure of what to expect. We walked down the narrow rocky tunnel. Often, there were gaps that would allow people or vampires to slip through, and sometimes I saw the flicker of candles, which indicated that there were other tunnels further in. It was a vast network. Every step made my ears feel as if they were pounding and my throat was even dryer. Balzar, with his hands on the back of his head, continuously glanced across at me from the corner of his eye. When I made eye contact, he only smiled, with the lingering knowledge that I was parched. Was there an apparent physical state which stated so? Did I look as drained as I felt? It only urged me to put a stronger facade on. I couldn't let anyone know how weak I was because it left me and the others in a vulnerable state.

I heard scuttling noises and people talking. Not people, vampires. I highly doubted that ordinary humans could live down here. The air was too thick and heavy to breathe. But for a coven, this was perfect for hiding. I imagined the reason Balzar was here instead of the other two sons was because he was the youngest, so would have the least control around the hunters. I wondered what Yolo might've been like before he gained his gift and was able to suppress his thirst. How bad could the thirst get?

Within mere footsteps of walking around the corner, the vampires silenced. I was overwhelmed at the sight of their numbers, but didn't allow anyone to notice my quick count and exit strategies. Some lounged on the sides of the rocky wall, with their head tilted up so they could inspect me closely. All eyes were on me, hundreds of pairs of eyes. When I thought coven, I didn't think of such high numbers. This was close to the numbers and army that Fier had within his Council, and the coven vampires were far less restrained than the Council members. Some were well dressed and groomed, and others looked like they hadn't left the tunnels for centuries. I had to get Dillian and Julia out of here.

"What is the meaning of this, Cesar?" A short man, who looked to be in his forties, stepped forward. "The coven has been restless the past few hours. We can smell hunters in here, but are given no explanation. Above all else we can smell another coven leader in here, he reeks."

Small snarls purred from the vampires, at the offense of my familiar. He certainly attracted a lot of attention, which I imagined he'd smirk in response to if he were here. "Above all, you bring a human to our attention," the man continued.

Cesar looked at Tythian with a gleam in his eye. "I told you they would think of her as human at first," he shook his head with excitement.

"Cesar, don't toy," the irritable, short man continued. A few murmurs began through the vampires. "Have you lost your mind?"

"Listen here, wee little Thomas," Cesar began. I shaped the vampire up who was called Thomas. So, this was who Tythian wanted me to kill. I side glanced Tythian, who watched his fellow vampires. "Maybe if you stopped asking so many questions, and theatrically speaking your claims, you might be given some answers. And perhaps, it might be in your best interest to step down, because you're getting on my nerves."

Cesar's threat was definite. With a moment of thought, Thomas simply crossed his arms behind his head and stayed silent. His stare most certainly directed on only me. I watched as the other vampires looked at me differently. Some curious, others obviously struggled to stay within the room, tempted to attack. They thought me their next meal. A small smile crept at my lips, I dared them to attack me, I would love so much to spill their blood on this rocky ground. I was humored to see, that no matter how exhausted, my love of killing vampires quickly replaced that thirst.

"Everyone, I would like to introduce you to my only biological daughter. She is not human. She is part hunter, and part vampire." Cesar let the words linger in the air. Many of the vampires whispered amongst one another.

"That is hogwash Cesar, there is nothing of her that would claim either to be true." The woman beside Thomas with short black hair at her roots and a deep purple mixing with the tips of her hair, projected. They looked similar, perhaps siblings.

"Are you calling me a liar, Lydia?" Cesar's leadership was absolute, and she quickly dipped her head in apology.

"I didn't mean to offend, Cesar, but understand where we are coming from," she said in pardon.

"I need proof," Thomas pushed further. I could understand why Tythian wanted Thomas dead. He was irritating me as well, which only pushed my smile further. Debating and initiating a fight, was something I was well equipped for.

"Perhaps your incompetence will be your undoing, are you stupid, deaf, or simply don't wish to listen to your leader?" I said blaze.' "Step up little mouse, and perhaps you will understand your unimportance in this matter."

"What did you just say to me?!" Thomas roared. Lydia held him back, amongst a few others as he went to charge me. Never for a moment did I let my antagonizing gaze break from his.

"Let me make one thing very clear, right now!" Cesar roared. "Everyone's priority until the day I die is to protect Esmore. If anyone has any issues, or wishes to debate me on the matter, I will behead you instantly."

The threat lingered in the air. I liked this position that I was in and the restraint that Cesar had over all these vampires. I had just walked in, and yet not one of them could lay a finger on me. Better yet, I could extend that immunity onto the rest of those I wanted to keep safe. With a smile, I walked toward Thomas. If anyone would give me a reaction, it was him, which was good because he was the one I had to now kill. I walked up to him, with such a smile, the corner of his eye twitched.

"Or maybe, I am just a silly human," I teased him. Lydia still held him back; her brown eyes darted back at Cesar, uncertain of the exchange. Thomas inhaled heavily, a fiery glaze burned in his eyes.

"Esmore, don't push him," Cesar instructed, but not as strictly as he had on the vampires in front of us. I danced in fire here, tempting them all, and being so close to their hungry fangs. But the inner hunter in me couldn't resist. Caution was in the past; here I could play with fire. "Inside our tunnels, contains her fellow hunter comrades, a male and a female. Her mother, who is my familiar," Cesar let that statement linger. Everyone's face's anguished with confusion. But Thomas' raged even further.

"I suppose, hearing your leader has a hunter for a familiar, must be a great deal of furious shock to you. You have nothing to say?" I pushed at Thomas, waiting for the final layer to break. I had to tempt him. He had to come at me.

"Esmore," Cesar growled. "And the other coven leader is Esmore's familiar. For the time being, he is welcome amongst these tunnels, until another solution is met." My lips curved into a smile, snapping the last layer to Thomas' control.

"Are you fucking kidding me?! He could be in here to ambush his coven onto any of us, what kind of rash decision is that!" Thomas roared and pushed his sister aside.

"Do not question me!" Cesar bellowed back. It was a stifling roar of command. One that had many of his vampires cringe from the tone. Thomas panted harshly in rage. He only needed a little further to be pushed.

"You know, recently I've discovered what it means to have a familiar," I purred, "and I would do anything for him. So shut your filthy mouth, before I rip your jaw off its hinges, and plunge my hand so swimmingly around your heart, that my face will be the last and only thing you see in your dark afterlife."

Thomas roared in a frenzy and pushed back his sister to grab for my throat. He was fast, and his nails scraped past my throat, only narrowly missing a firm grip. My whole body thrived in excitement and burned with pain from my exhaustion. My eyes glazed a purple, and I knew my hunter's eyes were present, as well as my fangs that thirsted to drive into his neck, and rip out his throat. Vampires gasped as they hid away from the fight, and my purple hunter's eyes.

I leaped at Thomas, grabbing his wrist and wrapping it around his back to break it. But he was fast and strong. With the same arm, he threw me back and leaped for me. I kicked him in the stomach, pushing him away, and lunging for him again. My muscles didn't contract as quickly, and there was a moment of pause from my body as its tiredness tried to keep up with my next sought out ambition and movement. I was weak and had exhausted myself already. The sensation of the Descendant knocked at me lightly, but I knew I was too weak to call it forth. Instead, I prepared myself for his pounce, ready to take a wound to trap him again. Would he dive for my heart, or try to behead me?

Thomas' feet dragged along the dirt from my kick. His calves flexed as he went to pounce. A shadow flickered behind him, and much to Thomas' surprise, he turned and tried to elbow his new opponent. But Chase was too quick and dodged him. Chase wrapped his hands around Thomas' neck and snapped it. Thomas' body dropped to the ground.

Lydia pounced on Chase. He grabbed her arms and flung her into the ceiling. By the time she had dropped onto the ground, Chase had snarled and sized up the room of vampires, who were now excited by the fight and wanted to join. His fangs were so large in comparison to mine. His fingers were bent and ready to fight to protect me.

Four vampires leaped toward Chase. I gathered my footing to help him. But he didn't need help; he was capable of looking after himself. He plunged his hand into the chest of one, ripped their heart out, dropped it at his feet, and prepared for the next attacker. The vampire's body fell to the ground, decaying into a black tinge, as its corpse began to rot.

Balzar and Tythian pushed another two back, and stood beside Chase in a protective circle.

"Enough!" Cesar roared. The last vampire halted his steps, but it was too late, and he was too close to Cesar. With one swift movement, Cesar flattened his hand and swept it forcefully across the vampire's neck, instantly beheading him. The vampire's head flew into a crowd of vampires. The vampire's body, blackened as it suspended on its balanced legs. Cesar kicked the decomposing body into the rocky wall, where it spluttered and dropped to the ground.

"I hope I've made myself very clear! No one touches our guests! And above all commandments, you protect Esmore or I will hunt you personally. I have kept you safe and alive for this long, trust my judgment. I do not take kindly to treachery. Now go!" Cesar roared. The vampires scuttled throughout the many tunnels. Within seconds, it was only us five and Lydia that remained. Lydia helped her brother Thomas up. He swiveled his head uncomfortably. Chase hadn't killed him, and I was embarrassed that Chase had to come to my rescue because I had ignored my weakened state. I was now worse and barely had the energy to move.

Thomas stared at Chase with disgust. "And so now the foreign coven leader has killed our own. How do you expect to cover that, Cesar?" Thomas said, still rubbing his neck.

"Be quiet," Lydia hissed. "Cesar, I am sorry. I apologize on behalf of my brother for his actions. Please forgive him."

"You and I are going out for a chat," Cesar growled to Thomas.

With a swift movement, Chase picked me up from my weakened stand. He held me close to his chest, with a fiery anger in his eyes as he continued to stare at Thomas.

"Fine," Thomas angrily replied. He and Cesar hastily exited the room.

Lydia looked over us before vanishing into one of the tunnels.

"Well, that was exciting. Nothing like killing your own coven members to protect some prick," Balzar said sarcastically and gave Chase a lingering stare.

"You failed," Tythian said to me, gesturing that my killing of Thomas was unsuccessful. But I would have never presumed my body was so weak. A snarl came from Chase's lips.

"If I find out the reason she was hurt today was because of some bargain…"

Tythian's presence vanished into midair as a black hole consumed him, and he teleported out of the room.

"I didn't need your help," I defied. Chase took a long breath before looking down at me.

"You're weak, Esmore. And you are my familiar. How long will you be on a suicide mission before you realize that when you put yourself in danger, you put me in danger as well? I'll always come and protect you, which is exactly why you're going to feast. Stop being so selfish and risking my life as well. You're no use to Dillian in this state."

I went to argue, but his sudden fierce demeanor forced me to stay quiet. It was no longer the goofy Chase that held me.

"I refuse to feast off Dillian or Julia," I grumpily said in defeat. I was so ravenous.

"No, of course you won't, you're beyond that now. You'll most likely kill the person you feed from because you're so beyond thirst," Chase said stubbornly.

"But I don't want to kill anyone," I argued.

"This is the state you've left yourself in. I warned you," Chase growled. With vampire speed, Chase took me to a solitary room. "You can't be around the others right now; you're a risk to them, more so now than before." A light tap on the door startled me. My hearing pounded and my blood burned. Yolo opened the door and carried on a tray, five bottles of blood.

"Here," he said, offering it to Chase. "I can't be long. The whole coven is in a frenzy right now. I best be protecting your friends, while Cesar and Thomas are gone. Tythian is posted close by for the moment. As soon as she is stable, you both best be coming back. We're safest in numbers here, in case the coven rally against Cesar's command."

"Thank you." Chase nodded and closed the door behind Yolo. He sat the tray in front of me. Without hesitation, I swept the first bottle and divulged in the taste. My fangs pounded in delight at the soothing serum that glided down my throat.

"If Tythian had you attack one of those vampires as part of your bargain, you were tricked, Esmore. He knew in your weakened state you couldn't have a fair fight. Being exhausted as a vampire is far different from being exhausted as human or hunter. If you exhaust yourself too much, some vampires drop into a coma-like state, until others can help rejuvenate and feed them blood. He knew I would come to protect you. You were tricked. It was a political statement. Because I'm technically the leader of a foreign coven, I'll most certainly be targeted from the inside now." Chase didn't sound upset or mad, just factual. I stared at him, infuriated that I had been manipulated in such a way, and I had endangered the person I most wanted to protect.

Chase pushed back a part of my hair, with a smile. "Don't worry about it. I'll be fine. What I'm saying is, from now on, you tell me everything. I'm the only one here who you can trust, and I do not have another agenda that puts your life in danger. I'm your familiar, Esmore, trust me." He kissed the top of my head. "Now hurry and drink, so we can return to the others."

I stared at him, wanting to feel guilty or displeased with my actions, but the sensations and feelings I once knew as a child, didn't come. The removal of my heart was the cause. I truly struggled to feel emotion like a normal hunter, no matter how limited it might have been. But it was necessary to return to the others as soon as possible, and I consumed the bitter cold blood, which I so much wished was fresh. How my body ached for its very nutrients, and for it to quench my undying thirst.

CHAPTER 5

MY BLOOD DIDN'T feel like sandpaper scraping my insides at every movement as I took my last gulp of blood. The bitter taste eased into my body like a washing relief and balm. Although it didn't entirely take away the irritation, it soothed me. With heightened speed, I joined the others in the room that was allocated for us. Tythian guarded the door. He didn't even bother a side glance at us. With such speed, I aimed to ram my elbow into his throat, infuriated by his trickery. But already, his gift consumed me, as he grabbed firmly onto me. We had vanished and now reappeared in a different area. Before Chase could stop me from making physical contact with Tythian, he had teleported us elsewhere. I coughed hysterically still not used to his gift, and this time I was unable to brace myself for it. Tythian dusted off his well-groomed shirt as I stumbled across the rough terrain.

"You lied to me!" Although I had drunk five bottles, I was still thirsty, and every heartbeat within the woods that we spoke in, pounded in my ear. I wanted to hunt, and I wanted to feast. I focused my attention on Tythian, not provoking the thirstier side of me to take over.

"No. I gave you the facts. Your opponent was a strong vampire, and you were weak. It was because of your arrogance that you still accepted. It's a political statement, don't take it so personally, no harm would have ever come to you."

"I don't care about what happens to me. My issue is that you purposefully put Chase in danger knowing he would race to my aid!" I tried to impair my rage, which urged me to pounce on Tythian, and rip his throat out.

"No, I simply started moving the pieces in this chess game. And, Chase is a large piece and factor in that game. He's made a direct attack on one of our own coven members. That won't sit well and will be questionable amongst the members here. We don't own the vampires like the Council, nor monitor their freedom. So something like this, such gossip will be spread eventually to the very ears I want them to. You see, sometimes Cesar's hands are tied in the movement of this rebellion. So, it is my job to step in and do what is required to be done." After a silent moment, I straightened my back. It infuriated me that Tythian was playing a larger game then I could comprehend because I knew nothing of this outside world. I thought through all my teachings within the Guild, hands on experience, and raids that I understood what the world was about. But the reality was, I knew nothing and could do nothing now. Not until I understood the larger game at hand.

"Whose ears are you expecting it to reach?" I asked. I wanted to know whose attention Tythian was trying to reach, especially because of Chase's rebellion. Was he trying to reach Fier?

"His coven of course. Whether Chase wants to claim his leadership or not, is no longer a matter of choice. We don't have time to play childish games. After telling me about his coven many years ago, I found and kept an eye on them. I know their size, which is the only reason why they've survived this long, leaderless. We need those numbers. We have many covens that have aligned with Cesar, but having the additive of Chase's coven as well..."

I cut Tythian off, vexed at the betrayal he laid on his friend. "You're trying to force him to take a position he has refused for years, he's never wanted it!"

"You do not get to make that decision for him. I know the reasons he's cowered from his obligation and hides in shadows from them. I've seen what they've done to him, as a young boy and his mother," Tythian said condescendingly. "When Chase first received the gift of his mind, he couldn't so easily control it, and accidentally transferred shards of memories from his human lifetime to me.

You forget little vampire, I've known him for many hundred years longer than you. I know of his peril intimately, but he can no longer escape it. He *is* a coven leader. You'll soon learn that the world you've been bubble wrapped and living in as a hunter is very different to the world of vampires. Justice does not apply to our rules. You are either the strongest or dead.

Thomas was the second vampire Cesar took in after me. He's old and powerful, and your pathetic attempt of an assassination will not be the death of him. I thought you would've heard my warning clearly and been more tactful. But that's a lot to depend on someone so naive and young. Despite him reciprocating the attack, Cesar will not behead him. I won't take you and your friends to the Guild."

"I did as you asked and promised," I snarled, infuriated that he'd dishonor his word.

"No. You failed. You, of all people should understand the consequence of a failure's result. Before you take up such challenges, I implore you to start understanding your new bearings, and how being a vampire works. Perhaps you can take a lesson from this, stop deluding yourself into thinking you're an equal here, have a say, and can instruct *me* of all people."

"I will tell Cesar of your lies, and have him force you to take me," I snapped, thinking of the devotion he held for Cesar. It was a low blow, but I was desperate to get the others to safety. Tythian's blue eyes narrowed on me. A gust of light wind could not ruffle his slick blond hair as it swept through us in our moment of silence.

"Cesar will not let you leave his sight. With everything you are and represent, he won't allow me to teleport you anywhere else. That was our own bargain, and me risking myself to have you satisfied. He will never allow it, which means without me, you are stuck there. So think of another solution that aids me and pleases me so greatly that I will re-offer this bargain to you." I flexed my fingers in and out, struggling against my rage. It was so heightened and fierce, I wanted to attack Tythian. Where had all my self-control vanished to? I refocused on my father's teachings, and began to count backward from ten.

"What must I do for that?" I hissed under my breath. I knew he was right. Cesar wouldn't let me out of his sight now, even though I was not his to claim, especially if my mother agreed that my protection was best under his wing. Protection: a ridiculous notion. I could more than anyone, protect myself.

"Something will arise. We're in a time of war, opportunities always arise. But I want you to fixate on a more personal task for me." After much silence and the image of Tythian looking away to hide his sudden irritation, he spoke. "I want you to go into the human compound with Yolo. There is a possibility, that on their scanner, you will appear as human. Neither your hunter nor vampire self is evident if you don't use any of your abilities. I want you to find Whitney's brother. I want you to relay the image of his face and every fine detail you learn of him, to me. And then, I want you to bait him out, and I will torture him, for as long as his pathetic human life lasts for, just as he had done to my own familiar. To Whitney, he took that lifetime away from her, and he took both of our happiness," Tythian hissed, in his most exposed expression. What a lengthy list Tythian had of people he wanted dead.

I wanted to kill Whitney's brother, just as much as he did for what he had done to the precious and joyful Whitney, but it was Tythian's right above everyone else's. It infuriated me that I was lied to, and he stole the memory and truth from Whitney. But I couldn't pass that judgment any longer in this deformed world. He did what he thought was best for Whitney. And her brother certainly deserved a lifetime of torture. While Tythian focused on him alone, I could kill all those that practiced on humans in such a way to try and create new hunters. I didn't care for the humans any longer. My last thread of commitment to them was severed the moment my own kind blasted a hole in my chest. But I cared for one human in particular, and that moment with Whitney was what would propel me into fixating on the human facilities. If not for Tythian's and my alignment, but for my own sought out justice and blood thirst. I wanted those humans dead.

"For all the time in the world you stand here and debate with me, you have left your friends exposed without both of our protection. We should be heading back." Tythian held out his hand and looked away as if my touch revolted him.

"I'll go with Yolo. I can do that," I agreed. This was something that we both wanted. For a moment, I thought I saw a streak of relief pass over the usually composed Tythian. I grabbed his forearm and was instantly thrown back into the tunnels, and in front of the door. Chase now guarded the front, his arms crossed over. I detested that he was left to guard the door when he was at risk of being overthrown by the vampires of this coven.

Stop doing that, Chase growled at me internally. He had no connection with me when Tythian and I went elsewhere. He opened the door. Connor and Yolo were impartial to his entrance.

"Well, baby sis looks a bit healthier with some color in her cheeks," Yolo said with a gleam in his eyes. I looked at my mother, still foreign to the idea of an extended family. She stood against the wall, finely narrowing a piece of wood with her knife.

"What is your plan of attack?" she asked quietly under her breath. It was very different to see my mother as she is now. We were never within the same group, even within the Guild. We didn't so often fight together. So to now have her by my side, and instead of initiating her own plan, she waited for mine; it was both an honor, but also a precautionary measure on her behalf—because I was a ticking time bomb. She had to follow my movement because she knew she couldn't restrain me. My mother fought by my side, but only because of her own purpose which for all hunters within the Guild, it was to protect humans, and we no longer had that. All of us hunters here had no purpose, and to follow someone who thought they knew what they were doing, seemed easier. My mother's task had been to hide my heart, now I was curious about what else she prioritized. I had no idea what the right path was, but I never doubted my steps. First and foremost was removing the hunters from this coven and finding a safe place for them, including Chase.

"I want to go to the human facility with you," I said to Yolo. "My first priority is finding somewhere safe for Julia and Dillian. If they can live amongst humans, then I would like to find out if that place is safe for them."

"A place where they experiment on humans and are trying to create new hunters; what makes you think they won't experiment on a pair of hunters?" Connor said distastefully. Connor's hatred and distrust in the humans blazed in his intense blue eyes. Even if I hadn't been informed of it, the hiss that came from the word 'human' on his lips was blatant hatred. His worst assumption of the humans was one I'd already considered myself. I had no intention of leaving Dillian and Julia with humans who were already so cruel to their own kind. But I had to make it look convincing. If I handed Whitney's brother over to Tythian, he would then keep his end of the deal, and I could go anywhere in the world to protect the others. That was my goal now.

"That may be true, but for the time being, it wouldn't hurt to scope out our resources. If it's an option, then I would like to have considered it thoroughly." After a long silence and exchange between Connor and Yolo, Yolo uncomfortably shifted in his chair.

"I'm really flattered that you want to spend some sister-brother bonding time, but Cesar would never allow it. There's no guarantee you will scan as a human for starters. If you trigger an alarm, it makes it harder for me to angle an excuse as well. I can't guarantee your safety in there. Not while I'm in my human form, I can't break my own identity if something goes wrong."

"Cesar doesn't own me. If you won't aid me in this task, I will simply leave and find my own solution." I crossed my arms, aggravated. I'd never been coddled in my entire life. I was a Token Huntress for goodness sake. I exchanged a glance with Dillian, who stayed quiet in the room. He and Julia out of everyone must have felt most displaced here.

"Good luck on leaving the tunnels. You obviously have no idea where we're located. Taking your little friends and surviving might be an issue," Connor said, and side glanced me. He was not rude or held sarcasm in his tone. Much like Tythian, his tone was dry and factual.

"And why's that?" I counteracted. Without hesitation, Connor sat up from his chair and began walking toward us.

"I don't like playing games. Follow me," he murmured as he walked toward us.

"Connor, you can't be serious!" Yolo shouted out from behind him.

"I tire of riddles and debates. We won't be too long, but perhaps this will give princess here an understanding of her current position. Maybe she'll realize that she isn't the one to be throwing demands around here." Connor sized me up as he walked past us, and then Chase with indifference. Tythian nodded his approval to Connor as he led us out of the room.

"If any movement happens, I'll bring you back straight away," Tythian said unflinchingly from his position beside the door. It rendered me speechless to see him in such a solider like role, obeying Cesar's every word. I wondered how often he was here back at the coven considering he was double-crossing Fier in his Council.

Connor lurked further into the shadows. At vampire speed, we followed him through alternating corridors and on an uneven elevation. I still had to adjust to my vampire speed. Although as a Huntress I was fast, it was like discovering a new level of speed entirely, and I clumsily used it to keep at their pace. Within me, deeper, I knew this wasn't the fastest I could go but managing it was something entirely different.

Connor halted, raising his fingers to Chase and me. There was a small crevasse, where only one person at a time could barely fit. An array of scuttling noises and heavy breathing could be heard. There was a light pouring noise of water, like a fountain. I went to step closer, but Connor grabbed my shoulder. Instantly Chase's hand was on Connor. Connor gave him a disgusted glance. He wasn't being threatening, but the touch seemed to repulse and offend him.

"I wouldn't step out past the crevasse if I were you," Connor said indifferently. I held my gaze with his beautiful blue eyes for a moment longer, before pushing past him to look further out through the fissure, without stepping through.

"The waterfall helps block the sun of daytime for them," Connor said in an informative low tone. Chase stood behind me as Connor stepped aside. I could sense movement outside. Even amongst the coldness, numerous amounts of body heat radiated from the creatures.

I would have been startled if I hadn't already felt the presence of the monster lingering against the wall. Large fangs that dipped over the vampire's lip crept out from the darkness. It sniffed hysterically, only centimeters from my face. Its glazed eyes searched for our presence, yet it couldn't see us, but somehow it sensed us.

"Sabers?" Chase asked, examining the same creature in front of us. Its one eye searched back and forth through the crevasse.

"It's one of the bigger packs we've come across. They rest here during the day, to keep away from the sun. Sabers are still affected by the sun. It might not kill them, but it near cripples them if they're in it for too long, unless it's an overcast day of course. We've only been here for six months. Cesar had his eye on this location for a while. What would deter any other coven or Council force, more than having to go through one of the largest packs of sabers on this continent?" Connor asked rhetorically. "However, this wasn't possible until Cesar found the hunter who had the gift of concealment. Once that was his, he was able to conceal our presence within the walls."

"I thought his gift didn't work if you were physically seen?" I asked, still watching the saber that sniffed in our direction. Its ghastly breath spread over my heightened smell.

"Sabers rely on their senses more than anything, mostly their smell. But granted, they are not blind. Cesar renews the concealment on the tunnels constantly. This is why, outside of this concealment, he cannot physically cover anything else. He can conceal smell and someone's presence, but not their physical state because all that energy is constantly washing over this coven. It's no surprise that he's weaker now than before, although still admirable and almost near impossible to challenge. He conceals the rocky walls and what dwells within them. Basically, he has bubbled this whole system from everyone's sight. Even the sabers, who physically peer into our eyes, cannot see through that bubble."

I looked at Chase, trying to study his reaction. But he only watched the saber with interest. When I looked back, the saber was no longer there, it had given up. Past it, I saw shadows of more and in the distance the sounds of a pouring waterfall.

"And if we were to step out of this crevasse?" I asked, already knowing the answer.

"Then you would be walking in the midst of their lair," Connor said impartially. "I wish you the very best, if you decide to take your hunter friends through there. There is another two-hundred and fifty-six meters until you reach the waterfall and break out into the woods. Also, keep in mind that these are not malnourished sabers that you might have challenged in the city. In the woods here on a completely different terrain, they're faster and stronger." That information sunk in. It would be near impossible to move Julia and Dillian out, even with hunter and vampire speed. With so many sabers we wouldn't make it out unscathed.

"Shall we return?" Connor asked, and gestured his hand in the direction, back toward the tunnels. That made up my mind. Tythian was our only way of escape, and for that, I had to push and make sure I went to the human compound to hold up my end of the deal. I would find Whitney's brother, and set flames to the rest of them that caused her harm or discomfort. I'll find Julia and Dillian a safe place to live, and one with purpose. A hunter without purpose was like the remains of a saber. Eventually, we would lose our minds and sanity. Especially Julia and Dillian who felt empathy toward the humans, they would soon be in disarray. It was in their genes. And I would do anything to prevent that.

I spared Chase a glance. He was watching me from the corner of his eye as he often did. We were both calculating, and though my first thought was Julia and Dillian, I had no doubt that he was putting my safety first. I had to find a way we could all make it out of this unharmed. I brushed my mind against his in a soothing manner. His lips twitched into a small smile. I had to be sharp in my approach to make sure that I no longer put Chase in danger or antagonized the vampires from within.

With your wit and my good looks, we'll find safety for them, Chase telepathically said.

I rolled my eyes at him though I appreciated his faint-hearted approach. He trusted in my judgment though I could sense he was blocking his thoughts and plans of action from me. I had no doubt my cunning familiar was up to his own games as well. And in some bizarre way, it comforted me.

CHAPTER 6

WAITING FOR CESAR was tedious; he'd now been gone for hours. As the leader, I wondered if he had decapitated Thomas or given mercy. Though, I imagined it was as Tythian said and the vampire would be allowed to live. We cramped within the small room, waiting. Everyone sat uncomfortably amid the odd companionship. Amongst all, Chase slept through it unbothered by the high-strung tension. When I prodded within his mind to see if he was awake, a smile crept on his lips, but he never opened his eyes.

Yolo didn't speak of the human compound any further. Ultimately, he knew it wasn't his decision and that when Cesar returned, I would ask to be involved with or without Yolo's favor. I noted that out of the four brothers, Balzar was the only one who was not here. Perhaps it was because he was unable to control himself around hunters. He was around one hundred and fifty vampire years, and yet he still found it difficult to suppress the urge to attack hunters and humans. How was I to survive in such an unexpected way and world?

Everyone jarred alert, with the heavy footing of someone walking in our direction. There was no mistaking it was Cesar. At vampire speed, I flew out the door to reach him first and make my request. A small breeze swept around me as I stopped in front of him within the tunnels.

Cesar let out a raucous laugh. "Ah, Esmore, you're as subtle as a rhino, dear, you really need to work on your vampire skills. I have a task for you."

"I have a favor to ask of you," I said forwardly. Cesar rubbed his orange beard as he looked toward the ceiling as if recalling a memory. He began a monstrous laugh. "They told me if I ever had a little girl, she'd be more demanding, but I didn't expect it so soon." After his inside joke with another ceased, he focused on me seriously. "I have a task, and you have a favor to request, this should be interesting. Let me go first. I want you to lead a team tomorrow. Members of separate Councils are starting to move for their meeting. One of my scouts has recently found a group of them, I want you to inspect it. I need to find out their numbers, which they migrate with, and whose Council it is." I could sense someone listening in on our conversation. They stood closely but hid in the shadows, for now. It was a conversation Cesar didn't mind this vampire overhearing.

"Is it Oppollo's Council?" Balzar asked. His face emerged out of the dark as he stepped closer. Well, he was equipped to be a vampire: lurking and creepy. A flash of rage crossed Cesar's face at the mention of the person named Oppollo.

"Who's Oppollo?" I asked indiscreetly. A long time swept through us as Cesar attempted to calm his facial expressions, but his knuckles whitened over his bones as he tried to soothe himself. Unlike other vampires I had met, Cesar could conceal his expression and distaste for particular things and fellow vampires. But not when this particular Council leader's name was mentioned.

"Oppollo is the vampire who turned me. He also slaughtered my entire village back in the day in the wee land of Scotland, a very long time ago before turning me as the sole survivor. To say the least, I've hated him for this long. He's the leader to one of the largest Councils, and I want him and his group eradicated from the face of this earth. I want him to feel dirt in his teeth, before I watch his corpse decay in front of me," Cesar spat venomously. I wondered how old Cesar was and how long he had held onto this grudge. From what I had gathered, vampires were bound in ways to their maker, so how had he escaped that? Or maybe it meant someone else had to do the killing for him.

"So why have me lead a team to inspect it? Wouldn't you rather have someone who has been within your coven for some time now, surely you already have an inspection group?" I asked, unclear of his reason. He must have an ulterior motive by putting me in such a position of power.

"Why indeed," Balzar grumbled. "Apparently, baby sis is the favorite."

I hissed at his referral of me being, 'baby sis.' The other three had implied and named me the same, but when Balzar said it, it forced me to cringe.

"You would be wise to watch your tongue," Cesar threatened. "Well, I thought it was obvious. The coven doesn't like the change of you living within the same walls as them, but they must learn your importance and who you are. Instead of waiting out and trying to wean you into the group, we simply put you at the top and make you leader straight away. I don't play games, they either follow or they don't. They know the consequences if they choose not to."

"They won't like it," Balzar grumbled.

"This coven isn't meant to be a little love nest for everyone. You either follow orders or you don't. Secondly, I know how hard it is for you, Esmore. To be a Token within your Guild, and to now be shifted here, powerless. I hope you stay with us, with your real family."

"This isn't my family. You are not my dad," I snapped. My fangs split my gums in the savage growl that rumbled through me. "My dad died, he was the one who raised me to keep this monster within me at bay, and you are trying to exploit it."

"I'm not trying to exploit anything. I'm trying to give you purpose. I know how mad hatter hunters go without any direction or order, I want to offer you that. And if you agree to this task, I'll agree to your request." I arched an eyebrow and crossed my arms, enjoying the sound of that.

The fellow three brothers communally joined the meeting, having caught up after I had fled the room so quickly. I could still feel Chase's presence, lying down comfortably across the bed, simply listening in on our conversation. The image was very different from the one where he always lazed in his hammock. Dillian and Julia were situated close to him, and sat at the wooden table, eating some fruit that she had retrieved from her bag.

"Before she suggests her request, I don't like it," Yolo presented, although half-assed. He said it in a cautionary tone, but his carefree nature told me he didn't care either way.

"I want to go with Yolo to the human compound. I want to see if it's a safe location for Dillian and Julia to reside within. I know there's a high risk that they would only experiment on them because they're hunters, but I have to see for myself. I can't cross out any options." Cesar sighed expectantly as if he knew this request was coming.

"There's no guarantee you won't register as vampire in the scans. You could destroy the whole infiltration Yolo has underway," Cesar said, rubbing his eyebrows together in a stressful gesture.

"Although I agree, Cesar," Connor interrupted. "With her also being a new vampire, she risks attacking the humans within the compound uncontrollably. With that said, I think we could also use this to our advantage. If she comes up as neither vampire nor hunter in the scan, she could focus on another part of the system. Yolo only has access to their records and medical procedures, it might not hurt to have her try and focus on other departments, perhaps even their military force. If they are in fact of the government from human time, they might still have a fair bit of gun power. Considering they're experimenting to make hunters; what if they're using some already, whether defective or not." I side glanced Connor suspiciously. I was surprised he spoke so much, but also that he defended me and further reasoned my purpose of going. Tythian stayed silent, which made me consider that Connor only thought of such a scheme because Tythian had already told him of why he truly wanted me to go.

"Am I the only one registering the word, 'risk' being used repetitively," Balzar sniped. "We got by fine before she came, we can still manage without her."

"Congratulations, Balzar," Cesar said jollily. "You've just been made second in command to Esmore and will follow her tomorrow as she inspects this Council group. You will basically be her lap dog and do every order she tells you to. If you don't learn to keep your sass to yourself lad, after I've already warned you, you're going to be punished like a child."

"Pfft." Yolo covered his snicker with his hand as he looked away. Balzar mixed with rage and the urge to say something else. But at the hint of Yolo's laughter, Balzar turned on him.

"I am going to tear you apart," Balzar growled at Yolo.

"Don't you have to ask for permission first, lap dog?" Yolo laughed again. Both of them ran into the tunnels at heightened speed. The two seemed close.

"Tythian, you seem awfully silent on the matter," Cesar said, crossing his arms and watching Tythian expectantly. It dawned on me that Cesar favored Tythian's advice.

"I think it's a risk. But I also think it'll pay off if it works and that we could use that resource. I'm in favor of sending her to inspect the Council group migrating. I'll teleport them, only a mere half-day run from the location. They can inspect and return by dusk tomorrow. It gives them a few hours to review and watch. If you take Lydia, she'll be able to decipher whose group it is. She has knowledge of those who publicly have gifts and might be able to identify the group by that.

In the meantime, I'll see if I am still welcome within Fier's Council; although, it is possible he might have already learned of my true identity and my false alliance with him. If he has missed it then I still have an opportunity to learn of their next move. I've already been gone for a day, perhaps my return won't be so unexpected. And then let the little vampire go with Yolo, to learn of their weaponry and such. Maybe we'll learn something Yolo hasn't already reported."

After a long pause of consideration, Cesar continued to rub his orange beard as he looked at me. "Do you even know how to act human, love?" I was taken aback by his question. "You raise your head too proudly, to be only a human. And they have that annoying thing, where their shoulders and back slouch. You need to learn that posture quickly and try to get a different air about you, one that says, 'I'm actually a good girl, and if you stole a piece of my cake, I wouldn't kill you over it,'" Cesar joked. I didn't understand his reference, but to his advice, I attempted to slouch my shoulders in. It was so uncomfortable that I thought my face was pulling expressions of its own accord.

Yolo clapped his hands, now coming back to the group with a smile on his face. "Kicked his ass." He laughed, pointing back toward where he must have fought with Balzar. "It sooo pays off not being the baby of the brothers anymore. It always used to be me; impaled to the walls in joking spirit." Tythian and Connor exchanged a certain gleam in their eyes.

"Never fret, the mastermind is now here," Yolo gloated. "Have her pretend to suffer amnesia. There are humans within the compound who study the brain and characteristics of humans. I once had a friend who suffered amnesia. They didn't recall anything about themselves, anything," he emphasized. "We could call you Ellie. I'll inform them that I found you knocked unconscious with a wound to your head, it explains my absence for the last few days. I could say I've been treating your wounds. The only thing you remember or feel comfortable with is weapons. Sometimes things come naturally to amnesia patients, this could be yours. It'll give you the chance to infiltrate their military sector. I'll try to organize for you to meet Sydney, himself," Yolo said, very proud of his plan.

"Who's Sydney?" I asked, impressed by his makeshift plan. Because this had been his mission, I imagined he wanted to hold authority over the matter.

"Sydney's in charge of that section. He trains a lot of the humans there and has a team. They're the ones who usually track singular vampires and sabers; take them down and bring them back for testing. They're rather elite, considering they're only human. If you can get within that group, it would be to our advantage to learn of their tactics. That way, you can inspect the area and deem whether it is stable enough for your little hunter friends as well. Since that is the focal point of this mission, correct?" Yolo antagonized. He didn't pointedly call me out as a liar, but I wondered how switched on the other brothers were to Tythian's partial plan.

I looked at Cesar expectantly, that plan could work. I could do all those things. I cringed at the thought of pretending to be human, but perhaps it wouldn't be as hard as I thought. I had already attempted it within the Council, and no one suspected otherwise.

With arms crossed, Cesar tapped his thick finger on his forearm. "My only request is that if you feel like you're losing your senses or control, you must get out of there, Esmore. You can't eat the entire camp. It'll jeopardies Yolo's work. You need to feast regularly, I mean every day. We can't risk you going on a frenzied feast," Cesar said. Before I could argue, Cesar raised his finger to me. "I know you think you have control over this, but it's not something you control, Esmore. Being a vampire is like being a wild animal, eventually you will be led by instinct alone, and your morals will come after that; after the damage you have caused, not during. I'll agree for now, but if at any point I feel like you are far from control, I'll remove your involvement. I'm only letting you go because you're part hunter, and I hope, that is the part that will help you keep in check."

There was a moment of apprehension. I nodded my consent at Cesar's advice. I felt the animal that he spoke about reflect already within me, trying to claw out at every chance it had. I'd always felt that within me, but now that I had awakened it, it was more prominent than ever.

"Now, move them to their new quarters, a little more room for you, and where you can monitor your friends at the same time. Afterward, Connor, could you show her to the team she'll be in charge of, and have them prepare for the departure tomorrow. Come and get me when they're ready." Cesar held out his hand past us. "Come along, love, you and I have much time for discussion," Cesar said to my mother, who had obviously been listening to our conversation beside the door. She walked through us. Before she grabbed Cesar's hand, she pressed a kiss to my forehead.

"I'll come speak with you soon, my beautiful daughter," my mother said with a stern expression, it reminded me of the mother I once knew. She took hold of Cesar's hand, and together, they walked into the tunnel's darkness. I still struggled to comprehend such a sight—my mother alive and with a vampire.

"You're starting to become an errands boy, Connor," Yolo joked. Connor's glare alone had Yolo running with laughter. "Well, that's my queue to leave."

"What makes this room safer than the one we're in now?"

"Because the rooms are part of Cesar's quarters. No one is allowed near them, unless permitted," Tythian said indifferently. "I'll aid you in escorting them."

When we opened the door, Julia and Dillian were ready. Dillian looked like he hadn't had one moment of rest. I didn't need to speak to him to know what he thought. Simply, 'enough messing around and let us get out of here.' Chase stood behind them, with a knowing smile.

"It makes it weird, 'doing it' in your parent's room," he joked. If I knew the sensation of embarrassment, I think my cheeks would have gone red. Dillian's eyebrow rose as if to say, *really, at a time like this?* And Julia, well, she reacted exactly how I imagine any faint girl to, red streaked across her cheeks.

The walk was ten minutes further into the tunnels. We took our time to take in the surroundings. There was a lot of scuttling and whispering from onlooking vampires, but like Tythian implied, none would follow past the first set of double carved doors. We were now in Cesar's personal quarters. There were a lot more candles lit along this narrow tunnel. There was one door on each side, until another set of doors were opened. The room was brightly lit with candles, and a chandelier hung from the ceiling with candles pre-lit. Beneath it was a long wooden table with complimentary eight wooden chairs. There were a few paintings that hung on nails, which were embedded into the rocky walls. There was one painting that grabbed my attention of a war, where men sat on horses and fought, in the background, there was seashore and what looked to be ships.

At the back of the room, was a large wooden bed and two rooms detached from either side. There were fur rugs on the ground and close to the wooden table, on the left, was a desk and chair. Beside the door on the left, was a small table which had a horse carved beneath, to hold the flat plank of wood. On top, was the same game that Yolo and Chase played previously in the day if I recall correctly, it was called 'chess.'

"On the left is another room, and in the right room, is a small stream of water, which comes from the waterfall in front of the tunnels. Apologies, little hunter, but it is not hot. Temperature does not bother vampires, however hygiene does," Tythian said to Julia. Dillian put a protective grasp on her shoulder, still uncomfortable with even Tythian, who had teleported us all from our inevitable death.

"Come along, Esmore, I'll show you to the group you will be leading tomorrow," Connor said.

"Can you please give us a minute?" Chase smiled charmingly. Connor looked between us. He nodded his head curtly.

"I'll be waiting outside," Connor said. Both he and Tythian left the room and waited outside the door.

Julia went straight to the steady stream of water that was revealed when she opened the door. Dillian was close behind her, and watched her as she splashed handfuls of water over her face with a relieved expression. The soot of smoke began to cleanse from her face.

"I don't like you doing either," Chase said, meaning both the Council and the human compound inspection. He reached out for my hands and pulled me in. "I might have to take you for myself and make sure you can't walk for days to prevent that," he charmed. I wavered a smile.

"I have to, Chase, you know I wouldn't do it any other way," I said. It was odd to be able to speak to him as an equal. In comparison, with James, the only other relationship I once had, I was repulsed by his constant attempts to control everything I did. It forced me to become secretive. Chase respected me for the fighter I was, and what I believed myself to be capable of.

"You're only a new vampire, there is so much more for you to learn. You are far from being in control, Esmore. You might have been in control of so much before, but this is one thing that can't be curbed. I can't be by your side for either, they won't allow me on the inspection team with you," he said, pushing back a part of my golden fringe.

"Because you are technically a coven leader?" I asked. Chase and I hadn't yet spoken about this in depth. His expression was both confused and saddened.

"Yes," he admitted. "No matter how much I push to be by your side, they won't allow it. Allowing you and three hunters in here, already changes the bounds of this coven. Having me be treated as equal will most certainly create a rebellion against Cesar."

"I would much rather you stay here and protect my best friend and Julia, I wouldn't so easily entrust that to anyone else," I said. I kissed the inside of his palm as he stroked my jawline.

"But you know, I like the fight," he grumbled to himself. I smiled at that, we both did. "I need to be able to teach you the basics of vampirism, at least, Esmore. You'll only be a risk to both Dillian and Julia otherwise."

"I'm not weak, and I will not be defined because of my new found vampirism. I am a Token still. And launching attacks and slaughtering vampires is what I do best. Secondly, I love and thirst for it more than any other sensation I can grasp onto right now. I've not much cared for human survival until now, so why would I worry myself about their presence, just because they are now a source of nutrients for me." I cupped his hand to my face. "I'll be okay." I saw Dillian watching us from afar. How different it must have looked to him, to see me comforting someone in such a way. These feelings of mine and openness were only ever evident when it came to Chase. "I have to go now," I whispered, and pressed a kiss to his lips. I went to walk away, but he pulled me back. His hand pressed hard on my back as he forced himself against me. His tongue melted into mine as he took a savage kiss. He left a nibble on my lip, which created a pinch of blood to appear where he had bitten me with a domineering smile.

"I'll be pissed if we don't even get to snuggle tonight," Chase joked as he let go of my hand.

"We shall see," I purred, infuriated at the hot mess he'd left me in. With that single kiss, I wanted to tear his clothes apart, and devour that glorious body of his. If it were not for Dillian's lingering stare, I don't know if I could've pulled away. With regret, I left my very tantalizing Chase behind, whose eyes I could feel on the shifting leather of my ass.

CHAPTER 7

I STUDIED THE distance of every turn and tunnel I took. I focused on the areas which concentrated the most noise. Vampires were clumped in certain directions, idly going about their business. Tythian vanished and left Connor and me to walk in silence beside one another. Despite his hard exterior, I could tell there was an unyielding loyalty that lay within him. Even further, the beast he would've tamed a very long time ago that unlike the others was so close to the edge, I could see it dance across his blue eyes. I pitied the humans for how much hatred he held for them, and all the ways I could imagine he'd torture them, as they did in his human life. I was not familiar with the 'Hitler time,' it was only listed as one of the human reigns that happened, and another incident where one person created a religion or belief and attempted to take more power than any human should have. It seemed to be a movement that was so gut-wrenching and disturbing, that Connor was the result and aftermath of the survivors, and that was pure hatred.

We arrived in a small room that reminded me of the weapons room within the Hunter Guild. Twelve vampires stood in front of me, all with mixed expressions. Some with instant respect and understanding that I was now their leader; and others with hatred or revulsion in their eyes. The one who glared at me the longest was Balzar, who stood beside Lydia.

I noted that already most of them, which varied in all different heights and shapes, were strapped with weapons. Perhaps Tythian and Cesar had planned this to happen a lot sooner than they led on. We weren't meeting. We were leaving *now*. I gave Connor a suspicious look.

"We couldn't risk the chance of your familiar trying to be a part of it, so we adjusted the time mentioned a little from overhearing ears," he replied unapologetically.

I scanned the distance to brush up against Chase's mind. It was easy to find him because we were so used to talking with one another, and I found him effortlessly. *We're leaving now. I'll be okay.* I heard the growl in his reply. Once again both of us had been tricked, and he didn't like being left out, especially when it separated us.

Be back before dinner time. And snuggle time has now been extended, he responded. I felt his warmth pool into me. We both reasoned he couldn't be involved and I relished the trust he resided in me. I didn't have to ask him for permission to leave, and his only request was to make sure I was back soon. *Be safe,* he said lovingly before I broke our connection. If I was doing this to gain Cesar's favor and enable access to the human compound, I would do it the only way I knew how.

"I need to know if any of you have gifts, anything that might be to our advantage. I need you to all be honest with me. If everyone is to make it out alive under my order, which everyone will, I need to know everyone's weaknesses and strengths," I commanded, easily slipping into my Token role. This was always who I was meant to be.

"No gifts," Lydia responded after no one else spoke up. They were still uncertain of what to say or who should speak. "And we have no weaknesses." Lydia surprisingly was calm. She responded well to command, despite the incident that occurred between her brother and me.

"Who was your Token before me?" I asked.

"We don't call them 'Token' here." Balzar tisked. I narrowed my gaze on him.

"My brother," Lydia responded when no one else did. "Thomas, for the time, has been demoted," she said indifferently. I had my reservations about her being okay with her brother's demotion, but not enough to convince that she'd defy me. I didn't trust any of them, but I recognized raw power when I saw it in Cesar, and I doubted any of them were willing to go against his word or oppose me by extension.

"Congratulations, Lydia, you are now my second in command," I said approvingly. She looked straight to Balzar, who tightened his grip on the spikes strapped across his knuckles.

"What? Cesar put me in second." Balzar angrily spoke, trying to keep his cool.

"And I've now dropped you, continue, and you will be the last on my list. I don't take kindly to backchat. Anyone else who exempts the same attitude will be removed before we leave. I take the security of my team very seriously. When you act childishly you endanger us all. When you act disrespectfully and put yourself in danger, you endanger me for trying to save your sorry ass."

"In all fairness, Esmore. Our previous leader, Thomas, defeated you before. You hadn't a fighting chance before your familiar stepped in," one of the fellow vampires said. She had a long sword strapped to her back. She was bald and looked to be only eighteen at most. She was small in size, but there was a certain gleam in her eyes that told me she was wiser and older than her body conveyed. Her particular style of ear, eyebrow, and nose piercings, and a vine tattoo with roses crept from beneath her singlet and over her chest, intrigued me.

"What's your name?" I asked. She looked between the others uncertain.

"Sharon, but my friends call me Shaz around here," she replied with a slight smile.

"That's an excellent question, and one that I would expect all of you to ask. There is no disrespect in that, and it's the kind of thinking I expect from this team. Please note, Balzar, you might learn something today," I taunted. From the corner of my eye, I could see that Connor was somewhat bemused. Although his expression never changed, I could see the sense of approval and amusement in the gleam of his eye.

"I was turned against by my Guild, and my ex-boyfriend blew out my chest. When I was first greeted by your coven, I could hardly walk. I hadn't yet restored my energy, which I have recently discovered can only be quenched in one way. But let me assure you, I am restored to my fullest and this task that I have been given, is what I do best. So yes, Balzar, within this group, I am called Token, and Lydia is my second in charge. I won't turn to see where you are all at, you are either competent enough to keep up with me, or you lag behind. Does everyone understand this?" Sharon gave a smile and rubbed her nose ring. The tension in the room was very different now to what it was when I first walked in.

"Now, let's go kick some Council ass," I said, turning on them and heading back into the tunnels where they followed me. Connor stayed by my side, leading me to where we first had to report to Cesar. Fellow vampires of the coven watched us, as my team of twelve marched through the tunnels confidently, untouchable, and unbeatable. I hoped in every way, that we could spill some blood on this very fine day. I felt rejuvenated, like my old self again. I never thought I would lead a team of vampires, but never had I felt so empowered.

Cesar met us in the circular room that I'd first arrived in, and met all four of his sons. My mother wasn't with him. It led me to believe that for some reason, Cesar didn't want her involved in any of this. I never thought my mother would be a woman to be told not to follow, unless she was doing something more important at the time. Although I felt distant to the woman she now was, I also longed to be able to sit down and talk to her.

"Well, don't you fit in quickly," Cesar said with amusement. "I have something for you, pet," he said, handing me over my sword and Barnett crossbow. The weight of them felt so familiar and comfortable. I wanted to start slicing through the Council vampires right away. It didn't bother me if I had to turn on the vampires behind me. But right now, this was a task directed to me, so my favor could be returned. I would not fail.

"Why so many vampires to stand behind me when we are simply spying?" I asked him. A smile spread on his face.

"You don't miss anything, do you, my daughter," he laughed. "Would you believe me if I said I was overprotective of you?" I stared at him irritably while I strapped the sheath of my sword over my back, and my Barnett crossbow comfortably slung over my shoulder. "Depending on whose Council it is, actually, I don't overly care whose it is. If it is only a small group migrating, say fifty or less, I want you to slaughter them all. We'll send a message. There are to be no survivors, so survey their numbers accurately. We can't have any one of them returning and announcing that a coven forced this assault. Times like these are testy before the Council gatherings, and with the war to come, they'll more than likely presume it was another Council. We need to rattle that, have them deciding whether they want to launch minor attacks before the meeting or not. Lydia has a large range of knowledge when it comes to identifying covens and Councils. Use her to distinguish whose group it is and then if possible, annihilate them." My blood pounded at the thought of being able to sweep through the masses of vampires and slaughter them. "I've given you my elite team. The youngest here is five hundred and thirty-two years old, excluding Balzar. You will only need the twelve to take down fifty or so of them."

"If I need their help, I will use them," I said arrogantly, receiving the reaction from Cesar that I wanted. If I had a team I would use them, but I wanted to see how he would react when I challenged his order.

"Now, don't go doing anything brazen or I won't allow you to lead again, you understand me, little miss?" Cesar opposed, but not as harshly as he had any of his sons. It was a desirable asset to be in a position of power when I had for so many years been watching over my shoulder within the Guild. I now realized I'd been branded a Token so Campture could keep a closer eye on me.

"Crystal clear," I said. "Well, we're ready when Tythian is."

Tythian emerged from a black hole within the wall. "Apologies, I assumed the fatherly speech, and overprotectiveness of his only daughter would go longer. Shall we? I can take two at a time comfortably." Tythian offered his hand out to Lydia and me. We both accepted it and were teleported into the bright orange haze of the sun seeping into the day. The fog around my feet vanished around me as our sudden appearance pushed it away. I squinted at the rising sun, uncomfortable by the itchy feeling it left on my skin.

"You're only a new vampire, aren't you?" Lydia asked inquisitively as she watched my reaction. "Keep to the trees, it helps block it out slightly. Try not to think about it, but it gets easier for some in time, eventually." The trees that surrounded us were half dead, with very little leaf coverage. I highly doubted they would block much sun. I recalled Chase explaining to me that vampires couldn't always walk in the day, but it was because of the human era and the pollution that went into the sky, that helped censor out the sun that enabled them to do so. Even then, he mentioned it could still be irritable. Mist swept over our feet as Tythian teleported the group in lots of two. Within the minute, all twelve members were with me. I looked at their sizes and weapons, assuming the best structure for the group.

"Okay, we'll go in an arrow format. I'll lead at the point, and expand further out. When we reach visual distance from where they're camping, I'll halt us. We stay as a wall and don't break structure," I commanded.

"Usually, we circle the unit when we're going to attack," one of the members stated.

"Which weakens our wall because we have thinned our line of attack. No matter your strength, it is much easier to be an efficient wall where we can help one another, then being spread out. Now, who was the scout that found them?"

A short man with long white hair stepped forward. "I did." His tone was crisp, and his body looked to be an old man's. Yet the wrinkles that covered his face were only an illusion of the years of fighting and tact he probably had.

"You'll stay close to my side and will lead the way." I gestured for him to position beside me. "All right, let's move out," I said, commanding the elderly vampire to start leading. The sun irritated my skin as we ran through the foliage amongst open areas of dead grass and sweeping fog. The irritation of my skin only worsened the higher the sun rose in the sky. I tried not to think about it, but the itching sensation of my blood boiling, couldn't be easily censored. We ran for hours until we came to a halt for a moment of rest. Running at vampire speed was far greater than my hunter team could ever acquire. We were still on the outskirts of the enemy's camp and took a moment to rejuvenate.

I sat on a log in the corner of my group, watching over them cautiously to ensure they stayed close, in case we were attacked. After scouting the area and having two positioned on lookouts, I was relieved to know for the moment, we were safe. I unsheathed my sword, admiring its shine from the sun. I never thought I would see this again.

Balzar approached and sat next to me, admiring the sword as I did. He uncomfortably shuffled, his back hunched over as he clasped his hands together.

"I'm sorry I was rude to you," Balzar said in a barely audible tone.

"What was that?" I asked. He shot me a daring look before inhaling deeply in defeat.

"It's just different. The coven doesn't like change, I don't like change. The coven is my family. It was my way of protecting it." He was quiet for a moment. After an awkward silence, he licked his lips and continued. "Did it hurt when you were turned, did you have to die first?" he asked curiously. I looked at him, surprised by his question, and the way he looked around at the other vampires to see if they were listening.

"No, it just sort of happened. I lost control and it sort of unearthed itself. Now I can't un-trigger my vampirism," I said honestly. He nodded, absorbing the information. "How did it happen for you?" Balzar's grip tightened on his other hand, the skin over his knuckles turning white. I couldn't gauge what the sudden change in his character was. All the brothers were different in their own way. I imagined Cesar didn't just turn anyone without a particular reason.

"I actually was team hunter once, a human, but I had believed in your kind and mission. When we tried to reclaim the White House and military resources in the year 2100, hunters and humans fought alongside one another. That was how it once was.

I was one of the soldiers there. The humans underestimated the Vampire Council. Or should I say, maybe they were just too weak. I was affected by one of the explosions. I was pinned by a part of the roofing; one of the metal poles pierced through my shoulder. I was bleeding out as I watched my fellow soldiers, both hunters and humans swarm around me in death or screaming in pain. I heard those who were in distant rooms being overrun by vampires. They cried for mercy, but the vampires didn't offer it. I could hear their screams muffled by their own blood. And I knew I was next. I would either be found by the Council or by sabers when night came, or I hoped that I would have bled out before any of that. Rather cowardly, I suppose."

Balzar looked up as one of the other vampires sent a questionable look our way. It appeared that Balzar streaked slightly red. "I'm embarrassed, okay. I acted like a dick. But it's so frustrating being the only one without a gift. And then your hunter friend came, and I thought it was easy for the taking. And then you were angry, so I got angry. And I get angry a lot, and I seem to apologize a lot afterward," Balzar began rambling.

"Tell me the rest of your story," I cooed him, interested in how it led him to Cesar and the others; it also subdued the red in his cheeks, so he could tell his story, instead of blubbering on in apologies. An apology I was surprised to receive from him, but didn't overly care for.

"My story…" Balzar continued. "I was bleeding out and was surprised when a blonde woman beside me, who was wearing the same human soldier gear that I wore; I thought her dead, got straight up and brushed herself off. I remember her voice as clear as day when she got up and dusted herself off. 'You've got to be fucking kidding me. No one told me I had to deal with bombs,' she'd said. Two vampires came into the room, hungrily awaiting and applauding the meal they were about to enjoy. I still didn't understand how she'd survived. She looked directly at the vampires and told them to 'back the fuck off,'" Balzar scoffed in amusement. "I thought, *how does a woman stand so confidently against them in such a way.* And then as the vampires lunged for her, I saw that the 'she' turned into a 'he.' It was Yolo. Within seconds, he ripped at their throats with his fangs. Before he leaped from the broken and blown up third level of the building, I reached out to him. I didn't fear challenging him, I was going to die anyway. *'How can you kill so easily? How do you have so much strength and justify it?'* I asked him angrily. I had always thought it was so unfair that these creatures of darkness could overpower us so easily with what seemed like an unlimited amount of strength.

It intrigued him, to say the least, because he crouched in front of me and just stared and watched me as if looking into my soul. I didn't fear him like I did the others, or maybe I just didn't care at that point if I died. With one swift movement, he ripped the pole from my shoulder and bit into his own wrist and fed me his blood. He threw me over his shoulder and within minutes, we were on the outskirts of the city. He dropped me in front of Cesar and said, 'we should keep this one.'

Before I knew it, Cesar had bitten me, injected his venom, and snapped my neck. I woke two days later during the night as a vampire." Balzar tapped on his hand, his tongue poking in his mouth as he absorbed his memory.

"It was only a coincidence that me and Yolo met, he was just there to monitor and see the results of the fight. To inspect which Council members were involved and which direction the humans ambushed from. I've learned a lot since being a vampire. I now know that the humans were in way over their heads and never stood a chance. But when I was born, the change in the human world had already happened, we were already at the bottom of the food chain. So to fight for that, well, we were raised to believe we had no option. Cesar gave me an option. He gave me a better life, on the winning side, and race that will sustain. I'll always be loyal to Cesar and the coven for that." I now understood why Cesar entrusted Balzar to fight within his elite group, despite his younger age. He was a soldier, tact and fighting was what he knew and comforted him most, such as myself.

"Esmore," the elderly vampire interrupted. "There's movement within the Council, they're starting to release their own scouts. Only three so far."

"Erase them, let's move forward and decipher their numbers. We'll then decide if we wait another day or attack now," I said, scraping my sword back into its sheath. "Balzar, stay on my right," I said. He accepted. For now, this was the only form of lenience and acceptance I could offer him. I would allow him to fight by my side. We held a comradery for having once both been tricked into fighting for the losing side. Even then, we were still soldiers that were sent out to a new mission. One that would ease our nerves as we fought on the battleground and were victorious in our own right. We both needed this, and I hoped that fate would play on our side today so we could.

CHAPTER 8

W**E HID AMONGST** the elongated dry grass. It was a prime position on top of the hill where we could look down on their campsite. It was a mistake on their behalf, to be within an open area that had little foliage. They were situated in a cave, but it wasn't a secure spot for them to hide in. Lydia crouched beside me and Balzar hid behind the tree on my right. The others waited further back. It was reported that their spotters had already been disposed of. Efficiently, and quietly, and had not yet set off their alarm. It only gave us a few minutes until they became wary of their scouts not returning. We studied them. Lydia looked majestic hunched over and carefully watching them. She was looking for any major detail of a certain vampire, which would indicate whose Council they were a part of and stipulate their numbers.

The vampires swarmed around the entrance, which forced me to presume it wasn't a very deep cave. I focused my exceptional hearing within the cave. I was trying to count the number of feet that shuffled, giving me a suggestion of the group's size. I couldn't hear as clearly as I would have liked, and if we were any closer we would give our position away.

Lydia squinted, her eyes situated on a particular vampire who now walked into the open. "See the vampire with the prosthetic leg?" she whispered so quietly that I would have missed it unless I focused on her lips. I squinted as she did and focused my sight. My senses took a little longer to hone in, unlike hers. She was used to her vampirism for over five hundred years. I, however, was just learning the advantages to it.

"Yes," I replied, spotting him.

"There is one vampire who was turned with a prosthetic leg, he is well known because he was considered a bit of a joke. It isn't Oppollo's Council, but it's Tracey's. Her people come from the frozen land, at the bottom of the world where it is glazed in ice and snow, formerly known as Antarctica. Usually, they dispatch a small team of thirty. But on occasion, depending on the task, she has been known to send half her fleet."

"Which could be?" I asked, studying them for a bit longer. Obviously, he'd lost his leg before becoming a vampire, or it would have healed and reformed itself.

"About two hundred," she said, with great consideration.

"Esmore," Balzar interrupted. "I can only guess, but I doubt there are that many. Their footing inside the cave suggests there to be less, and to have two hundred vampires in there, they would have a lot more spotters than three." I considered this. So Balzar was using the same tactic as me.

"What would they be so far inland for? It isn't yet time for the separate Councils to form and have their meeting. And if Tracey, their leader, isn't with them what other reasons could they have?" I asked.

"Well, we haven't yet confirmed if Tracey is or isn't in there. But my guess is there has been talk for a while, that she wishes to relocate her Council. They lack in food and resources. So, perhaps they're trying to find a new area to call home."

"Hmmm," I pondered. "I think we could send a nice message."

"If Tracey is in there, Esmore, it's a serious offense to kill a Council leader," Lydia said. She wasn't alarmed by it, just offered the facts.

"Declaring war is a serious matter," I purred, with the thought of slicing through them all. I turned to the other vampires who hid behind me. "We have less than an hour, and the numbers aren't yet verified. The Council leader, Tracey, could be in there. But I say that Cesar wanted us to send a message. If we kill every single one of them, no one will know it was us, but will only think it to be a direct assassination from another Council. I suppose, we could return and report, or... we could have some fun. What do you all say?" I arched an eyebrow as I opened my arms wide, suggesting for them to step out.

The smiles and nods in agreement were overwhelming. Their fangs gleamed in the irritating sun. Some had already begun to pull out their weapons. I turned to Balzar, who tightened his strap around his knuckles with a certain smugness. Lydia stood beside me, unsheathing her own blade. No one opposed. This was what we loved and thrived for. If we were to live forever, then why consider the consequences.

"No one is to survive. Those who allow someone to escape will be beheaded. I don't take failure well," I said. I cracked my neck to the side, unsheathing my blade and tightening my grip on my crossbow. The thought of the taste of their blood, the splutter of red over my blade and face, consumed me. My blood pumped for the assassination. I protracted my fangs, their piercing sensation through my gums like an elixir. I felt relieved in this form, like my true self. I opened my eyes feeling near to ecstasy, my vision hazed with the purple of my hunter's eyes. "Kill them."

The swarm of my vampires propelled around me, as I let the wind from their speed sweep past me in satisfaction. This power was beautiful, and this dark luscious form was my own. Not wanting to miss out on the fun, I launched myself into the hill daring to kill all those who opposed me. Even if they screamed for mercy, they would be at the end of my blade.

I launched forward, daring to test my limits and how far I could now go. The Council vampires were ready as soon as we made our attack, but not prepared enough. I watched my force go down and make an impact, like a giant wave from my extension. They were under my command, this power and pure driven lust of killing—they were an extension of my blade. They towered over the others, both on my left and right.

I came in strong and smiled at the first vampire who challenged me. I dipped away from his sword as he attempted to bring it down on me. I swirled behind his back and brought my sword up through his spine. But it wasn't enough, he wasn't damaged enough. I had to break him. I threw my blade into the air, to free my hand. I plunged my hand into his back as he tried to turn on me. I ripped his spine out of his back and enjoyed the crunch of his vertebrae as I broke them between my fingers.

His body sagged, no longer able to stand upright. My sword swung beautifully in the air and down toward me, where I caught it perfectly. Before he hit the ground, I crouched and sank my blade deep into his chest, before his spine could self-heal. His corpse blackened and decayed over me.

Another vampire came for me from behind. I rested my crossbow over my shoulder and shot her in the chest, killing her instantly.

Another vampire came at me on my right with a giant hammer. I pulled my sword out from the corpse of the first vampire, cutting it up and through its shoulder. I braced my sword in front of my face and challenged the hammer's strength that came down on me. I smiled, enjoying how many vampires provoked me. I flicked the hammer away and spun into a standing position, kicking him across the face, and forcing him to take a few steps back for balance.

Behind him, Balzar, silently crept up and plowed his bladed knuckles into his back and reefed out his heart. The vampire's body began to decay. Balzar had a certain gleam in his eye. When I looked around, all of the coven vampires did. They were thrilled and enjoyed the kill. I threw my sword toward Balzar's face, surprising him as he thought I was aiming for him. Well, maybe I was going for a little of a scare tactic. The vampire, who stalked him from behind, dropped instantly backward when I pierced him in the chest. I winked at Balzar, tormenting him.

His attention was grabbed by the Council vampires who ran up the hills. I mounted my next arrow and aimed my crossbow into the distance and shot them one by one. All six of them would've been deployed to report to their leader. Balzar covered my back and fought off any vampires who might have thrown off my aim. Once all six were shot down, I ran to collect my sword out of the corpse, to finish the job. From such a long distance, I hadn't hit all of them accurately in the heart. My new heightened senses overcompensated my angle and distance. Three of them, upon the hill, ripped out the arrows. Few of them still fumbled on the ground. I was going to enjoy bringing down my sword and piercing it into their chests.

The first one couldn't get up in time and still groveled on the ground. I had shot him only centimeters from his chest. I'd been so close to my mark but not close enough. With one swift movement, I plunged my sword into his chest with great satisfaction. I ran at the second vampire, who was on his feet and ready to run. I pounced on his back and wrapped my legs around his waist. He grabbed one of my legs, peeling it off and threw me into one of the trees. I flipped in the air and crouched against the tree. My calves flexed, and I propelled myself forward and my sword deep into his chest.

I couldn't see the last vampire. I honed my hearing to listen out for his footsteps. He was running amongst the dead trees. With a wicked smile, I gave chase, exhilarated by the run. He knew I was pursuing because he'd stopped. He was close, but I wasn't sure where. I stopped in amongst the trees, trying to pinpoint his location. Silently he dropped from above and onto me. He took a bite of the flesh from my collar bone. I felt his sharp teeth graze the bone. I kicked him off, irritated by the bite and the blood that oozed from me.

"Who are you?" he snarled. "Do you know who we are?" I arched an eyebrow at him, humored by the idea of his superiority.

"I don't care for titles, but do you know who I am?" I purred as I stood up. "I'll most certainly be the last thing you see. I am your death." I shot two arrows at him, but he was fast and dodged them. He ran toward me and pulled three daggers out, darting them at me. I dodged two and swiped the last one away with my sword. He jumped on me and tried to punch me. I sidestepped him and lodged my sword into his ribs. He was frozen, unable to move as I pinned him. I enjoyed that moment, where he was frozen at my mercy, with nowhere to go. Slowly, I continued to edge my blade further up toward his heart. He was struggling. He wanted to keep fighting but had nowhere to go. Too far to the left, he'd slice his own heart. Too far to the right and well, the sword was too deeply imbedded for him to unpeel himself. This disgusting vampire had no chance against me now.

"I wonder how long until my tip pierces your chest. Shall I sing you a lullaby to sleep?" I relieved him of his pain, reefing my sword out from his ribs. I wanted to toy with him a little longer. He tried to claw at my face with such a sluggish speed while still recovering that it was almost commendable. I stepped back. With one clean sweep, I severed his head from his body. His head flew into nearby shrubbery. I stood there for a moment, allowing the irritating sun to burn at me like a wave of victory. I wanted more, I needed to kill more.

With vampire speed, I raced back to the bloody field, but the coven vampires had already slaughtered them all.

With blood smeared across her face, Lydia walked up to me, greeting me with an accomplished smile. "Sixty-two was the number of vampires here." I was disappointed there was no more to toy with. We must have been fighting for only ten minutes, at most.

"I killed eight, but let us not keep track," Balzar toyed with the others. They began calling out the numbers they'd killed today as if it were a competition. I was disappointed that I hadn't any more. I searched my team's numbers. No casualties, they were as superior and efficient as Cesar had said.

"Then let us not keep Tythian waiting," I mused. I sliced my sword sharply through the air to flick the blood off before sheathing it again.

"Yes, Ma'am, I'm so parched after that," one of the vampires said with a gleam of victory. I too smiled, it was a victory, and the team I lead was safe. But I wanted more, that irritation burned more than anything. I needed more. My fun had been over far too quickly.

We waited for Tythian at the meeting point. I was irritated that we'd already achieved our goal so efficiently, that we now had to wait for him impatiently. Finally, he arrived. He summarized our bloodied faces and weapons.

"Right, so it went that way," he said. The vampires laughed amongst themselves, but Tythian lacked in humor. He took the vampires in pairs, leaving Balzar and me until last. In that brief moment of us being alone, we both looked behind into the trees. There was a new presence that surrounded, more vampires. I could feel their very presence animating, and they were slowly surrounding us.

Tythian teleported back, and before he could grab either of us or say anything, I raised my finger to him to be silent. He gave me a scornful look, before noticing we were not alone.

Tythian teleported elsewhere. There was an outburst of voices, who claimed to have seen something in the trees. More than likely, Tythian was inspecting the group.

"We're leaving," Tythian said, teleporting back to us.

"No, we're not," I snarled. If there were more to fight I wanted the delicious thrill as a private treat. But it was too late, he'd already grabbed Balzar and me. The nauseating sensation of being swept through darkness consumed me once again. Tythian had returned us to the coven. "What was that?" I demanded, shoving his hand off of me. *I could have had a glorified blood bath*, I thought uneasily, with the satisfaction and pleasure it would've given me. My skin wanted to glow under the many corpses that I was victor too.

"Get over yourself. That was not your fight or mission. That was Chase's coven. That's his problem," Tythian said. I snarled at him, my fangs wanted to dive into his neck. I lunged for him, but the difference in our age and speed was evident. He slammed me against the rocky wall. One hand firmly grasped around my throat, the other casually hung over my head as he leaned in to speak to me.

"Control the monster you've become, look at yourself," Tythian scorned disgusted. Before I could respond, I fell back into the wall. Tythian had teleported me and dropped me into Cesar's room.

"Esmore?"

I snarled in a foul mood at the person who dared speak my name. I spun, baring my fangs, and froze when I locked eyes with Dillian who stared at me mortified and cautiously. I looked over my positioning, which was ready to attack. I looked like the sabers and vampires that had attacked us many times before.

"Aww, my baby vamp girlfriend returned. Let me handle this, Dillian," Chase said with a charming smile. "Grab Julia and take her to the other room. I'll handle this." With great hesitation as to whether he should move, Dillian turned his back to me. He reached out to Julia who sat at the wooden table, petrified. Chase walked over to me and crouched to my level.

"Somebody had a little too much fun today," he mused with a mischievous smile. He trailed a finger over my cheekbone, which shot flares that danced against my skin. I wanted the flames to fulfill a much deeper urge in me that hungered. I slammed Chase into the closest wall, wanting him entirely. Chase was mine, and I wanted to claim him all over again. He didn't seem shocked by my movement, but only laughed at my dominance. Just as quickly, he flipped me onto my back and pushed me into the jarred and rocky wall.

He traced his fingers over my lips, his eyes burned with the same desire. "You make it hard to say no, Esmore," he purred. I nipped at his finger and drew blood in a playful tease. I rolled the taste in my mouth, savoring it and wanting more. This is when I felt closest to Chase.

"But, unfortunately, my love, I can't have you in this state. Don't get me wrong, I like it rough." He cupped his hand under my ass and raised my heat to his hard shaft. "I want you more than anything, in this state." He licked the salty taste of both blood and sweat from my neck. My body thrummed for him, and the thirst was almost excruciating.

"We need to keep you in check. I can't have you like this. Not now, when you have no control." He smiled sweetly and kissed down my neck and collar bone. I could feel him intruding in my mind. He raced a calming effect over my entire body. I wanted to fight him and push away the peace he placed over me. I wanted to ravage him, and I knew he wanted the same. Gently, he let my feet touch the ground. I swallowed shakily. His tranquility pooled into my eyes.

"We can't here, not like this Esmore. I'll only take you when you're in control," he said, kissing my forehead softly. With the softness of his lips and influence in my mind, I felt relieved. Slowly, the monster that had taken over today was receding into a quieter place, where I could now properly think. I furrowed my eyebrows in confusion. How had I let myself be taken over without even realizing it? I had reveled in the thought. I retracted my fangs, my vision now clear as my hunter's eyes vanished.

Chase grabbed me and held me close to his chest. With vampire speed, he took me to the other room and placed me gently into a small stream of water. I couldn't rid my internal disgust. The sensation of being a vampire and how good it felt had overpowered me.

"Just because I'm being chivalrous, doesn't mean I don't want to scrub your back." Chase winked. He peeled my leather shirt off and gulped at the satisfaction he had when looking at my bare chest. He grabbed a cloth and began to rub away the dried blood. "Now, you naughty little thing, tell me everything that happened."

CHAPTER 9

I INFORMED CHASE of the assassination, which came as no surprise to him. He already knew I'd thirst in such a way. Chase and the brothers had predicted I'd have little control in such a position of power. I soaked in the water, enjoying the sensation as it passed over my naked form. I needed to refocus on what was important, and my ultimate goal before my desire for power consumed me. I was too quickly overcome and ravished by the monster within. No, not a monster, my vampire self.

Chase had rolled up his jeans, so he could dip his feet into the water. He lay back comfortably on his elbows, looking at nothing in particular. "You have something else to tell me, don't you?" He hummed in assumption. I finished scrubbing my hair and began to braid it. "Come here, Esmore, I can do that for you." I drifted over to him, the water around me rippling.

"You can braid?" I asked with a promiscuous smile.

"I used to for my mother when I was younger. Even if she were ill, she still had to look presentable when entering the village. And, I'm practically amazing at everything I do, so don't be so shocked," he teased with a cocky smile. I tried to picture a younger Chase who cherished his mother so dearly. I turned my back to him and gave him my hair. He began to comb through my hair with his fingers. I hadn't told him everything. I was wary about how to tell him that the coven he'd been avoiding for his entire vampire life, is still hunting him.

"Before we left with Tythian, only Balzar and I remained. There was the presence of many more vampires that swarmed around us, after the assassination. Tythian wouldn't let me further inspect the matter myself. He'd teleported us both once he confirmed who it was." Chase continued to braid my hair. He slightly paddled his feet in the water while listening. I stopped him by placing my hand on his and looked over my shoulder. I needed to see what expression he would show. "Chase, Tythian confirmed it was your coven."

Gently, Chase straightened my face to look forward and continued braiding. "Oh, is that so? Well, I am thankful to Tythian for taking you out of that environment."

"Why are you thankful to Tythian?!" I snapped and tried to reface him. But again, he readjusted my posture so I was looking forward. He continued to braid my hair. I felt his presence hover over my mind again, enforcing his calm self. Was I really unable to control myself that much?

"It's not Tythian's fault I avoid that coven. It's mine alone, so don't blame Tythian. I would have asked him to do the same thing," he said calmly.

"But, why? I could have helped you with that problem. I can fight them, Chase, if you—"

"No." He pulled back on my hair lightly. I looked up at him. His gray eyes pooled into me calmly, yet there was an edge of protectiveness in them. Chase and I had an uncanny knowledge of how one another felt, even one another's thoughts without relaying words. Was that the power of being one another's familiar, or simply because we were so comfortable together? "I *forbid* you to make contact with them. This is not your fight, Esmore. Although we'll always aid in fighting each other's battles, this is one I must conquer myself."

"Why do you fear me helping you? What do they have over you that has had you running for so long?"

Chase pressed a kiss onto my forehead. "That is a part of my past, Esmore. That is something only I can challenge and defeat. I don't see it as simply, a vampire fight and going in for the kill. That coven represents the demons of my past, the decisions I made, and the life I once had.

And still I am too weak to face them. I do not fear challenging them. I fear accepting what I've become. I never wanted to be a coven leader. I didn't know of those rules and leadership regulations. Even if I had known, I would have probably still murdered that vampire who stripped my mother away and into a vampire. I don't want to be a coven leader. For now, I am content to aid you in whatever way you need me. My only focus is on you, Esmore. To me, that coven is only a step back and a distraction. I've made no claim to them in the past, and want nothing to do with them now."

Chase gently placed my freshly braided hair over my shoulder. I flicked it back and forth, considering his words, *his previous life*. It was so surreal to have the same body and look the same, yet to now feel entirely different, like a completely different creature altogether. I had no idea who, or what I was anymore. And Chase had lost himself over four hundred years ago.

"You are beautiful." Chase kissed my cheek and slowly spun me around, creating ripples through the water. He held out his hand to help me out. "Let me remind you of what you are here for. You are here to help your friends Dillian and Julia. You will find them a place where they are safe. What happens after that is your choice. But for now, that is what you are focusing on. Your next step is to go to the human compound with Yolo. This was your decision, and I support it, as long as you feel like you have full control." Chase pulled me out of the water and held me close to him. I inhaled his intoxicating smell.

"You always know what to say to me," I purred. For all my independence and strength, I found myself to be further lost by every step I now took. Chase was my only solid foundation that connected me to reason and my hunter self.

"That is because I am basically a God." He smiled sheepishly. I punched him in the stomach in flirtatious play. "Now put these on, some fresh clothes for you, and go talk to Dillian. Remind him that you are still you, and that you're safe to be around."

"I think he'll fear and hate me by how I reacted before," I said, self-conscious of my actions. I broke my physical contact with Chase, which dispersed that awful sensation of emotion.

"He won't hate you," Chase said, tucking part of my fringe behind my ear. "Esmore, you won't win if you try to hide from your vampire self, you need to find balance and learn to control it. Don't deny that it's a part of you. You need to be honest with him. Now go," Chase said, slapping my ass. "And come back to me later, to remind me of how amazing and handsome I am." He began walking out of the bathroom.

"Where are you going?" I asked, collecting the clothes from the ground.

"To find and talk with Tythian."

"You can't go out there by yourself. What if the others find you and—"

"Are you worried about me, Esmore?" Chase cooed as he rested his arm on the doorframe. "I am no weak, lost puppy. I can look after myself. And don't forget, I am as stubborn as you. You can't tell me what to do." He winked, before racing out at vampire speed. If I weren't entirely naked, I would have given chase. But he was right, I had to make amends with Dillian and Julia. I needed to refocus on my prior goal and stay connected to my hunter self. Dillian always advised me and looked after me. I had to depend on that stability and do my best for them. They were in this situation and underground labyrinth because of me.

I flicked my braided blonde hair over my leather sleeveless shirt and walked toward the other room. The door was closed. I knocked on it lightly, waiting for Dillian's permission to enter. Cautiously, he permitted me to do so.

I could feel the tension in the air. There wasn't much to the room; a spacious bed, wardrobe, and corner chair. I leaned against the back of the door and closed it. Julia no longer held fear in her eyes at the sight of me. It was Dillian's expression that hurt the most—that I was affected by most.

"I'm sorry about before. I'm struggling to adjust to this new *part* of me," I said honestly. Dillian said nothing and only watched me. There was something that I needed to know, something I had to ask him. I wasn't yet sure if I was prepared for the answer, but either way, I would make sure he and Julia were safe. "Do you hate me now, Dillian? Finding out that I'm part vampire, it's something I can't change. A hunter's natural instinct is to kill vampires, and that feeling still resides within me. But, I can't deny the presence of my other self any more. Do you hate me and want to kill me?"

Dillian looked at Julia, who prompted him to speak. The numerous bars in his ear reflected against the small candlelight.

"I don't hate you, but it's hard, Esmore, as you said, it's our natural instinct. But, I still see you as my friend, not a disgusting vampire. I'm scared for you because you are my friend. Don't prove me wrong in that matter. Don't rely on that ability, rely on your own. You're one of the strongest huntresses I know. You are a Token Huntress, Esmore. You are also my best friend. I had made amends with losing my life that day when you rescued Julia and me. But now being here, I feel more stuck and tortured than ever, and I feel weak because I can't completely protect Julia or do anything."

"That's not true." Julia gasped and grabbed Dillian's hand. "You know I would have chosen to go anywhere you did. I'd rather be stuck here with you if only for a few weeks, than lose you to Campture."

"You both don't need to speak in such a way," I said, wanting to dispel their misconceptions for their safety. "I've already vowed I'll protect you both and find you refuge, that's my main focus. It's not going as quickly as I'd like, but I have to play by their rules to get anywhere. Tomorrow, I'll be going to the human compound. There I'll see what I can find and study their structure. If that's not deemed safe then I'll convince Tythian to teleport us to the human camp near our old Guild."

"Just help us escape, Esmore, we can handle it from there," Dillian said confidently. He was a fine warrior indeed, but I wasn't entirely sure whether they would survive on their own. Not because I doubted Dillian's strength, but I doubted Julia's. Her plant enhancement and growth ability would sustain them for food, but Dillian would do anything to protect her. If a formidable group or sabers attacked them, I was confident he'd protect her at any cost. She wasn't trained to be an elite warrior as we were.

"I considered the same, and I'd have joined and protected you both nearing the Guild. However, there's no way of escaping, other than Tythian's teleportation. The entrance to these underground tunnels is also the home to a large group of sabers. We'd never be able to escape through such a passage. Cesar's gift enables him to cloak our very presence from them. It's also a deterrent for foreigners to attack. Tythian is our only option, but he's withholding his generosity until I do something in particular for him."

"Sabers?" Julia gasped in surprise. Although it was a shock, it also made perfect sense. Cesar was a clever leader, but that could easily go down like a double-edged sword if he were severely weakened for any reason.

"Give me a few more days. I'll find us some place to go. But, please don't fear me. Now that I know the extent, or should I say, lack of control over my vampire side, I won't let that happen again," I said. I wasn't confident that I could learn to master it by myself, however with Chase by my side, he'd never let me lose control to it again. In this sense, I had to admit I was entirely indebted to Chase for being the only person able to pull me out of such a frenzy. Not even I had the control to do that. Footsteps approached Cesar's room.

"Someone's coming, stay here," I hushed. I closed the door behind me and guarded the double wooden doors.

"Oh, hey baby sis," Yolo gleamed. "I saw Balzar and thought you might be here. Cesar wanted an updated report, but it appears Lydia already told him. Good job, that's a decent sized group to take down on your first outing. I bet Thomas is going to be pissed when he hears about it." Yolo began laughing to himself. "Also, your familiar shouldn't really be walking around by himself. I saw him with Tythian a little while ago, but still."

"My familiar does whatever he likes, I'm not his keeper," I said, crossing my arms over my chest.

"You're so cold to me." Yolo's eyes teared up theatrically. "And here I was, coming out of the kindest of my heart, to see if you were thirsty—"

"I'm not," I said, cutting him off.

"Well, that's rude, you should let one finish their sentence first. I also came to talk about tomorrow. So stop giving me sass and start respecting your older bro," he said with a lecturers tone and then a wink at the end.

"You're not my—"

"Yea, yea, whatever. Tythian said you lost control and turned into a savage. I can't risk taking you in like that. You understand that, right? The goal of what you did today and what you'll be walking into tomorrow, are entirely different. You cannot act out of accordance for one second, you'll have to act entirely human. Although the weakest on the food chain, humans aren't entirely dumb. I can't have you risking what I've already built." I tried to interrupt, but he raised his finger to me. "Like you're trying to protect your comrades and family, Esmore, I too am doing the best for mine. You're the only thing right now that will jeopardize what I've built for that goal. I will only take you if you honestly believe you're in control. If you break my trust, lose it, and destroy all that I've gained, let me assure you that I can do the same. I don't take kindly to liars and those who lack restraint. I'm a very reasonable guy, but this will depend entirely on you, as to whether your hunter friends survive within here or not. Mmmmkay?"

At first, my body was thrilled at the threat and challenge, but this was exactly what Yolo was talking about, this inexperience of mine. I gulped down that sensation, which too quickly came to the surface. He had every right to state so. "I understand, but I won't lose control."

Yolo looked at me for a moment thinking, entertaining an idea. "Okay, well, we need a safety word or something. If you are fixating on their military sector, while getting a feel for their function, to see if it's safe for your hunter friends, we won't be together most of the time. You can like mind read and stuff, can't you?" His bouncy attitude was giving me whiplash. It reminded me somewhat of Kora and Kasey. It was overly tiring.

"Sort of. I can communicate with Chase fluently. However, unless in a dream, I can't speak to others in such a way, only if they permit me and open their mind to me. Then I can do so." Yolo gave me a pained expression. Obviously, the thought of him opening his mind to me scared him. We all had our demons to fight and secrets to hide. "Besides that, I can send influential thoughts and such, but in a subtle way so they don't know I'm manipulating them."

"Well, that's kind of quirky. Just slam it into me. If something happens, find me and hit me hard with something so I know. Can you send me like a brief panic signal so like I'll be overcome with panic, and know that you're in trouble or something?"

Implementing the idea, I focused on Yolo's mind, like I would anyone else's. It was still a new skill to conquer. It surprised me how everyone's mind was different, and somehow I could decipher them apart from one another. It was fascinating that their mind was in a way, the same feeling I had of their personality. Yolo's was goofy but kind, experimental, but practical at the same time. He wasn't the most level headed person, but he was dependable. With a huge rush of panic and sensations of torture, I pressed them onto him hard. Yolo's eyes widened in fear. I dispelled the sensation. I now felt slightly connected to Yolo. What an odd experiment. Yolo took a few breaths and then began laughing. He scratched the back of his head.

"Holy shit woman, that is terrifying. Could you imagine if you like did that to a whole hoard of people? People would freak the fuck out." He laughed. "That would work. Can you do that from long-range, without looking at me?"

"I think I have a feel for you and can decipher you from others now," I admitted. I was still not fluent in my gift, only that of which Chase had shown me. I scanned over into the next room and was instantly connected to Dillian. Perhaps I could easily find those that I'd already connected with or had an implied impression of through their personality. I had never used my ability on Julia, yet I had the sense of her warm, innocent self, it definitely represented who she was in physical form.

"Okay, sweet as. Well, meet me at the same spot that Tythian had teleported you from this morning. You remember how to get there?" I almost tsked at his imprudence. Of course, I had been mapping out the place and inner tunnels.

"Yes."

"Okay, so eight hours? I know there's no clock, but when you are a vampire, you kind of have a sense of the day and when the sun begins to rise and then..." Yolo began to blabber on.

"I'll find my way, Yolo. Thank you for allowing me to come. I understand the hardship you've faced to get into that position, I won't fail you," I said sincerely. I had no option but to succeed if I wanted to please Tythian and find a way for the others to escape. I wanted to be left alone and rest for a time. I wanted to be surrounded in darkness where I could close my eyes and just simply be, while all the commotion in the previous days caught up with me.

"Okay, sweet, see you then, baby sis." Yolo smiled before walking back within the dark tunnel. I slipped down the door, resting against it for a moment and listening out for any other footsteps. I had to practice and remember my contact with humans and decipher how to *act* as if I was one. I exhaled, feeling exhausted. There was still so much to do, and time wasn't in our favor. It would only be a matter of time until the vampires within the coven turned on us and sought out Dillian and Julia. Maybe even Chase. I slumped at the door and closed my eyes, guarding it as I dove into a moment of silence. I just needed one second to myself.

CHAPTER 10

CHASE LAUGHED THE entire night as I practiced my impersonation of a human. I slouched, stumbled, and tried to slow my pace and speech. He enjoyed it far too much. He constantly asked me questions, where I had to respond as a person who had no recollection of whom they might be. He laughed at my obvious discomfort in trying to be the very creature I despised. Humans were so defenseless and vulnerable. That was never something I'd been exposed to, and trying to reflect that characteristic was frustrating. He didn't mention what he and Tythian spoke about. I was relieved he came back, without any other vampire attempting to attack him. He mentioned a few vampires who watched him from afar, but none approached. For now, Cesar's threat and orders were indefinite to this coven.

We even mock fought. In the likelihood that I was attacked by another human, I had to belittle my strength to match theirs, so it wouldn't be questionable. It felt to the equivalent of being air, instead of using any of my force. I had to pretend to be human when Chase brought me to the Council, but it didn't seem as difficult there, or so I presumed. I simply had to restrain myself. This was entirely different, and I didn't know what to expect.

"Are you thirsty? If even in the slightest, you should drink before you go or the temptation will be too great," Chase warned seriously.

Admittedly, I was. Chase smirked, susceptible to my agreeance. I didn't want to fight him on this matter when he only did it for my own good. He grabbed a bottle of distasteful blood for me and watched as I gulped it down with dissatisfaction.

"It tastes horrible," I admitted.

"Better you getting used to it bottled than fresh. Come here, you messy eater." Chase smiled, grabbed my hand, and tugged me toward him. He sat on the edge of the bed, his legs either side of me. He wiped away the smear of where the blood must have dripped.

"Chase, how do you view me now?" I asked. It must've been different for him as well, to see me now like this. Had he become comfortable with my hunter self or did he prefer that I was tainted as well?

"I think you're as sexy as always, and that I want to piss you off even more, now that you have the strength to match me. I like the fight." He winked. "Or I could convince you simply." He grazed his fingers up my abdomen as he stood up and looked down at me. His eyes held such pure passion that I knew I was entirely ensnared in his. He cupped the back of my head and licked the edge of my mouth where the blood had been. I parted my lips to match his. The fire he swelled inside of me was unmatched to any other sensation I could compare it to. He pulled away and smiled wickedly. "Very simple, Esmore, I am the one person you need not worry about judgment from. I'll always be yours and your first line of defense. I'll protect you no matter what, not even just you, but what we have. You're now, my only focus and entirety. So today, please be safe." He kissed my forehead and took the empty bottle from my hand. "Now go, it's time. I'll watch over the others. I trust that you won't blow your cover and hurt yourself. Come back to me, okay?"

"If you're lucky," I teased. He smiled cockily at the response and grabbed my hand, placing it on his belt.

"Or do I need to convince you in another way, to make sure you come back to me," he teased, arching an eyebrow. Before I was tempted, I pushed him away.

"I don't have all day to tease and play, Chase. When I have you, let me assure you that a few minutes will not be to my liking. We will need all day, *dear*," I teased as I walked away and out from Cesar's room.

I was hyper-aware of other vampires as I walked through the tunnels. I walked past a group who fed off a human, her eyes were glazed and almost nearing death. They fought over her like ravished animals. "Stop, you don't want to kill her," one of them said and pulled her away and into the shelter of his arms.

"I'm still starving," the other growled, but looked content as he patted his belly.

"Oh, hey, Esmore, whatcha doing?" one of the vampires asked me. I recognized him. He'd been a part of Cesar's elite team I'd led yesterday. The other vampire looked between us with uneasiness.

"Nah, she's cool, man," the other vampire said with a childish beam. "I'm telling you what happened yesterday is the truth. She ripped the spine from one of them and crushed it in front of him, she's badass." I ignored the praise and continued walking as if I hadn't seen or heard anything. That was something I didn't need to reflect on, however there was a part of me that smiled internally from the comment 'badass.' That obviously amused my vampire self, how egotistical it was.

Footsteps approached me from behind. I stopped and turned, waiting for this familiar and unpleasant vampire to seep from the shadows.

"They praise you as if you are some kind of leader now," Thomas snarled from the darkness. The short, black-haired vampire, walked out of the shadows. Lydia and Thomas were very different in approach and manner of speaking.

"Oh, you are still alive. What a shame, what a shame," I purred. "Did you come out to play childish games or do you have something to say that actually concerns me?"

"You're a smug little bitch aren't you?" he seethed, his fangs bearing. But I wouldn't mirror the image of him. I would not resort to my own inner vampire, no matter how much I wanted to. It begged me to let that part of me free. I had to prove to the others that I wasn't like this, exactly what Thomas looked like, an uncontrollable, furious, and dangerous vampire.

"I am a factual huntress who looks for results. I pity you if you're envious of what I achieved."

"I am not envious," he spat sharply.

"Oh good, because everyone took a liking to how I ran things. It seems that your presence is easily replaced, so it makes me feel at ease to know that this doesn't disturb you. Have a nice life," I said and turned my back on him. He leaped for me. He was fast. But I was strong too and at my full health once again. Not of a vampire, but of a huntress. This was the part of myself I had to rely on.

I avoided his grasping hands and kicked him to the wall. Before pouncing on his position, he too had already moved. He reevaluated me, it wouldn't be the same outcome as last time when we had fought.

"How long do you think you can keep up your little pretense of being in control of your vampire self? You're a new baby vamp who has no control over it. How I pity your little hunter friends who believe your lies. And when you're in a frenzy eating the very people you swore to protect, nothing will give me greater pleasure than to watch. Then when you are at your absolute peak, I will destroy your familiar in front of your eyes and slit your throat and behead you." I remembered my father's training of counting to ten, which quickly calmed me. I had to remind myself of those tactics and take his threat lightly.

"I'll kill you, I just don't have time for you right now. You see, I have a list of priorities, and you, Thomas, you're currently at the bottom—like you are right now, within this coven."

He lunged for me again with a wicked snarl, but I avoided him.

"I'll kill them all, your smug mother, I will rape and devour—" My sanity switched off at the mention of my mother. Before I could delve into that darkness that would relish in nothing more than to savor his blood and torture him to death, a hand caught Thomas' before he threw the knife he unsheathed from his belt.

"Is that a direct threat to your coven leader's familiar, Thomas?" Tythian asked. His grip was firm around Thomas' wrist. Behind him was Yolo in female form, with arms crossed over her bountiful chest.

"You put her up to killing me, didn't you?!" Thomas barked at Tythian. Tythian kept his composure, looking like a proper gentleman.

"My dear, Thomas, when you play a game, you play it tactfully and elegantly. And, you move your pawns at the right time. Esmore, is not one of my pawns, but a very purposeful piece on the board. And you are not.

"Your simple presence is an embarrassment to this coven. But don't worry, our father still has a use for you, like a dog almost. Maybe that's why he hasn't killed you yet. But I don't know, if after such an open threat." Tythian began to tsk. Thomas' expression continued to flicker between anger and composure. He understood his position here. "See, denying your true intentions until the very end of the game is how someone truly plays. So, as to your previous accusation, I have no idea what you're talking about, and if you dare speak to Cesar with this assumption, I might comment with your open threat of his familiar.

Somehow, I dare say that won't end well for you," Tythian remarked.

He threw Thomas' hand out of his grip with repulsion. He grabbed a silk handkerchief from his chest pocket and began wiping his hand.

"What's going on here?" Lydia hurriedly crept out from the tunnel where Thomas had entered, quickly analyzing the situation. She measured us all evenly, her brother in the center of the commotion.

"Nothing," Thomas snarled. "Let's go, Lydia." Thomas walked past her and waited for her to catch up. Lydia looked between us cautiously and followed him. We waited until they vanished. I wavered over Lydia's loyalty. Which would she chose, her coven or her blood relative? That one I couldn't yet predict.

"Take his threat seriously," Tythian said, still wiping his hand. "But don't be alarmed. He won't do anything now. He's not in a position to, but Thomas is tactful and clever. He also has a lot of say over other coven vampires within these tunnels. Try not to get too involved with him. Know that your mother is safe. She's the last person within these walls any vampire would dare to touch. Besides you, she is our top priority to protect, until she has been properly introduced into the coven."

"She wants to be a part of this?" I asked, surprised. I hadn't the chance to speak with my mother yet. So much was happening, like a whirlwind of different games being thrown at me and I had to learn the rules to every single one. Everyone had their own ambitions, and I was simply being used in the process, hoping that I was playing my own game to best benefit me and the others.

"I don't know. I take orders, I don't take particular interest in one's feelings. You can ask her yourself when you return. I'll let family matters remain with you." Tythian held out his hand to both Yolo, in his beautiful womanly form, and me.

Yolo offered me his hand with a beautiful and charming smile. It was hard to remember this stunning woman was the same person as the goofy male Yolo. She looked to be imported from an entirely different era of elegance and radiance that contrasted with this world's darkness. "Are you ready, Ellie, to be introduced to the human compound?" Her voice was silky and endearing.

I grabbed Yolo's and Tythian's hands at once, being sucked into the darkness and into a new place that I'd never known or knew what to expect. I was now Ellie, the human—I wondered how smoothly this would go.

CHAPTER II

TYTHIAN WAS ONLY there for a mere second, a glimpse that his existence was ever present. We were surrounded by dry and dying foliage. The mist poured around our ankles and cockroaches infested the crevasses that were in the ground. I could sense that the pollution was thicker here. The sun rose from the corner of the Earth, breaking into dawn. The sensation of it crawled over my skin. I wondered if this irritation from the sun would always be there. I questioned how severe it might be if I were fully vampire instead of only half. I looked at Yolo's slender shoulder's from behind, in his woman form, was he still affected by the sun's rays?

"It will take us two hours at human pace to reach there. Don't act out of character, this is the border I found that they didn't keep surveillance on, their weakest corner. It's a lot larger than you would expect," Yolo explained in his sweet womanly voice. "Follow my exact footsteps, Ellie, there are traps for vampires specifically around this area. If this goes sour, and when you walk through their security gates, the alarm goes off, and you're found out to be vampire, you must deal with it on your own accord. I can play naive, but don't ruin what I've built here."

"Wait," I said, pausing and trying to remember the façade I would now face as the human woman named Ellie. "What is your name again?"

Yolo smiled charmingly, he was in fact a beautiful woman. "I'm Jenn Cadolwadt: engineer and specialist at the Human Activist and Regaining Existence Movement. And you, Ellie, have suffered amnesia and the only thing you feel comfortable with or can connect with your previous life is that you're good at swordplay and crossbow shooting."

"Why don't we have weapons now? Won't they find it suspicious if we walk there? What if we get attacked?" I asked, pushing aside a tree branch and following Yolo's hurried pace. I noticed that he, or I mean, Jenn, was following a manmade trail.

"Don't worry about being attacked, there are enough booby traps around here to contain sabers or stray vampires. We've only ever had two incidences of our kind being taken. This entire field is a weapon for the humans. Besides, I always walk upon dawn, which reduces concern for being attacked. Although once, I only had to step twice to my left, and the saber was snagged within netting and thrown into the air." I looked into the high trees. The dead-looking trees didn't seem as if they could support such action.

"As for my living domain, it's somewhat unquestionable. There are a few other humans who were once outsiders such as myself, and slowly incorporated into leading roles. Some decided to live within the compounds, I however, didn't, for obvious reasons. Although it's a terrifying world, freedom is still an option. Don't get me wrong, I've had many male members gloat about how they could protect me and such," Jenn said. She flicked her hair over her shoulder, smug like. It was hard for me to remind myself that this was still Yolo. Sometimes I saw his personality shine through, but then other times I had to concede that he was truly the master at pretending to be human.

"But I don't need protection. My results as an engineer are highly praised within the compound, and they assume I have a system set up at my own lodgings. I was raised in the technology era, and it surprises me by how little the later generations know. I praise them for their efforts, a lot have self-taught or learned from generations before. As far as I understand, the compound was created a little over two hundred years ago. Since then, it's been formed as a safe haven, but also a prison for vampires. The humans have learned from them, simply by watching and examining them. I assume it's because they want to retaliate against the Vampire Council, but I haven't been told that directly. I'm not within their political hierarchy or circle. However, if you can learn a lot from their military sector, it'll be an absolute gain," Jenn said, giving me the thumbs up.

That was the part of Yolo that shone through, I imagine for only me to see. "It's been within the last fifty years that they've adjusted their methods and began experimenting on both vampires and humans. For example, Whitney, Tythian's familiar." He let the words linger in the air, so I could absorb that awful truth. "I help within that department, well my expertise does. It's disgusting watching it, but I can't make one single move against it unless instructed by Cesar. I wonder if he'll want to take the entire establishment down. But why, I say, when the Council can do it themselves. When I linger around this border in my usual form, I can sense others around. I think it's being closely watched. And as far as Cesar is concerned, if others are interested, we should be as well."

I continued following his footsteps along the very narrow path.

"You want to see if this is suitable for your friends?" Jenn said, pointing her chin higher. "My advice is not to bring them here. They're obviously hunters, because of their eyes. I think for certain, they'll become nothing more than an experiment. But if there is a glimmer of hope, I do hope you find it."

As Yolo predicted, it took us about two hours walking, at an irritably slow pace. I acknowledged Yolo's superiority in his patience. With hunter speed, I could have been there within minutes. The sun was now bearing down on me, which only agitated me further. I could feel my fangs wanting to slip out and snarl at the sun as if it were following only me.

I focused my gaze forward, ignoring the irritating burn. I could hear shuffling of feet which indicated there were people ahead. They wouldn't notice if I used my superior sight, smell, and hearing. These were the only things as a huntress I could rely on within this human compound, without giving myself away. I struggled to get through the pollution. There was so much mist that rose, even around my face. It usually wasn't so thick in the parts I'd come from. But it was clever and set as camouflage for their camp. I approached very tall fencing. It reminded me of the layout of my old Hunter Guild. The fence was tall and shrouded with mist and plant vines. The haze crept up the cemented walls, stagnating around its enormity.

"Please grab my hand, Ellie," Jenn said, offering her hand out to me. "You can trust me, it's safe here." I grabbed her hand and allowed her to lead me. In any other circumstance, I imagine no human would be able to see. Jenn grabbed hold of a rope, which led us onto a very thick piece of metal that acted as a plank. I pretended to be blinded by the mist and walked unsteadily.

"Try to grab hold of the rope on your left, Ellie, and watch your footing, this can be at times rough," she mused. I did as she said, pretending to miss the rope next to me a few times. Jenn grabbed a piece of rope that was lowered over her head. With a large tug and a moment of waiting, the piece of metal slowly began to lift. We were being escalated up the cemented wall. The higher we got, the thicker the mist seemed to get and then suddenly, as if revealing a whole new world, the mist vanished. I peered over the tall wall, which was higher than even my own Guild's. Two men pulled down on levers, which had slowly elevated us. They both stared at me, skeptically.

"It's wonderful to see you back safe Miss. Cadolwadt, who do you have with you?" one of the men asked. They were heavily guarded in metal armor. I tried to hide my eye roll as if such armor would protect them from vampires.

"Yes, my guest here has suffered from amnesia. I found her on my return to my home and have looked after her since. I'm shocked sabers didn't attack while she was lying down, unconscious. Bless the poor darling. I named her Ellie."

"She'll have to go through the scans, and you'll have to advise Mr. Richard," the man said. He returned Jenn's smile, blushing slightly. Obviously, Jenn had her techniques of flattery and manipulation. I wondered if Yolo had a laugh about how he could wrap these full-grown men around his finger.

"I will, thank you." Jenn smiled, stepping off the platform and onto the cemented wall. All around the large circular wall was wide enough for three people to comfortably walk along. I was surprised to see so clearly now, after the extent of the mist that cascaded below and against the wall. "This way, Ellie."

"I'll escort you, Jenn, we've had a few attacks while you were gone. It's always safer to be precautionary," the same guard announced. "Lower the escalator back down," he commanded to the other guard.

"From vampires?" I asked inquisitively. It wouldn't seem like such an odd question, from someone who would have been recently educated on vampires. Jenn gave the guard a nod in reassurance.

"I apologize, Ellie, I only told you of the vampires. There are other creatures within this area, specifically. In the old world, when war broke out, a lot of radiation and miasma were the result of that. We're safe within the compound, and if we don't stay too long in the mist outside, we're fine. However, there were animals from the human world that were affected. They have in a sense mutated to survive their environment. The guards on patrol here wear such heavy armor because the animals sometimes try to invade them. A few of our own have been picked off and eaten."

I looked between them, in what I imagined to be my best attempted expression of shock. I was surprised to hear this, Yolo hadn't informed me sooner.

"What form of animal is it derived from?" I asked, wondering if I'd be able to relate to the memory of the creature, or if I had even made contact with its breed before.

"There are a few," the guard said openly, as he continued to escort us on top of the wall. "The ones we have issues with most are a form of rodent. However, because of them, it also helps with the sabers, as a sort of repellent. They're singularly no match for the sabers, but I've once seen a pack of them take down a lone saber. They can efficiently look after themselves."

"You saw that?" Jenn gasped. "How brave." She put her hand on his shoulder in comfort. I tried not to smile. Jenn made it look too easy. How easily the humans had fallen for Yolo's charm.

I'd never heard of such mutations on creatures, in what part of the world were we? I looked down at the uneven cemented ground, and then over to my left where there was a thick metal. I couldn't see anything that was within the human compound from up here. It seemed to be a large dome concealing and protecting the inside. Along the wall, I had now seen three harpoons. I assumed they were used in defense against enemies and the rodents if they tried to scale the walls. It reminded me much of the tactics Cesar used. Better to keep a few enemies close, then the real ones closer. How presumptuous, yet clever at the same time. The humans assumed they could handle and kill the animals living around them, more than the monsters that lurked and waited to destroy this compound.

"The roofing is a thick layer, it helps us conduct more electricity when we eventually have thunderstorms and such," Jenn said, educating me as we walked.

"You make it sound so simple," the guard said as he strolled behind us.

"There are only a few things, Ellie can understand and recall, so I like to inform her in such a manner. However, I've found she's good at handling a sword and bow. I plan on taking her to the military sector after I give her a tour. I hope Sydney will be able to find a use for her."

"He won't just add anyone," the guard said begrudgingly. From his response, it might be difficult to weave my way into their hierarchy. Whoever this Sydney person was, I had to impress, which wouldn't be hard if I reined it in at human comprehension. I could test the limits of showing my skill, but to such a weak extent that they wouldn't be suspicious of my human self. Hand to hand combat was one of my greatest strengths, if I had to put on a show for the humans then so be it.

"You're grumbling again," Jenn teased, flicking his nose. We approached cemented stairs, where Jenn permitted the guard to leave. She gave me a wavered look, which advised me that we were approaching the scan. The remaining question lingered between us regarding whether I would be perceived as human, huntress, or vampire. I wasn't sure how their scan worked, but if only physically, I was recognized as human. I'd already thought of my missing heart to be of concern. But, Yolo had previously mentioned that with my mother's gift, a replacement of sorts was made. So, within the scan, it should still look as if I had a proper heart pumping and circulating my blood.

I followed Jenn further into the rocky foundation. After twelve steps in, one of the doors behind us closed abruptly. Low lights illuminated from the ceiling. It reminded me of the Council, they didn't use flames or candles, this was electricity. On my left was a well-lit white room, which had one male and female, who sat with items I had never even seen before. Was this what they called technology? The male typed vigorously on the board below his fingertips and continuously looked up at a screen. Was this a computer?

"Good Morning Miss. Cadolwadt, I see you've found a human. Please step her aside, she'll have to go after you. Protocol, of course." The woman smiled.

"Just watch after me, Ellie, it's safe," Jenn reassured. It was exactly how I imagined someone would treat a patient with amnesia. I tried to recall my contact with human children and how fearful they were of everything. I felt as if this was how Jenn treated me.

On either side of the narrow walkway, there were two large white poles. I could see long into the distance that there were small holes within the walls. I imagined that if a vampire walked through the scans and failed, no matter how quick they might be, that this would undoubtedly trigger a trap or their certain death. I looked behind me and noticed the same form of holes. If I was irregular on their scan, there was no way for me to escape unscathed.

Jenn walked between the two scanners. I wondered if Yolo had feared walking through for the first time, uncertain if his woman self would be competent enough for the scans. His gift was truly amazing, to be able to change his entire physical structure. I wondered if he stayed in that form permanently, if it aged and was only mortal.

Rays of small light beamed from either side and glowed over Jenn's skin slowly. The lights flickered green, and the man who watched the screen gave her the all clear. Jenn stepped out and turned to face me with a smile.

"Your turn, Ellie." Jenn smiled and gave a quick short glance at the holes within the walls, advising me of the trap, if I hadn't already seen it. She then looked down at the flooring. Exactly below where the scanners were positioned, I noticed the slight distortion in the ground. If I didn't move quickly enough, I imagined there was a trap door, and I would plummet into some form of pit. This whole walk was a trap for outsiders. The exchanged glances that Jenn had given me were so quick, that the others hadn't seen. But, I knew what she meant, what Yolo was relaying—be wary.

I stepped between the two white bars, inhaling deeply. *I am human, act human*, I reminded myself. The small white lights projected on my skin. I stood still, very still as if any movement might trigger a reaction. I focused looking forward, and prepared for the light to turn red. If it did, I had to run at vampire speed through to the entrance and jump off the top of the wall. Even as both vampire and hunter, I wondered if that would stun me for some time until I healed from such a massive fall.

The lights turned green, and the lady spoke through the glass. "Miss, what is your name?" I looked at her for a moment, surprised that I was permitted through. For a moment there, I thought I'd have to run. So on their scans, I was considered as human?

"Her name is Ellie," Jenn interrupted. She pulled me through by my shoulders, comfortingly. "For now until she regains her memories, she's an amnesia patient. I'm going to inform Mr. Richard. I hope to make a recommendation to Sydney, to put her in the military sector."

The man tapped at the little board underneath his fingertips and continued to stare at the screen.

"It has been noted," he murmured.

"Thank you," Jenn said with a wavering smile that he hadn't noticed. Jenn placed her hand on my lower back and paced me further into the tunnel. She gave me a side glance, which conveyed she too was just as surprised as I had been. I had to remind myself that her glance and touch was all Yolo. His hand on my lower back was what I imagined a family member would do in such a comforting way.

"Now the tricky part, to find you a place amongst us, Ellie," Jenn said with a smile as we approached a metal sliding door.

CHAPTER 12

T HE SLIDING DOORS opened and revealed bright pasty white walls. There were many doors on either side of me, which had various numbers on them. Other halls led in separate directions. Jenn walked me to another pair of metal sliding doors; the whole tunnel had an eerie silence. Using my sensitive hearing, I couldn't hear any living creature residing within the rooms, and I couldn't decipher what all those empty rooms might've been used for.

Jenn placed her hand on a large white button beside the door. The doors opened and natural bright light irritated my eyes. The sun bleached my eyesight for a moment as I squinted, trying to readjust to its brightness once again. Jenn stepped onto the white marble floor, where we were within a glass tunnel. Above us, the sky beamed down that oh so irritating sun.

"It appears they've pulled back the dome," Jenn mused. "We try to have it open for as long as possible, but for security measures, it's closed most of the time. To see the natural sunlight within here is a rarity. It often gives the generators a break."

The air was dense within the glass tunnels. Everywhere I looked, outside of the glass tunnels, humans walked. Some with books in their hands, others were chatting and laughing, some children were even training with wooden swords. There were cemented paths throughout the well maintained green grass. There were four glass tunnels in total, including the one we walked through. They all connected to the center, where a large statue of a man stood.

"That was the founder of this place. A bit embarrassing to have a statue made of him, in my opinion. Resources surely could have gone toward something else," Jenn murmured under her breath so only I could hear. Two men approached us. The well-fed bald man wore a white coat that hardly clipped around his belly. The other, in complete opposition to his companion, wore thick leathering, with weapons strapped all over him. They seemed to be in an argument. I could smell them before they'd even turned the corner, and into our tunnel. I could see them through the glass, as they turned from theirs, circled the statue and walked toward us. The sweet smell of their scent and light sweat paused me for a moment. I could hear the pulse of their blood pumping, inviting me to take a bite. I counted to ten, as my father had taught me. I couldn't act out here, I'm only human I reminded myself.

"Well, you'll do as I say. You can't just be a feral outside the walls all the time. You need to be interested in the studies of experiments as well," the man in the white coat said to the other, who seemed irritated. "Ah, Jenn, it's nice to see you again," the man with the white coat cheered. His eyes rolled over me and lingered on my inner thighs before his expression reached my eyes. "Who's your friend?" I clenched my jaw and paused my every instinct. This man smelt distasteful. My natural predisposition was to lunge for him and rip out his eyes, so he could never look at another in such a vulgar way again.

"Mr. Taine, how lovely to see you," Jenn said with a fake smile. I could read her particularly well right now, and she didn't like this man either. "This is my guest, Ellie."

"Lovely to meet you, Ellie," the bald, well-fed man held out his hand to me with a smug expression. Still clenching my jaw and fists, I looked at his hand. I refused to shake such a repulsive man's hand. I looked him dead in the eyes, with an expression that stated so. Although I denied my darker self that wanted to rip him apart, I could still express my distaste for him. The other man, who was very broad in size and had sandy brown hair, watched me intently. He wasn't as fixated on my body but more my expression. I could see him in the corner of my eye, studying me. He rubbed his light stubble around his jaw. A large scar down his neck caught my attention, forcing me to make eye contact with his blue eyes.

"Please don't mind her," Jenn said with another charismatic smile. "I found her. It would appear she has amnesia."

"Amnesia or not, a woman should know her place and show me some respect," Mr. Taine hissed. I clenched my hands, trying to contain the shaking fit I could feel coming on. I wanted this man dead, he needed to be dead. What defused me was how intently the other man watched my every action, studying me. Not like Taine had, but as I would someone else, summarizing them.

"That's enough," the leather-clad man growled. "Shut your mouth and show me this damn thing you so urgently wanted me to see." His voice was rough and domineering.

"Well, does the girl not speak or something? Is she disabled?" Mr. Taine insinuated. Still within human speed and reflex, I grabbed his arm and twisted his face to hit the glass with force. I knew I was dabbling in very dangerous territory, but I wouldn't allow some low life to speak to me like that, no matter what form I took.

"Ellie!" Jenn snarled. I looked over his neck with such temptation, but even I couldn't be compelled to dive in deep with the repulsive odor that reeked from his every pore.

"She speaks," I said calmly in his ear. I looked into the glass and saw the reflection of the other man who did nothing. His arms were crossed over his chest as he held back a twitching smile.

"Ellie, let him go!" Jenn yelled, more seriously. I looked out beyond the glass to where a few people had now noticed us. This wasn't exactly going within character as to who I was meant to play, but as long as I did everything with human pace, Jenn couldn't lecture me for breaking some rules.

"Disgusting," I said and threw him to the side. He took a few wobbly steps, trying to catch his footing.

"I'll throw you to the sabers, you dirty—"

"That's enough, Taine," the other man said. His voice was rough and sharp, like a bark. He stood in front of me, his broad shoulders blocking me from the view of my prey. "You want to act in such a way, of course you're going to get your ass handed to you."

Jenn came to my side, her eyes like a wild storm. I looked up again at the dome that now began to close. Yolo will most certainly lecture me for this later.

"Don't worry about it, Jenn. I'll make sure this isn't reported," the other man said, looking over his shoulder and at me.

"That would be appreciated," Jenn said, patting over her skirt. "I actually needed to find you in regards to Ellie. It seems she's good with crossbow and swords. And well, this kind of behavior as well."

So, this was Sydney. He was much younger than I had anticipated, considering he was the man in charge of their military sector. He looked me up and down, not repulsively, but in measure.

"You look only small, if I hadn't seen you move so swiftly just now, I wouldn't have considered you." He turned with his hands crossed over his chest. "I'd like to see what you can do, and I'd hate to be disappointed."

"I don't think I am one to disappoint," I said, keeping my gaze locked with his.

"That's a bold statement coming from someone with amnesia," he said, smugly.

"I'm still trying to find myself. But being weak or shy is not something I can sense in myself," I said, forwardly. I felt relieved almost to have met Sydney and to find him to have such a strong personality, even for a human. I felt I wasn't as closed off or pretending, that a part of me could stay, even as I pretended to be human.

"Bring her to my training grounds this afternoon. The usual time," Sydney said to Jenn. He measured me one more time with a distinct expression of appreciation. "Don't disappoint me."

He walked off, ushering Mr. Taine, to be quiet. Mr. Taine threatened and spat every filthy name he could conjure at me. By the time they'd walked further into the tunnel, the dome was completely closed. Small lights flicked on all over the grassed grounds and within the tunnel.

"What the fuck was that?" Jenn said. "You can't be acting like that in here. What did I say before we came in?"

"I made a good impression, didn't I?" I shrugged. "I won't attack anyone. It's fine, I'm in control."

"You just attacked someone, not even two minutes ago," she growled.

"I'm sorry, I just...I couldn't not attack such a filthy man. There is something not right with him. He smells...odd to me," I said, frowning and unsure as to why that was. "He's not right. He's not a man who should live."

Jenn's face scowled at me as her foot tapped on the marble floor. She gave up, looking away and back at me. "He is a repulsive man, and there are not so nice rumors about the way he has treated young women here. But, you can't do anything, Ellie, this is a serious role."

"I know, I'm sorry. The only way I could control myself was by doing something, instead of nothing. I'm sorry." It was a peculiar notion to apologize profusely, but I understood how much this pretense meant to Yolo. I couldn't break it.

"Believe it or not, I was worried about how we would impress Sydney. So, you acting out might have been a blessing in disguise," Jenn quietly confessed. When she saw my smug expression, she snapped on me. "But, never again or I am booting you out." I nodded in agreement.

"Now come along, I have yet to introduce you to Mr. Richard, and show you around."

We reached the middle of the tunnels, where they connected in the midsection. We walked around the largely built statue of a man with a mustache holding a book. Again, my impression of humans was that they were egotistic.

Jenn led me down the first tunnel on our right. Humans were still walking on the outside of the tunnels, entering through other doors from the circular-like layout. Jenn pointed in the direction across from us. There was one large open entrance, which looked to be a residential area. Beyond it, I could see many steel rooms connected to one another. It reminded me much of the Guild, where very little space was available to the individuals. The structure continued up four levels. Some people were climbing up ladders to reach the door to their room.

Once the glass tunnel ended, Jenn clicked on the large white button on her left to open the metal sliding doors. Again, there was a white marble hallway that forked off into other directions.

"Down on the left is where the training, education, meals, bathing, and connection to the residential areas are," Jenn said. "In front of us is the sector I mostly work in. This is where experiments and such are conducted. Down on the right is where prisoners are held." She gave me an even look, which conveyed that they weren't just any prisoners, they were vampires.

"Can I see it? Before we go to the labs?" I asked. Jenn considered it for a moment. She looked around the area and saw that no one was approaching.

"Since you've never seen a real live vampire, Ellie, I'll show you. So you know how dangerous they are and don't get involved," Jenn said, keeping up our pretense. Pretending to be affected by amnesia was a clever plan derived from Yolo. We continued to walk down the hall and into the first set of doors. A small glass room contained two humans, similar to the layout of when we first scanned into the compound.

"I've come to assess their characteristics and also show this new member their cells," Jenn said. "She may soon be a part of the sedation rounds."

"Actually, Jenn," one of the ladies interrupted. "The member who was supposed to check in and do the rounds hasn't yet shown up. Would you be able to by chance, sedate four of them? I don't want to wait too long, just in case it causes alarm," she said.

"Of course," Jenn agreed. The woman opened the door and gave Jenn a small suitcase. Jenn opened it, and assessed the four syringes, that contained a bright silver liquid. It looked like it contained liquid silver, one of the only weapons that truly weakened and exhausted a vampire. The woman handed Jenn a board, which had a list of cell numbers and highlighted the four that were due for their sedation. I wondered how long these vampires had been captive.

"We won't be too long," Jenn smiled. She led me down the corridor of white walls and bright lights. I noted all the traps and holes that were within the walls, if any managed to escape. They wouldn't even make it out the door. We walked through another two sets of steel doors; I noted they became thicker as each one closed behind us. Above us were tiny holes, but I couldn't decipher what weapon it was, they weren't thick enough to be darts.

"It's a gassing system, in case they escape," Jenn said. She waited patiently outside one of the doors. She stepped onto a small platform beside the door; it was so small that only one of her heels could properly fit. "It goes by a weight system. We haven't been able to reproduce surveillance cameras, so we go by weights," Jenn said. "When I approach the door and stand on this platform, it relays that weight back to the main room, the sector where we had grabbed these syringes. They can then tell if we are ready for the door to be opened or not."

I stared at her for a moment, mixing around the phrase, 'surveillance camera' in my head. "What is a surveillance camera?" I asked. Jenn looked at me from the corner of her eye and smiled. It was a Yolo smile.

"Never mind. With the lack of knowledge on the old world, I'm surprised your Guild survived for so long," Jenn murmured.

"We were only educated on certain things, it appears that was not one of them," I said. I slumped my shoulders inwardly, remembering that my straightened posture was not one of humans.

The door slid open and revealed numerous glass rooms on either side. The hair on my arms spiked within the hostile atmosphere. There were various vampires, one detained in each cell. Most were sluggishly slumped in the corner of their boxed prison. There was no item within the rooms, just hard floor. I was disgusted, yet had no remorse. At the Guild, we used to tie them to chairs before we tortured them.

Jenn scanned through the numbers on her page and spotted the first one she had to sedate. She followed the numbers, stopping at the first. I looked into the glass room where the barbaric creature laid, its left leg twitching.

"You keep sabers in here?" I asked, surprised. A small crack was evident on the glass next to the door. She opened the door. Both of us walked in, and she closed it behind us.

"That crack was from a previous saber, someone missed their duty to sedate it, and it was a little rough for the next person when it tried to escape." The creature's leg continued to twitch, its elongated claws slightly scratched at the cement floor beneath it. Drool poured from its mouth and onto the cement, it was both saliva and blood. Its eyes pinned on us and it growled. But that was the most effort it could extend. Jenn grabbed its deformed arm and injected the first syringe into its arm. The creature's eyes pinned on me before glazing over into a white color. Its pants became shallow and near non-existent.

"How are you able to sedate them, what's in that syringe?" I asked. The saber's heart rate dropped dramatically. If it weren't immortal, it would be dead for certain.

"The particles in this syringe make it very difficult and time-consuming for the vampire to recover. Although they have unbelievable healing time, there is a lot of silver in this. It thickens the bloodstream and takes a long time for the healing properties to remove the silver. By the time the body is close to doing so, we've already injected them with another shot."

Jenn placed the empty syringe back into the suitcase and exited the room. She looked over the numbers to see who she next had to sedate. I looked over the allotment of vampires and sabers, which were compacted in tiny rooms. How did they get themselves caught? I could admit that I had satisfaction in killing vampires, but this felt almost foreign. We tortured within the Guild to pull information, but never for something like this. This seemed far more unbearable than death.

"How long do you keep them in here?" I asked, walking closer to one of the vampires whose eyes were glazed over in white. They sat in a corner, frozen and stared at nothing in particular. One of the veins in its neck was a deep blue and bulged out. "Do they ever feed while in here?"

Jenn looked up from her board and walked across the room to see which one I was looking at. "That one has been here for three years; she's specifically being tested for biodegradation, to see how long her body will last until she decomposes, if she does. She hasn't been fed once, and will continue to be in that form until she dies naturally, which is something that won't happen. But, that is the test subject they wanted to do the trial on, so simply she will be like that forever.

"Vampires within the wild can become similar to this. If they exhaust themselves or starve, they'll go into a coma-like state until someone else can hand feed them blood to help recover. Some in here are fed, depending on what they're being tested for."

I walked over to the next room which had four large and tall containers. All of which were glazed over in ice. The whole cell looked to be chilled inside.

"Those contain four vampires, one within each. It's only in its fourth round of testing. The first four died. The ice was too intense and created shards within their heart and exploded. The second ones broke out. The third were killed by an insider who lost his mind and tried to kill all the test subjects. He was thrown out into the wild after that, only minutes after I heard his screams myself. Something got to him. And this is now our fourth; they've been frozen for about nine months now. It simply seems like they're sleeping. Because of the temperature that reaches beyond something a vampire could usually handle, their brain cells freeze, so, they cannot think nor heal, and are put into a slumber of sorts."

"Can a vampire really be affected by being frozen?" I asked, with myself in mind. I was no longer as sensitive to the temperature as I had once been, to think that I could freeze wasn't something I'd considered. There were a lot of possibilities I now hadn't deliberated.

"Vampires can sustain in any environment, temperature is no issue. However, this is adjusted beyond those temperatures, this is manmade, Ellie. No matter how extreme the world might be now in environment and temperature, this is far more severe," Jenn said, moving away from the glass. "Ah, fuck," she said, looking at the next number she had to sedate.

"What is it?" I asked, looking over her shoulder. She stopped at the numbered cell which matched with the one on the list.

"Stay out here. Whatever you see, don't believe or be influenced by it, he's gifted in illusion," Jenn said. I looked at the vampire who didn't seem sedated at all. He looked at his nails while sitting down with one arm perched on his bent knee. He had fiery red hair with a blond goatee. He was also naked and sat on his clothes.

With a charming smile, he looked at us. "Can you imagine my disappointment after sitting here naked for twelve days and still having no tan," the vampire said.

"Are you going to play nice today, Lincon?" Jenn asked, still hesitant to enter the room.

"Oh, darling," Lincon said as he rose to stand tall. I looked away at his naked form, his very *hard* naked form. "I always play nice."

"When are you going to give up on this game and escape?" Jenn asked, with hands on hips.

"You think because you're on the other side of that glass, I can't affect you?" Lincon laughed. Suddenly, I was surrounded by snow and all the rooms that existed, vanished. Snow particles fell from the sky, and the sun beamed down on me. It was so cold and yet the burning sun clung to my skin.

"Ellie, don't be fooled, it's a trick—" Jenn's voice vanished. Where she once stood, was now nothing but pillowing snow. Lincon stood there proud and naked. Determined not to look past his eyes, I stared unimpressed. How had they captured a vampire who held a gift to this magnitude? And although all the other cellmates seemed sedated, he was not.

My sense of smell heightened, and I clung to the familiar scent of blood. Behind me, there were humans drenched in the bright red, massacred on a forest floor. Sabers tore them apart, enjoying the taste of their flesh. I licked my lips, my fangs tempted to slice through my gum. But it was my huntress self that saved me, that was instinctually wanting to kill the sabers. This had to be a trick. I stood there, reconnecting my gaze to Lincon's.

"Interesting," he purred. "You know, within my first encounter with Jenn, I was quickly able to see who she, or should I say, he was. You'd be surprised how people react to certain things. It gives away their weakness, or even sometimes, what they might truly be under the surface."

The field of dead people vanished, and then a bustling scene of confusion burst in front of me. The only thing I could refer it to was the technology era. I stood in the middle of an intersection, where cars chaotically drove around me. Buildings were tall as people walked in steady streams. Cars beeped at me as they drove toward me. I sighed unaffected, if this is an illusion, then I will not flinch under his amusement. A car swerved straight for me, still I stared directly into Lincon's eyes. The vehicle swept through me, and the scene around me vanished.

Lincon smiled. "I think I like you. Do you know how many of the humans in here I've forced to drop to their knees? It's rather fun actually. And none of them will report it, because they'll look like the insane ones. I'm a sedated vampire, how could I possibly be able to use my gift?" he said sarcastically.

"What are you doing in here?" I asked.

"Free buffet obviously. With all my tricks and illusions, I make them sedate me with only how much of that shit I actually want in my bloodstream, sometimes I do it so I can have a bit of a high. Other than that, I just feed off them until I've had my fill. They all think they had a daydream and don't say anything. Everyone is different, but you're not human, you have a different feel to you," Lincon delighted. "And everyone reacts to something that they see. It's what always gives them away and feeds me the answers as to what sort of person they are."

His entire body continued to shift, his face and body, morphing into different people. His features and clothing continuously changed over several centuries. After flicking through twenty-three various forms, which only my hunter speed could follow, my eyes rested on the slender eye slits of whom I thought to be Pac. I snarled in response, accidentally breaking my façade.

I felt a hand on me, and suddenly everything disappeared. Jenn was holding my chest in alarm. My vision had hazed purple, and my fangs had pierced through my gums. I couldn't save Pac, who was part of my Guild raid team that I led. I now knew that it wasn't Pac, but only someone who had looked like him. But it had still sparked that recognition within me and given Lincon the reaction he was after.

"Holy shit." Lincon sparked with life. He slithered back against the wall in delight, watching me intently. "What are you?"

"Calm," Jenn said. "Don't worry about this, I slipped too." The vision of my huntress's eyes disappeared, alongside the haze of their purple. With my fangs no longer revealed, I looked at Lincon angrily. This was only a game to him.

"All right, love, you seem pissed off now. Let me guess, you're in love with an Asian boy, and you're all protective of him. Wait, could it even get better, is he human?" Lincon toyed. "That Romeo and Juliet shit gets me every time."

"I could rip you to shreds if we weren't within these walls," I hissed. He only laughed.

"Please, quit the tough girl act. I am fascinated by you. Let me just say, the day you leave here, I'll follow you. You've grabbed my attention, and seem like a whole pile of fun. Do you know how long it's been since I've had fun? All right, Jenn, give us a hit," Lincon said. He talked at such a speed that it was hard for me to consume his words. He walked over to the door and opened it himself. He held out his arm to her.

I couldn't believe that of all the vampires within here to trick the humans, it was someone so loony. The other vampires were so easily trapped and stuck within these walls for a lifetime. But this one particular vampire was beyond measure. Jenn began to inject the silver until only a small portion remained. She seemed to space out for a bit and her hand cramped, she dropped the needle. Lincon was obviously doing something to her.

"That'll be enough love," Lincon said with a painful grunt. He stumbled over to sit back on his leather jacket. "It hurts like a bitch, but that should give me a buzz for a few hours."

"I wish you wouldn't play those games on me every time," Jenn hissed.

"Well, I can't trust you, sister," Lincon said with a slur. "You sedate every other vampire within these walls without issue. I doubt if I told you to stop nicely, you'd actually do so. Now rack off and let me sleep."

Jenn picked up the needle and sprayed the rest of its contents on the floor. She emptied it only tiny droplets at a time, so it wasn't evident on the floor. Lincon clicked his fingers at me.

"New girl, come back and see me. I think we have a lot we can discuss. You'll need me soon you know," he said cockily before he began to laugh and the drugs and silver were inevitably affecting him.

"Stay away from that head case, Ellie," Jenn said, ushering for me to continue doing the rounds with her. We continued to do so, all other vampires lacked in the expression of life. It seems that the only one capable of ever escaping would be Lincon.

CHAPTER 13

J ENN CONTINUED TO watch me over her shoulder. I reassured her I
was all right and sane. A trick as small as Lincon's would not be my
undoing. After sedating the last two vampires who slightly shuffled
and appeared to make a pathetic attempt to fight back, we walked back
toward the prison's entrance. There were so many traps and holes within
the walls. Jenn informed me that if a vampire had escaped its room, the
weight scheme and scanning system would trigger various traps and
weapons. It appeared that even if a human was taken down in the
process, they didn't care. I had no sympathy for the vampires, but I was
disgusted in the state they were left in. As a hunter, we contained and
tortured a few, but never preserved them. It was always, kill on site.

Jenn returned the suitcase with empty syringes inside and signed off
on the four that she'd sedated. Apparently, Lincon was of no issue
because he liked to pretend and play dead.

Jenn led me through the tunnels and toward the sector where she
worked. Like the other entrance, this too was exclusive, and only
authorized members could enter. I wondered if everyone within the
compound even knew to what extent the experiments were taken to.
They were cautious about allowing me to enter, but Jenn insisted that I
was now her personal assistant. Hesitantly, they let me through.

"Mr. Richard is the person in charge. Although he dabbles in all departments and overlooks them, he's also the leading scientist here and orchestrates most of the experiments," Jenn said as she led me down cemented stairs.

"Remember when we enter, you have to keep it together. What you will see down here isn't nice. You can't react to the people you meet down here either, Ellie. Whitney's brother is within this department."

I tried to contain my distaste. It would be hard for me to keep my calm around him. But I had to report this to Tythian. This was his right and kill. I couldn't take his right of revenge away. This was my only bargaining chip. If I could find out the identity of Whitney's brother, then Tythian would take us to the human camp near our Guild, where I could possibly find closure for Dillian and Julia. "I will be fine," I insisted. I had to be.

After walking down numerous stairs that continued to spiral, we finally stood on solid ground. A loud scream rolled over my spine. I cringed at the mechanical noises that came from that direction. It sounded as if someone were sawing against bone. I refocused. No matter what I saw, I had to contain myself, even if there was blood.

Jenn continued walking, unfazed by the noises. There were four distinct rooms, and a part of me didn't want to be curious about what was behind each door. Another howl of a scream echoed through the hall, it was the furthest room on the right. Was that a vampire being tortured, or another human being tested on?

Jenn stopped at the first door on the left and opened it. There were three beds, and numerous glass tubes filed in boxes on wide shelves beside me. Two people were lying on their beds. One was being injected with something into their arm. The man pulled a twisted expression of discomfort before telling the man in the white coat that he was feeling okay. It smelt wrong in here, the very atmosphere smelt mutilated. I cringed at standing in this very room and the possible monsters it'd birthed before. A very dashing young man who was administrating the syringe, peeled back his white mask and looked at Jenn and me.

"Miss. Cadolwadt, what brings you and your guest to our department's area?" he asked with a smile. He sat on a chair that had wheels beneath it. He grabbed another syringe and flicked at it to make sure it bubbled. He then moved on to the next man sitting down. "It'll be fine," he reassured. He injected the man, who gave the same uncomfortable grimace.

"We were looking for Mr. Richard, actually," Jenn said, seemingly unfazed by the human experiment that was happening. "I'm certain he was in his office. He was here earlier." A presence from outside interfered with my calmness. I recognized his disgusting smell. I inhaled deeply, remaining calm. *I am a Token Huntress, nothing will break me*, I affirmed to myself.

Mr. Taine walked in. He recognized me with an expression of disgust. He walked past and said nothing.

"Any changes to report, Charlie?" Mr. Taine asked the young man with blond hair.

"No. The first admission went well. So I sped the process up on the second. We should let them rest for a time however, and have them report in a few days. I would consider—"

Mr. Taine cut him off and now fixated on both of us. "Any particular reason why you're interfering with my progress with your new friend?" Mr. Taine asked, crossing his plump arms over his chest. I imagined he hadn't reported my assault on him. One thing I'd learned about humans was that they were very egotistic, and I was certain he wouldn't want others to know that he was manhandled by a woman this morning.

"Can I please have some water," the first man who'd been administered asked, with a raspy voice.

"Of course," Charlie said and offered him a glass of water. Yelling poured from the staircase. I recognized the scent and voice to be Sydney's. The woman who permitted us through continued to warn Sydney that he was not allowed within the department without being escorted.

Sydney flung the door open and summarized the two men. He walked up to Mr. Taine, slamming his elbow into his throat and pinning him against the bench.

"I told you that you couldn't administer them without my consent!" he growled.

"Sydney, it's fine, we told them it was okay," the first man said, his voice rasped. I looked at him, his face had begun to melt above his eyebrow, and his lip began to dip on one side. "Can I please have some more water? I am so thirsty."

"Of course," Charlie calmly said. He stood up and walked over to a small red button and pressed it in. The man noticed this and looked up mortified.

"I feel fine. You don't have to do that!" he shouted, scared.

The other man jumped from his bedding and hid behind us, mortified. "Please don't let that happen to me!"

"Max, it's me," the other man said. "I feel fine, I swear." His voice seemed more of a whimper and plea. He tried to sit up from his bed, but part of him slumped back. "Syd, you gotta' believe me. I feel fine." The man choked hysterically. Blood poured from his nose as he looked at us all wide-eyed. "It's just itchy here." He panicked, as if not noticing the blood that continued to stream from his body. He clawed his chest, where underneath, I could see blue bruising and what looked like something squirming beneath his chest.

"Get everyone out," Sydney said, slamming Mr. Taine one more time. Mr. Taine was not affected by the man's condition at all and proceeded speedily out. I continued to watch the effects the admission had on the man. Was this the same they'd given Whitney? Was this how they were experimented on? I heard footsteps marching above and pooling down the spiral staircase.

Sydney ushered everyone out, so he was closest to the man.

"I'm so sorry," Sydney said, his voice rasping. He pulled out the sword strapped to his back from its sheath.

"It's inside of me," the man desperately cried out. I could sense the change within him.

"Ellie, come out," Jenn said and grabbed my elbow. Everyone else had left the room. Sydney lined his sword with the man's chest. But, as quickly as a switch flicking over, the man snapped. He was no longer human; I could sense that within him, his consciousness was gone. This was the same presence as a saber.

Sydney plunged his sword toward him, but the man, no not man, saber slapped it away and against the wall. He lunged for Sydney and pinned him against the counter. Sydney plunged a dagger into the man's brain. But it was beyond that, this was no longer a human. I yanked my elbow out of Jenn's grasp and slammed the door behind me. The group of warriors they'd alerted and pounded down the stairs would never make it in time, not before he'd ripped Sydney apart.

The saber lunged for me. I skidded under the first bed and lifted it within human might, still maintaining my fake profile. The saber fixated on the others outside. I used the distraction to my advantage. I lifted and pinned the bed against him, trapping him for a moment. I could sense

Sydney busily working behind me. The saber tried to break the bed apart and twist on me. Before I had to fake weakness and let the saber escape, Sydney jumped over the other bed and pierced his sword through its chest. The tip of the sword went through the saber's back and tipped into the glass door.

I looked out to where five men in leather were watching as blood sprayed everywhere. Sydney reefed his sword out, and the saber began to decompose. I looked over my shoulder at Sydney, who had blood all over his face and down his chest from when the saber had first pinned him. He gave me a firm nod of appreciation and tapped my shoulder that I could now let go of the bed.

"Thank you," he said in an unyielding tone. He grabbed the bed and ripped it away. He opened the door and stepped over the corpse of the saber.

"He was one of my best!" he snarled at Mr. Taine, who stared at the corpse, his eyebrows raised as if it disappointed him. I looked at the other man, who watched what was once his friend mortified. Jenn held out her hand to him.

"You'll be okay. Come on, I'll take you somewhere you can be alone for a while," she said.

"He needs to be put into containment." A new figure approached us. An older man with wispy gray hair and a honey voice said.

"Mr. Richard, I hadn't known that it would progress this quickly. If you might look at our previous results, you'll see—" Mr. Taine began pleading his case, but was quickly cut off.

"You've killed this man, do you have no remorse? Two injections within a day of each other, are you an utter idiot?!" Mr. Richard shouted. "You're not to experiment any longer until I give permission, you've disappointed me."

"But please, sir," Mr. Taine continued.

"Get out!" he yelled. The others silenced around him. So, this was the man who was in charge of the human compound. He crouched to Max's eye level, the man who had also been experimented on.

"We'll put you in there for two days, just to make sure you don't react in the same manner. If it goes well, you can go back to your family. If he was pressuring you into taking another admission so soon, you should have come to me. I'm sorry it had to be this way," Mr. Richard exasperated.

"But, sir, I feel fine. If I could just rest in my home for a bit, I think it'll be okay," Max said reassuringly, pleadingly.

"I'm sorry, Max, but I can't do that. Take him to the containment area," Mr. Richard enforced his power and commanded the soldiers.

"No, please, I swear I didn't do anything wrong!" Max yelled as he was dragged away. Few people had now opened their doors from the other sectors, watching the spectacle and wondering what had happened.

"Charlie, you too are in the wrong here," Mr. Richard condoned.

"Yes, sir," Charlie admitted.

"Come and see me in my office in half an hour. I'll decide what to do with you then," Mr. Richard instructed.

"Yes, sir," he said and walked off, mumbling under his breath.

"I want this cleaned up!" Mr. Richard shouted to the onlookers who now hid, regarding the deformed half human, half saber body. So this was one of the experiments they did.

"You two follow me." Mr. Richard gestured to Jenn and me. "I have some issues to discuss with you, Jenn."

"Of course, sir," Jenn said, unaffected by the commotion. Leaving distance between us and Mr. Richard, Jenn whispered so only I could hear her words.

"From the information I've gathered, Charlie is Whitney's older brother." The significance of that one sentence left me thirsting for a slaughter. I looked over my shoulder into the direction where Charlie had left. He was still experimenting on humans even today. With little concern for the harm he was inflicting on others or even he'd placed on his sister.

We walked up the stairs and followed Mr. Richard. I had to plead to my darker self to calm, to not give chase, no matter how infuriated I was. This was not my kill, this was Tythian's claim.

CHAPTER 14

THE WOMAN WHO tried to prevent Sydney from running down the stairs began apologizing to Mr. Richard. He raised his hand uninterested in her excuses.

"Sydney has no access to those rooms without being escorted. But today, we're lucky he was there. Who knows how many of the scientists down there might've been killed before the concealment team was able to apprehend the test subject," Mr. Richard said to both Jenn and me, as we followed his dreary pace. He side glanced me curiously. "It was reported to me, that you aided Sydney in stopping that very saber, and you are?"

"This is Ellie, I found her near my lodgings. It appears she's suffering from amnesia. However, we've discovered she's good with a crossbow, sword, and it would appear that her reflexes are very sharp and could contribute to Sydney's aid within the squad," Jenn said swimmingly. We continued to walk down the narrow white corridors. The air within the whole compound smelt richly clean. It irritated my sensitive nose. Before reaching the intersection which led to separate parts of the institute, Mr. Richard walked to one of the doors and stood in front of it, rummaging through his numerous keys.

He opened the door and switched the light on as we walked in. In comparison to the rest of the compound, this room smelt of dust and old books. In front of us was a large wooden desk, which had papers messily sprawled over it. Two dirty mugs which had been emptied and smelt like the rarity of coffee beans stained the desk. The whole room was surrounded by bookcases and sample jars which were separately labeled.

"Please take a seat," he said, offering the two seats, which had piles of books on them. Jenn picked them off and slumped the pile onto the desk. For a leader, he was very unorganized. I followed suit as Mr. Richard sat down opposite us.

"I suppose it makes it hard to ask about yourself, if you don't know who you are," Mr. Richard began. "But I take Jenn's advisement seriously. If she thinks you should be pushed toward the military sector, then we can organize something. However, I'm not imprudent to Sydney's wishes and the team that is already solidly built. So, if he has no use for you, then we'll need to find another department where you can be of use."

"I completely understand," I replied. I side glanced Jenn. Yolo had indeed infiltrated this compound because without hesitation, they believed his story about my amnesia. It had been the same with Tythian. He'd infiltrated the Vampire Council for years. I had some respect for the long game Cesar was playing. If they lived forever then I supposed they had the luxury of advancing a well thought out tactic. I felt as a hunter, almost inferior with the little knowledge and scope we had on the larger scale of things. I'd learned more in these rapid few weeks then I had my entire upbringing about the truth and rules of the human and vampire world.

"Perhaps we should organize for her to be an all-rounder," Jenn said, crossing her leg over the other. "She's already done a round with me this morning, administrating our subjects."

Mr. Richard raised his eyebrows in surprise. "That's a confidential section."

"I'm aware, but she had no recollection of what a vampire or saber was. I was rather perplexed to meet someone who had no understanding of the dangers in this world. I almost felt like it was my obligation to do so," Jenn said. "I would much rather have her as a personal assistant than fighting, however I cannot deny her skill. And for the compounds benefit, I think she's best positioned there."

"A personal assistant, you say?" Mr. Richard mused. "Well then, perhaps she can be exactly that until Sydney makes up his mind as to whether he wants her as part of his team or not."

There was a heavy silence. I tried to contain the irritation of being locked into another small white room, which had no window or even perception that there was an outside world. I didn't like these rooms where they experimented on humans. They seemed to avoid the sun just as much as vampires did. This entire compound felt as if it were a prison.

"Sir, about today. What do you intend to do with Mr. Taine? I must admit, upon meeting Ellie, he acted in a disturbing manner. I fear he might be withholding too much stress, and his overall mentality is becoming a bit distorted," Jenn pressed. Mr. Richard only sighed in response as if it had already been plaguing his mind.

"You know I've been waiting for you to come back. While you were gone during these four days, we came across something. I need you to help me contain them, with your expertise in engineering, I need you to craft me something that will keep *them* locked inside."

"Them, sir?" Jenn asked cautiously.

"On the outskirts of our compound, Sydney and his team found two hunters. Because they were already manufactured and products of manipulation with vampire blood, Mr. Taine wanted to study them further. The results were more receptive than we'd imagined and hoped."

"You tested on them?" Jenn interrupted, boldly.

"Well, yes, I never had the intention to. I wanted them to aid Sydney. But the two had a particular attitude that forced me to believe they were a danger to the compound. So I granted Mr. Taine permission to see if he could make progress. All our human subjects thus far haven't been receptive to the testing. Some have lasted longer than others, but no real result. They were our breaking point. Their bodies which are already engineered by vampire blood, took to it well. We have been successful in our first creation. We've created something greater than the hunters themselves. We could have them right at our disposal to use. However, there currently seems to be a prominent side effect. They can't be sedated, every time one of the members tries to inject them, they can propel the syringe away. They've killed four of ours already. It's resulted in us having to gas them every few hours, but their healing rate is phenomenal. We need to create a new way to contain them for now. We can't continue using our gas resources."

We sat there, somberly. I feigned no reaction, though inside it infuriated me that he so easily discussed hunters being tested on. There was no line to their curiosity. Whether human, vampire, or hunter, they'd experimented on them all in the name of hope and overpowering the outside world once again. How small-minded humans were. With all these resources, they could've focused on something better and maybe even bigger, but instead, they fell into the pit hole of their ancestors who turned to experimenting and crafting the first generations of hunters themselves.

"Max and Troy, what were they injected with?" Jenn asked. Her expression was lifeless. I questioned what Yolo might've really been thinking.

"We were able to take samples of the hunter's blood and inject them with that as a bi-product. The results within the first few hours went swimmingly, they were significantly faster, stronger, heightened senses—everything. I told Mr. Taine to wait for a few days until the next dosage so we could gather results. But as you can now see, these are the consequences of him acting out of accordance."

I sat there, as if not registering any of the terms or conversation. After all, I had to act as if I hadn't ever seen a hunter before.

"May I see them? The hunters, I've never seen one before," I said daringly. "Aren't they meant to be our saviors?" Mr. Richard scoffed. I tightened my grip only slightly in my lap. This disrespectful human so audaciously disrespected our kind even when our very life was dedicated to finding and protecting them. Jenn side glanced me with slight discomfort. Perhaps, I was pushing my boundaries. But I wanted to see the hunters. I needed to see what they'd done to them. I came here under the pretense that I wanted to inspect the compound to see if it was safe for Dillian and Julia, not a place where they would be experimented on. I quickly understood that this would only be another prison for them, if not, a more dangerous one. At least with vampires, we often knew what to expect, they only wanted one thing—blood. Whereas humans weren't even sure what they wanted until dumb luck struck them, and they found it. And through that, they were willing to test on anything or anyone.

"They no longer look like what they use to be, dear. The hunters are now 'special,'" Mr. Richard began to explain.

"If you don't mind her being with me while I look at their current enclosure, I would be interested in assessing it now. I'll put aside my scheduling and current project to focus on this one," Jenn offered.

"Ah, of course, that would suit very nicely. If you don't mind her being introduced so freshly to her seemingly scary new world, I can permit it. Yes, I think we'll make her your personal assistant until Sydney has made up his mind about her," Mr. Richard mused. I was alarmed by the carefree nature that was installed into their leader's mind. The things they discussed and were doing were inhumane. As a huntress, I had slaughtered and tortured many. But, I would never dare to experiment in such a way, even if the resources were in front of me. It was a sick and twisted thought process, when they thought this was how they gained strength. Was this why the humans were so easily overpowered in the technology era? They fought against one another in their own wars and struggle for power, and had ignored the vampires, which were closing in. It was why their very world was taken out from beneath them. I was educated, that they were experimenting on humans and vampires alike all those years ago. Three hundred years and generations later with limited resources, they still found the means to do such disgusting things. Was this how the human mind was built? Were they born with such darkness and corruptness?

I silently listened to Jenn and Mr. Richard speak lab talk as he walked us back into the four laboratory rooms. Two women now scrubbed the pool of blood with wet cloths. Drag marks of the saber's corpse had not yet been cleaned. What had they done with his body? The drag marks led toward the very door we followed Mr. Richard too. Beside the second room, next to Mr. Taine's, there was another door. Mr. Richard used another key to open it. I noted the thickness to this door as he slid it open, indicating it was in defense against vampires. It was clean cut silver, I avoided touching it as best I could. More stairs spiraled down. The further we walked down, the dimmer the lights became. We were consumed in darkness, where only a few lights enabled us to see. I continued to pretend to fumble for the railing as we walked down like a clumsy human would.

"Is this room not enough to hold them in? I created the door and dart system, specifically for gifted vampires down here," Jenn said as she reassessed her work. I was intrigued that she'd handed over such power to them. I suppose that was her way to make herself valuable and gain the trust within the compound.

"Amongst the various other set-ups we have in here, it can contain them. But I want another one implemented specifically for them," Mr. Richard said. "Tell me how much manpower you need, and you'll have it. I never want these two to escape. I have another team working on a project now as we speak. We're working on ways so we're capable of controlling them."

"Controlling them?" I asked, intrigued. If he thought the hunters were giving them attitude before, he had no idea what he was in for. With a lifetime of them being encaged, they wouldn't go down easily, no matter what Hunter Guild they were from.

"Well yes, we want to use them for military purposes of course, to slowly gain back our world. To restore it, so humans can live comfortably, and we can fight against the plague of vampires and sabers alike. We must be in utter control, so we can create more and see to what extent we can push them. But first, they must be subordinate."

The rounded stairs began to thin the further we ventured down. I could see that on this level of the stairs, there were large slits all around the room. I focused on a small droplet that hung there. This was another set-up. I could assume that the prisoners had weights on their feet and if they escaped, water would release from the gaps in the wall. By doing so, it encased them and would drown them until another plan could be initiated. I had studied such a tactic during my Guild years in only the first few years of my studies. This was no longer used by hunters, only in the olden days, when we studied vampires ourselves. The world couldn't possibly afford to have such tactics anymore, we couldn't waste such resources. Obviously, what was contained in this room was deemed very important. I questioned where their resources came from. How did they feed, have water, and sustainability? The world was damaged, but the resources could still be found if properly searched for. Perhaps, the founder had created such an ideal sanctuary for them, that they had all these resources unconditionally.

"If you don't mind me asking, sir," Jenn interjected. "You said Sydney's team captured them, how was that and what were his thoughts on this?"

"Ah, yes, Sydney. He reported that they were surveying them from the border for a while, one of them ensnared themselves in one of the traps, and the other wouldn't leave their side. It appeared they had some gift of some sort. However, as soon as the first one was darted and put to sleep, the other seemed ineffective. It took our team seven hours to capture them, but eventually, they did. I must admit, Sydney has gone above and beyond his measure. It's a shame what happened to his father, but he's capable of helping this project much more promisingly than his old man had been. The boy has a natural instinct like a hunter himself. It wouldn't surprise me if his mother had been one and he had some throwback gene. He wasn't happy about the experiments, but some things have to be motioned to make progress, and with a heavy heart, it's up to me to make that decision."

"Of course," Jenn agreed somberly.

Mr. Richard pressed his hand against a white button, and the whole room lit up. There was a concealed square in the middle of the room, surrounded by a thick silver box. He then pressed another button, which pulled the silver up and revealed see-through glass. "Don't worry, they can't get to us. This is the thickest and most impenetrable of glasses. Even bullets can't seep through."

The hunters snarled at the bright light and hissed as we approached. I froze on the last step before my feet touched the cement. It couldn't be? I recognized both of them.

"We're planning to test a pair of twins next that we have within the compound," Mr. Richard began. "They're only fourteen, however, the two hunters here are twins, and were well receptive to the treatment, so perhaps something within the gene of twins is the answer we've been looking for."

Kora and Kasey, two of my huntress's from my Guild Team snarled at us. Their majestic coral eyes shot up at me with recognition and shock. Large fangs hovered over their lips and nails that tipped as long as a saber's. Their usually clean-cut pixie hair was now shoulder length. The collars that once bound their necks, to help our team decipher them were torn apart. The only way I could tell them apart was because of the small scar on Kora's chin.

"Esmore," Kasey whispered. I slammed a huge charge of intent and the word *"Stop!"* into both their minds. They both scrunched their faces, unsure of the sensation that would have swept over them. Mr. Richard and Jenn looked between me and the twins.

"Do you recognize these creatures?" Mr. Richard asked.

"No," I said, keeping my gaze locked with theirs. I couldn't help them if they gave away my fake identity.

"Do you know this girl?" Mr. Richard asked them. Kasey spat at the window, directly onto the glass in front of Mr. Richard's face.

"Ask me in here you filthy piece of shit!" Kasey spat. It now made sense as to why they would've been captured. They were a part of my team, and my team was not weak. Kora's gift enabled her to take away mobility and Kasey's ability was an enhancement of that, where she could have projected it further into a bubble to protect them both. If Kora was the one ensnared and knocked out, then Kasey could only use her combat skill. Depending on the extent of the human's military equipment, there were only so many she could have fought off, even as a huntress. By the time they woke, they were probably already chained, tortured, and gassed. Eventually, they would've experimented, resulting in the fangs and claws. But they didn't have the mindset of a saber, only part of the physical effects. They still had their hunter's eyes, and as Mr. Richard had previously mentioned, they couldn't inject them anymore. The propelling of the syringes was probably the two projecting protection around themselves.

Mr. Richard began laughing. "As you can see, this is why we couldn't reason with them. But I'm so happy with the results. They can't break through the glass, and are still a bit drowsy until the next gassing. You should watch them for a while, look at the area and think about what you might need. We've written records of their movement, so you can better study that. They're in my office, so come and see me once you're done," Mr. Richard mused.

"Of course," Jenn said, watching the twins as I did. They stared at me, unimpressed and predatory like.

"Before you come, please take Ellie to Sydney. I'd like to discuss some things in private," Mr. Richard remarked, before walking back up the stairs.

Jenn glared at me as I watched Mr. Richard leave and waited to hear the click of the door close. I hurried over to the twins.

"What are you doing here?" I asked.

"Esmore, please get us out," Kasey pleaded. These two girls were a pain in my ass the whole time while on my team. Although only twenty-two, they had an issue with taking command from me because I was younger. Kora had her arms crossed over her chest, trying to convey ignorance. But I knew these girls, they didn't deserve this. Even if one was so stubborn that she'd never directly ask for my help.

"So you do know them," Jenn said, her small heels clacking toward us slowly. Kora snarled at her and Jenn only tsked.

"Well, aren't you a broody bitch," Jenn said. In her tone, I could hear that Yolo's façade had dropped for the moment. "Like don't get me wrong, I feel bad for what has happened to you, but then, oh wait, you're a hunter, and I don't give a shit."

"Yolo," I snapped. Kasey clawed at the glass closest to Jenn's face. Jenn's was smug and didn't flinch. "They were on my team, I have to get them out."

"Who is this woman to you? And why are you even here in a human compound?" Kora interrogated.

"It's a long story—"

"Well lucky for you, it appears I have all day," Kora snapped between a snarl. "And when did you turn into such a pleading girl, Kasey. She won't help us, she turned her back on us a long time ago."

I snarled at Kora, the haze of my eyes flickering to purple as my hunter's eyes and fangs appeared. Jenn gave me a warning glance before I calmed myself. My body acted on its natural instinct. And insult and betrayal was not something I took lightly.

"I never turned my back on you, and I *will* get you out. I highly doubt the Guild will take you back now with your deformities," I simply stated. It was the truth, they would be killed instantly.

Kora laughed. "Guild? What Guild? After the stunt you pulled with those sabers that ambushed us, everyone separated. How do you think we got into this mess in the first place?"

"I never started that! And you attacked my familiar!" I snarled.

"Oh, that's right, your vampire lover because that doesn't sing out traitor!" Kora scoffed. Jenn put her slender hand on my shoulder. I was growing angrier as the darkness within me so swimmingly edged to the surface. Jenn was gentle as she slowly pulled me out of my sensitive state.

"I wonder if they overuse the gases just to shut them up." Jenn offered them a devilish smile, only riling them further. Kasey again swiped at the glass as Kora lunged for him. Her shoulder smashed into the glass, the impact propelling her back. "Savage. I'll write that on my notes as I create a dome for you both to live in for eternity. Maybe I'll add sun. Oooh, I bet you haven't seen sunlight in this form, it's very cozy."

I pulled Jenn back, realizing she wouldn't help the situation at all. A small opening from the roof dropped, and a circular object dispersed on the ground. Kasey and Kora cowered in a corner where they projected protection around themselves so the gas couldn't reach. They could only surround themselves for so long; eventually that gas would reach them.

I placed my hand on the glass and grabbed Kasey's attention. "I will get you out of here, I promise. No matter what you think of me, you know I never leave any of my team behind."

"We are not a part of *your* team any longer, Esmore," Kora snarled. "Read and understand the new dynamics. Your role as a Token Huntress is dead. And I'd rather be dead too than live as a human guinea pig for these disgusting humans, who we sacrificed our lives for upon every mission."

"Esmore," Kasey interrupted, her majestic coral eyes pleading. She placed her hand against mine, a motion that Kora snarled at. "Please get us out. I've never feared anything in my life, not even death. But this is worse. What will they do with us?" her voice quivered. This was the shattering moment that snapped me out of my retaliation against the Guild, smelling fear on a huntress. We were a breed that specialized in having no fear and a lack of emotion, and yet my former huntress was periled in thought. The Guild might've turned on me, but how could I turn on them?

"We should go now," Jenn said. She began to walk back toward the stairs. "You have to meet with Sydney now." I looked back at Kasey, whose long fangs spiked over her chin. Kora no longer stared in my direction.

"I don't know. But I'll get you out, I promise," I said, before walking away.

"It's futile," Jenn said casually, not looking over her shoulder at me as she climbed the steps, her hips happily swaying. I was so angry with Yolo but maddened at myself for ever thinking we'd share the same camaraderie. I was only permitted here to serve the coven. I would have to figure out a way by myself to free them.

I'd hated the Guild, ready to kill all those who opposed me and tried to kill Chase and me. But I couldn't pull away from the sense of duty and belonging I had to protect and save my previous comrades. I now had a purpose beyond finding Dillian and Julia a safe place. In this human compound, perhaps I could do some good. Perhaps somehow, this could work to my advantage. I just had to figure out how.

CHAPTER 15

J ENN AND I walked in silence. Whatever Yolo's thoughts about my interaction with the hunters, he kept them to himself. It would be to my advantage if I could have his assistance in their escape. He knew the compound and was the very person allocated to best conceal them. Hopefully, it would also enable me to somehow create an exit strategy. But I would have to figure out a way to somehow convince him and even then, much like Tythian, he would probably want something in return. I just had to figure out what that might be.

We walked back through the laboratory rooms where I first saw one of their live testings that ended in disaster. The blood had now been cleaned up. The smell from the cleaning chemicals covered the incident as if it had never happened, though an eerie silence remained in the other rooms, where scientists quietly went about their work. If I hadn't looked up at the door's glass where Sydney's blade broke through, and the bed hadn't scratched along the flooring, it would have looked like the evidence had been entirely covered up.

We walked past Mr. Richard's office and continued on toward the intersection of glass tunnels. Jenn led me toward the area she'd noted previously for the residential, food, hygiene, and training sectors. I could hear numerous voices and feet shuffle within the sector. The distinct noise of children playing and laughter sounded unnatural. I don't think I'd often heard a child laugh. I could hear and smell someone chopping meat, the fresh hint of blood made me feel as if I were starving. I contained the urge that wanted to come over me, I wouldn't allow it to overpower me so easily. *I was in control.*

Jenn looked over her shoulder and past the blonde fringe that covered some of her eyes. She was evidently on edge as she continued to eye me reassuringly to make sure I wasn't acting out uncontrollably. A lot had happened today, and I had no doubt she was becoming weary of my tiredness. Being surrounded by this many humans and activity was new for even me as a huntress, let alone when I had to suppress the vampire within from attacking—another foreign desire to me. Instead of looking at them as the creatures I once had to protect, I now looked at them as some sort of unquenchable nourishment. The thought continued to make me sick, though my instinct troubled me to pounce.

Jenn exited the tunnel and took the first right closing in on the prominent sector where I could hear people actively going about their day. She led me through numerous steel rooms that were on either side and triple-layered with ladders. Three children ran between us playing with a ball on the dirt path. I sidestepped out of their way before they ran into me, giddily trying to keep up with the older child. On my right and on the ground level, an older woman was sitting outside on her doorstep, watching them as they played. The room within had a small light on the wall and a single bed with a small shelf beside it. And that was it, quite the opposite to the extreme measures of resources and usage put into the rest of the compound. The residential dwellings were enough to indicate the people were secondary matter here.

The rows of structured dirt paths and people lazing about in their sectors continued for the length of the wall. I could only see elderly, wounded, or children. Everyone had their part to play within the compound.

Jenn continued to briefly glance my way. "Good afternoon." She politely waved to an elderly gentleman who mumbled through his lack of teeth. His eyes were sunken, and his skin was surprisingly tanned and wrinkled. I hadn't seen such an old human before. He continued merrily, holding a canister of water. He walked over to the old woman who was watching over the children play. She blushed a deep red as he offered the water.

The structure of the compound had consistency, and the tunnels didn't change much. Whoever mapped this out made a very distinct separation between purposes of the space used. We forked right again and came to a steel fenced-off section. Jenn pressed the white button to open the door, where a large field of dead grass and rocky turf opened before us. My eyes squinted at the irritating natural sunlight that beamed down on me. I twisted my neck to the side, vexed, and wanting to scratch all over. I tried to ignore it as best I could so I wouldn't arouse suspicions.

The area was still within their wall but an outer section that wasn't protected by the dome. A group of twenty members various in sizes, both men and women, ran around a purposefully painted out circle that extended along the wall. At different marked sections, they would drop and do strenuous exercises, and then run again. One man watched over them, yelled at them to continue, and to pick up their pace. The smell of endorphins and sweat bombarded my senses. This reminded me of my training days within my Guild.

Clatters of metal grabbed my attention. On my left, another ten members challenged one another with their swords. I couldn't resist the smile as I saw four of them using fake ones. Within the Guild, we had dummy weapons for our first year of training as young children. After that, we used very real weapons. If your opponent wounded you, then you were forced to only train harder because of your lack of focus and stamina.

On my right was a long-range archery field—my personal preference of weapon. As a young apprentice huntress, it was the weapon I quickly homed in on and efficiently learned to handle. There was a small fenced-off arena, which had silver chains cemented into the ground. There were bloodstains on the ground surrounding it, both black and red. I assumed this was where they trained within the walls against real vampires. They more than likely chained them and forced new members to challenge them. The blood didn't seem fresh—I could now distinguish what was old or fresh—and this had no smell to it at all. It was a mere memory, that training sector hadn't been used for many years now so I wondered why it was left there as a sentimental reminder.

"Ellie?" Sydney said, interrupting my thoughts and drawing my attention toward him. He eased his breathing from what looked like an intense run. Sweat dripped over his naked torso. His scar that started beneath his jawline continued down his neck and over his hard chest.

"What about me?" Jenn teased with hands on hips. "As agreed, I brought her here. I have business with Mr. Richard, so if I can leave her in your capable hands, that would be great. I need a decision made within the day. I'll be leaving again within a few hours before sundown, so you only have a few hours of assessment."

"Leaving so soon?" Sydney asked as one of the members threw a towel at him and he wiped over himself. There was one drop of sweat that continued to stay on the tip of his eyebrow.

"Mr. Richard has proposed a new project to me. With so much drama happening at the moment within the walls, I won't be able to offer efficient planning unless I am within my own compound to think. I'll bring Ellie with me every day, however. I'll not leave her here though. I've found myself oddly attached." She smiled and looped her arm around mine with a cheesy smile. I froze under her intrusive touch. I fought off the urge to throw her over my shoulder from guarded reflex.

"Well, isn't that a decision for Ellie to make? She doesn't seem exactly comfortable," Sydney disdained, watching me as he crossed his arms over his chest.

"I'd like to return with Jenn." I tried to relax into her touch, though it felt more awkward to do so. "I'll go where she goes." I sounded as if I were some lost human child.

"Have you ever met anyone who doesn't like me, Sydney," Jenn said, poking her tongue out at him. "I'll leave her in your capable hands." She rested her hand on my shoulder. "Ellie, if you need me, *call* me." She said the word 'call' stressing our previous agreement. If I were in any form of trouble or felt like I was losing control, I had to signal her with my gift. "Go easy on them, okay." She winked.

"Thank you, Jenn," I said and watched her leave back toward the compound. I envied her pale complexion that sunk back into the shadows and protection under the dome as she entered, instead of straining under the tormenting natural sunlight. *So itchy.*

"I'd like to thank you for this morning," Sydney said. "Assisting me with—" He cut himself off, unable to finish the sentence. He cleared his throat. "But it doesn't mean I'm accepting you yet. My people here work hard. How you act today will give me an indication as to what sector you'll best work in. We have those who watch the wall, a collective team who gather resources, and then there is my team—you'll only ever need to concern yourself with what we do if you're shortlisted onto the squad."

I deliberated my cocky response. I knew I was capable of any mere task he would set before me. I'd proven myself time and time again with numerous trials that made what the humans had to offer look like child's play.

"Understood," I mused as a subordinate human. "So, what do I need to do to prove myself to be on that delightful team?"

"Ahhh, you have a sense of sarcasm. I don't like it, give me fifty push-ups," Sydney chided. I arched my eyebrows. It'd been a long time since I'd taken orders from anyone but Campture. I pulled away from the natural instinct to challenge him. Pretending to be so low on the hierarchy was foreign, and especially to submit to a human's whim.

"*Just* fifty push-ups?" I asked, not able to bite back the taste of irritation completely. He raised one eyebrow as someone approached him, asking for permission to speak. Sydney stepped closer, the steam from his body radiating toward me. The pulse of his neck was tempting as the blood pumped effortlessly through his muscular, healthy frame. I gulped harshly, unable to now meet his eyes as he looked down on me. I reined in all my power of self-control. But his closeness was too tempting, and I found myself digging my nails into my hands and focused on the irritation of my skin.

"Make it two hundred." He breathed hastily on my face. "Your mind may not remember who you are, but muscle memory is a very real thing. We'll see what you were capable of before you hit your head, Ellie." I could smell the endorphins by being so close to him. It tempted me to grab the back of his neck and pull him in to feast.

"Sydney?" The other man interrupted. It snapped both of our attention away from one another and my fixation of his neck. I looked to the ground, reminding myself to focus on everything else but his pumping blood. My nails had begun to dig into my hand so tightly that a few marks of blood remained. I quickly wiped them away on my leather pants.

"Let me clap for the first fifty as well," I mused, unable to contain my confidence in my physical strength. Sydney's lip slightly curled. He looked away so I couldn't see the smile. He continued to watch me intently as I did my push-ups while he spoke to the other member.

I listened in to their conversation, bored out of my mind. It was all about practices and exercise regimes. I gave the humans a clap for their extreme measures to stay fit. It was close to the extent of what I forced my raid team to do every day but in a different extreme. It only confirmed the difference between humans and hunters. However, I couldn't help but ponder over what Mr. Richard had said about Sydney. That perhaps his mother had been huntress. Even then, if a child was not born with hunter's eyes, then they were discarded into a human camp. They have no extended strength or senses, but perhaps it aided them slightly when comparing to standard human beings. It wasn't something we ever looked further into after they were removed from the Hunter Guilds.

After my first one hundred of clap push-ups, which I slowed in pace and pretended to strain like any human would, I paused for a moment to take a breather. Sydney crouched in front of me, his companion now ran with the others. "Why aren't you sweating?" he asked, curiously.

I started on my next hundred push-ups, making sure to do them at a slow pace. "I don't know, perhaps I'm not working hard enough," I anguished with feigned breathlessness. I found pretending to be a human comical, and so almost every instruction offered to me was somewhat humorous. There was a comfort I found in Sydney, which I hadn't had with most. It was like being within my Guild, training again before my mother was announced dead and I, a Token Huntress. I always accepted those who challenged me, and thought me incapable of certain tasks. It reminded me of what I had once been, pushing myself to advance my skill and superiority every day.

"You have a big mouth for a little girl. You look to be what, eighteen?" He stared into my eyes, intently. I didn't look away. "But you seem much older when I look into your eyes. I wonder what past life you had, Ellie, to have seen so much and been built as you are. People with the same expression in your eyes all have one thing in common, and that's trauma and a natural instinct to fight. When your memory returns, please share it with me, I'm very interested to know who you really are."

I very much imagined he wouldn't like to know who or what I really was. It did intrigue me that he associated me with people he'd come across before. He called it trauma, I considered it a necessity if you wanted to survive in the outside world.

"That makes two of us," I gasped through another push-up. I was pretending to have amnesia, of course I would want to know of my previous life.

He smiled and stood, no longer crouching over me. "Once you finish those, we'll practice at the archery range, a lot of those who are on the wall are accurate with a bow and arrow."

"I don't want to be on the wall," I grumbled. Instead of lecturing me in his overruling tone for defying him, he surprised me.

"And why's that?" he asked as he studied the rest of his members who ran around and continued to struggle under the heat and hours of strenuous training.

"It seems boring. When I saved your ass from that saber, I guess I realized I liked the thrill." I half-laughed as if straining through my push-up. This exercise was ridiculous to me.

"You think you saved my ass?" he mocked.

"I imagine a good leader would take it in stride," I reasoned. There was a part of him that reminded me so much of my trainer and previous Token Hunter, Drue. Before I was named in charge and Token, he was my teacher and leader. He didn't train me personally, but he pushed me because of my superior attitude. We played such idle games of taunts and challenge continuously. Finally, I had pin-pointed why I acted toward Sydney in such a strange way. He reminded me of Drue. I stood up, now done with the boring push-ups. "Now, let's go to the arrows."

He studied me for a moment and then presented his hand outward for me to walk first. I grabbed the bow that sat on the ground and strapped the bag with arrows over my shoulder. I looked at the distance, which was only about twenty meters, an easy shot. Though I preferred my crossbow the standard bow was still just fine. I pulled back my first arrow, it would be a perfect shot even with the wind that rushed past, and I'd already taken this into account. But I couldn't make it look so easy, I had to be human, and humans made plenty of mistakes.

Sydney stood behind me with arms crossed over his chest, looking at the aim himself. I let go and watched it hit near the center, but not dead on.

"You need to consider the wind, lift your next arrow," Sydney said, watching me as I aimed in the same position. He tipped my elbow slightly and angled it. It was an accurate perception, considering he himself was not shooting it.

A bellowing alarm grabbed everyone's attention. A surround system of numerous speakers all along the wall sounded in alarm.

"Everyone to the wall now! Take your weapons!" Sydney shouted. "What section?" he yelled at one of the guards who stood atop the wall above us. He squinted at Sydney, obviously unable to hear him. The guard beside him lined up the harpoon and began to shoot. Something was down there.

Everyone began to scale the roped ladders along the wall, with swords and bows strapped. I followed Sydney, watching the two guards on top as they shot below. There was no way they could see, the mist would be too thick. They must've been shooting aimlessly. I honed my hearing beyond the wall and heard the scratching noises of something scaling the wall. Not one, but four. The members that gathered were enough to handle the three that lumped together on the left, but there was one further on the right that climbed separately to its pack. I looked into that direction that had no positioned guard. That creature had now stopped scaling the wall, and I could smell fresh blood. Had it already overcome the guard who was once posted there?

I ran into that direction, annoyed by my pretend human pace that limited me. I jumped for the ladder and scaled the wall. I threw myself over the jagged cement and balanced elegantly atop. Still hunched over, I stared at the creature that now feasted and devoured the guard's stomach, who only minutes ago was alive. The fresh smell of blood ensnared me. My ears pounded, listening in on the lack of beating from the fresh blood. It was nothing but emptiness, but still the blood enticed me. It was still so fresh. My purple hazed eyes fixated on the steady stream that pooled out of the guard. I was revolted in myself. This guard wasn't alive, his blood no longer pumped in his veins. I savored for fresh blood, *alive* blood. I couldn't be tempted by some blood smeared on a pavement. My fangs retracted. I stood detailing the creature. So this was the rodent they'd previously discussed.

Its sharp fangs ate into the corpse savagely. There were bite marks around the guard's face. It looked as if the creature had lunged for his head and snapped his neck. The beast was the size of a horse. It had smaller legs and a thick tail, its fur matted, with chunks missing. The creature with red eyes looked up at me, snarling. Its ribs poked out of its transparent skin, where patches all over its body looked as if it had melted from a long time spent near radiation.

I raised my arrow, aiming for its head. What a disgusting creature. The creature slammed into the side of the wall, unable to run straight. I continued to follow it with my arrow, lining it up until I shot it. I hit it, dead center between its eyes and jumped over the wall, so it wouldn't run into me. I caught the rope and balanced my feet on the side of the inside wall, avoiding friction on my hand as I slid slightly down. The creature continued to scrape against the cement, of where I once stood. When it came to a stop, I propped myself up two footsteps and looked over the wall.

I looked up at Sydney who gazed between the dead rodent and me. The creature was dead at his feet. I'd been aware he was there the whole time. I had my back to him the entire time so he couldn't see my fangs or hunter eyes. What I made sure he witnessed was a lasting impression done within human speed.

"Sydney, three have been taken down. We can't see any more." One of the women came panting as she ran along the wall.

"How many were injured?" he asked, unimpressed by the remains of the dead human in front of him.

"Three," she said, "and one fatality," she continued when she saw the guard's body in front of Sydney.

"Report this to Mr. Richard. I want double on the wall, stick within rotation. Over the next month, everyone will be working double time. We can't risk losing anymore, they've been getting cocky lately," he instructed. She curtly nodded and pardoned herself. Sydney crouched down above the rope that I hung from. He held his hand out to me. I grabbed it, accepting his aid to lift me up.

"I'm still not sure about you. But your body moves as a warrior, and you have no hesitation or fear," he said somberly in thought. We both looked down at the rodent who had an arrow embedded between its eyes. It could've been slightly more to the left to be perfect, but it was still a good shot. "I'll have you by my side on my team. I don't know how long Jenn plans on skipping out again, but in two days' time we're going out to look for some resources beyond the wall. You're either here, or you're not," he warned. "Continue practicing on your archery before Jenn comes and collects you. You were a little off center."

Instead of being angry at his comment on my archery, I almost wanted to laugh. It had been a long time since anyone commented on my less than perfect skills, especially coming from a human. I said nothing as he walked past me and gathered the remains of the corpse that had been devoured. The guard's blood dripped down his still shirtless frame. I looked at the rodent, its red eyes still open. My aim had been close to flawless. Sydney climbed down the roped ladder with the man on his back. Blood was smeared all over his face. I could only imagine that his disappointment was not in my aim, but in one of his members being taken while under his command. The shuddering thought of Kasey and Kora came to mind. I had lost many on my team recently. Well, what remained of my team. I wouldn't allow myself to reflect the same expression that Sydney did. I couldn't feel emotion, but a sense of duty was the closest thing I could recall that was similar. It was my last duty to the world and life I once knew as a huntress.

CHAPTER 16

MEMBERS WITHIN THE compound remained silent that afternoon. Even the children had stopped playing and laughing as they'd been ushered into their bunkers. A few younger members continued to train with a new resolve, and those who remained guarded the walls. Jenn returned two hours after Sydney had left. She intently studied the high security on the wall and then me.

"I'm fine. I didn't lose control," I said. I wasn't willing to admit, for only a fleeting moment, I had. But, no one saw, so it was as if it had never happened. I also didn't want to diminish the trust Yolo had invested in me. If he truly had been concerned, he would've been by my side the moment the attack happened.

"They have a lot of fighters in their military section," Jenn praised. "There's another department that specializes in guns and bombs. This is only a small portion of their numbers. It surprised even me, how heavily guarded they were. But they only use old-styled weaponry for the borders. They're saving the rest for when they plan on making a move against the Council, which in incidences like these seems counter intuitive."

Jenn silenced when a member walked past. The man looked her up and down in admiration, before advancing toward the wall. Humans raced about frantically, even though it happened hours ago. The members of the military sector were vigilant, but the mentality of the others was not as controlled or strong. Somehow, even after all these hundreds of years, there were humans who survived, despite not being natural fighters or the fittest. Natural selection had immensely stripped them out but not entirely.

Jenn led me through the glass tunnels. We only crossed one armored human who was making her way to the wall. Humans had fled into their residence or further into the compound in fear.

Even as we walked throughout the glass tunnels and hallways from the way we'd originally come in, it was silent. We entered the initial scanning area where we were reevaluated before we left. We both received the green pass, but the guards gave us skeptical glances. They urged we stayed the night after such an attack. Jenn wouldn't allow it, patting the burly man I'd been introduced to this morning on the shoulder, flirtatiously telling him we'd be all right. Jenn often argued the importance of being in her personal lodgings where her brilliance could only strike.

"You are a fearless woman, Jenn," the guard from this morning commented. He looked at my bow and arrows with an intrigued look.

"I have Ellie for protection. I feel safeguarded," Jenn mused with a warm smile. Hesitantly, they lowered us on the outskirts of the wall. I was curious as to how Yolo was able to charm them into being let in and out and being trusted in for doing so. We found humans and kept them within the human camps for their own safety. Whereas surprisingly, the human compounds evoked way of free movement, well, except for those who were being experimented on. It was twisted in so many ways.

The sun was sinking as we started our two-hour human paced walk. "I'm concerned that they'll want you to stay within the compound," Jenn announced during our walk. "I fought very hard to have the ability to slip in and out, but I'm worried you won't have the same luxury, especially after leaving such an impression on Sydney. He might want to keep you close."

"I'm sure it'll be okay. We can organize for Tythian to teleport in at certain times, couldn't we?"

"Absolutely not," Jenn snapped somewhat territorial over her project. She recovered herself quickly, clearing her throat. "I don't think he'll enjoy the thought of being a babysitter and our means of transportation. Even if you had to stay within the compound, you wouldn't necessarily have a separate room. And, Tythian's never physically been within the compound so he won't know how to visualize the location he's attempting to teleport into."

I had the impression Yolo didn't want Tythian's interference with his hard work, but twisted it in a way of where it might be an inconvenience to Tythian. "I feel confident in being able to hold my own ground, no matter what way the leaf may sway," I said. "Though my core focus doesn't change from Dillian and Julia's escape, I'll make sure to find a way out of that compound."

Jenn came to a stop, we were now noticeably on the border of where their monitoring and traps ended. It was now night, the soothing sensation of the moon felt like a balm on my skin.

"What exactly are you after now?" Jenn asked harshly, her façade completely vanished. This was now Yolo speaking. "You've seen it isn't safe for your hunter friends. Are your only interests in the military section to help the coven, or are you apprehensive about your previous comrades who tried to kill you and are now trapped because humans outwitted them?"

My rage bore down on my shoulders, wanting to leap for Jenn's throat after a day of irritation from the sun and my inability to completely hide my fangs and hunter's eyes. A crunch in the nearby distance alarmed me. My focus changed. I sensed two presences close by. I slammed a strong urge of being watched into Jenn. She clutched her hand to her stomach as if a wave of nausea hit her and then looked around alert. I wasn't sure if in this body, Jenn was oblivious to Yolo's vampire senses, it was like he was completely side-blinded to being watched.

I pointed one finger to the ground for her to stay. "Human pace," she whispered. In case it was someone from the compound. I ran toward the two that tracked us. They began to run, and their pace was beyond that of human capability. I didn't announce that to Yolo however, I wanted to find the suspects before he did. What if it were somehow Chase's coven? What would I do if I made contact with them again? What if they were a part of Fier's Council, and how did they know we were here?

The two shadowy figures continued to run further into the woodlands. I enjoyed the thrill to chase after them at such a delightful pace. It felt like I was finally stretching my legs after a day of sluggish pretend enthusiasm. I cornered them and had them in my sight. A womanly figure turned, and flames splashed in front of my face. I dodged the attack before it had the chance to hit my skin. An arrow shot at me from the treetops, and I dodged it as if dancing. Oh, how I missed being on the offense. Flames flickered by my side again, before I realized amongst my dance that I knew those flames.

"Teary?!" I exasperated, still evading the flames as I tried to get closer. The flames and arrows stopped, descending into ashes on the ground. Like a wall had been dropped between her and me. My well-respected previous comrade stood across from me. "By the heavens ye still alive." She gasped.

"Esmore?" The apprentice's voice came from the trees. Tori peered down at me. I was ashamed by my form and retracted my fangs, the purple of my hunter's eyes clearing.

"I saw ye take a blow to the chest," Teary said in disbelief with her thick accent. Tori scaled down the tree efficiently and crept closer toward me.

"You are really alive! I told you Teary, I told you she couldn't be killed so easily!" the young sixteen-year-old apprentice said, clapping his hands in triumph.

"What are you two doing hovering along the border of the human compound?" I asked now alarmed. This wasn't a safe area for them to be. Why weren't they with the majority of the Guild, or had they been broken up as well after the ambush?

"We were following we' Kora and Kasey to see where they were goin,' but they got caught. We hav' been trying to find a way to break them out eva since. They were taken in a rather aggressive way, which to me would state they were taken against their own will. For all their attitude, those two girls hav,' I'd still use my own life to save them," she said insightfully. "And ye?"

I was cautious. Were they still comrades or were they baiting me into some trap? Could I trust the two? But their survival meant so much. If the compound wasn't an option, wherever they fled to maybe Dillian and Julia could join. It was much safer for a group of rogue hunters to band together, unless Teary would take them straight to Campture.

"I was trying to find a safe place for Dillian and Julia," I admitted, reading their reactions. It didn't matter if Campture found out they were alive because right now, they were locked away in a place she could never reach.

"They're still alive?" Tori mused. "Where are they now?" he asked, looking around.

"Not with me," I said abruptly. Teary and Tori shared a confused expression.

"Now, listen here, we Token. With what happened in the Guild, we neva' supported it. That's why Tori and I fled in separate ways." I could hear Jenn's voice calling out to me in the distance. She'd caught up to me. I doubted it wasn't long now until Yolo would resurface from irritation and refute me if I took too long. I didn't want him to know about this meeting. Teary and Tori's survival changed a lot of things. It meant that possibly, I had an angle that the coven wouldn't know about. There could be another out.

"I can't explain much now. But I'm trying to get the twins out as well, I have access into the human compound, they don't know I'm a huntress."

"Or vampire?" Teary asked me, slightly confused. They had been there when I protected Chase. They saw the mixture of my form. She was calling me out for the subject I wanted to avoid the most.

"They don't know that either," I said hesitantly. Aware of Jenn almost upon us. I hurried along. I didn't have time to discuss that. "Can you stay around the borders, but don't go further than this, they have traps set up. I don't know how long I'll be. But I don't trust those I am with right now. I don't want them to know of you two or our meeting. Can you hide for long enough around here? If you can, I'll find you in a few days," I promised.

"Ye don't give us much to go by, Esmore," Teary said with a lack of trust. "But in saying that I hav' vowed to be by ye side and listen to your command, I won't say no to ye."

"This isn't a command," I said so quickly it surprised even me. "I'm no longer deserving of my role as your Token," I said, defeated.

"It doesn't matter whether the Guild is still within place or not, Esmore. I made a decision the day they strapped ye and your vampire lover, that I would not follow Campture anymore. I don't know exactly the details of what ye might be, but if ye can assure me ye are the same, I will still follow ye,'" Teary said respectfully.

"Me too," Tori rattled. "I know I was a pain in your ass when I started on your team, but I owe much to you. I know we aren't meant to show emotion, but no one else cared for Fam or Pac's death. You still protected me, no matter how much lip I gave you. And Teary has saved me countless times since we escaped the Guild. If she follows you, then I will too."

I felt lighter by their words. I hadn't realized how much their gesture alone could work as a repellant to the darkness I'd let feed off me this entire time. I'd thought I was a monster, but at their expressions alone, it empowered me in the briefest that I could still fight this off. There was a chance that my huntress form could prevail. She wasn't entirely gone.

"You both must go now. I'll find you, be safe," I added. Within seconds they vanished, the mist around us billowing behind them. I ran back toward Jenn at my human pace.

"You're annoying, little sis," Jenn said, unimpressed and panting. "These breasts are beautiful, but they hurt to run in. What was it?"

"I lost them at this 'human' pace," I lied. "Do your senses really not work in that form?"

"What implied that?" she asked. I studied her for a moment. Did she know I was lying to her? Had she listened in to our conversation?

A pillow of the mist encasing our ankles vanished as Tythian arrived. "Good evening." He grabbed onto both of us, and the nauseating sensation of being pulled through darkness swept over me. Suddenly, we were within the coven again. Cesar, Connor, Balzar, and my mother waited in the central room, where I had first met all four brothers. The small chandelier swayed slightly from the wind of our sudden entrance. My mother took a step toward me in relief but stopped to hide the emotion, a natural thing for a huntress to do.

"Nice of you to be around," I said somewhat angrily. I had hardly seen my mother since all of this commotion began. I'd been on numerous tasks already and where had she been?

"Watch your tone," my mother said equally.

"Yolo and Balzar leave the room. Go and relieve Lydia from her guard," Cesar ordered. Jenn reformed into the shirtless Yolo, whose shoulders slumped tiredly.

"No, 'oh hey, how was your day?'" Yolo teased. With a firm look from Cesar, he waved his hand. "I get it, I get it, adult talk now. C'mon Balzar."

"Report to me later, Yolo," Cesar yelled out after them.

After the two left, Cesar looked at me with a mischievous smile, ignoring the tension between my mother and I. "So, how did my little girl go on her first day as acting human?" He stretched his hands out to hug me. I stepped back, impartial to his theatrics.

"Don't touch me," I said, not wanting such unnecessary contact with him. I was only in this mess because he had dragged us back into this coven. I wasn't here to play happy family. "I can confirm I've made an impression and was approved for the military section. However, as Yolo predicted it isn't a place for hunters. I found two of my comrades within the compound, both have been mutilated and affected as test subjects. I want them out," I stated bluntly.

"Who?" my mother asked, no longer sitting in the chair. I bit back my irritation. What had she been up to this entire time? She was a woman of action and rebellion, I had no doubt she was setting her own moves into play, but we hadn't spoken enough for me to have a better understanding of her goal. I trusted in my mother, but she now had a long line of secrets she'd been hiding from me, and I still felt violated from her taking my heart without permission with so little of an explanation, as if I were still just a child. Though, if anyone could convince Cesar to help me extract the twins from the compound, it would be her.

"Kora and Kasey. They've mutilated them, and their appearance seems to be physically part saber, but still have their hunter eyes, ability, and sanity."

Connor growled in the corner that he leaned against. "This is why I hate humans. Can't we just kill them?" Connor had such an impression that if he wanted to fade his presence into non-existence, he could, even when he was standing right beside you. Tythian was silent beside Connor, simply watching. It reminded me to keep my thoughts and questions for my mother at a later time. I didn't want any of the brothers or Cesar being a part of that confrontation.

"Be patient, Connor," Cesar hushed. "I need you for something else. You too, Esmore, I'd like you to be a part of it. I'm sending all five of you, my children, out for this task."

I was tired of these ongoing tasks, yet it was the only way I could find numerous options to suit our escape. If I outright told Cesar I planned on leaving with my hunter friends, I doubted he'd let me go. But he also understood the detriment to keeping them here for so long. Again, another person who was playing at his own hand. We all had ambitions that we personally favored, and in it, I would find my opportunity to escape by using theirs.

"What is it?" I asked, curious as to why he would send all five of us. I wasn't necessarily going to accept unless it would benefit the protection of the others.

"I went back to Fier's Council today," Tythian interrupted. "He seems unsuspecting of my involvement. His ego is rather easy to please and blinds him." I had no doubt it was also the skill and charm Tythian had about him and how he convinced me to make so many bargains with him. It angered me to realize I was yet another addition to his cunningness. "They assume you and Chase are dead, by the way, after leading the sabers to your Guild. He actually thinks he got the better of you. It was rumored that a small team of Oppollo's will be moving toward the meeting place within a few days before Oppollo goes personally. We need to intercept them."

"Why? What is your obsession with *his* Council?" I asked, recalling the name from our previous discussion. Cesar's expression changed, and he gritted his teeth.

"Because he has the biggest Council, and he'll most likely reign over the rest of them if it comes to an all-out war. I won't allow that. Until then, we have a few things that need to play out. Your familiar," Cesar paused, holding my gaze, "he cannot stay here, nor your hunter friends. The coven is moving restlessly, you've impressed a few with your leadership on the assassination, but that'll not hold off the rest. There's only one way he can weave in and out of this coven. And that's if he reclaims his coven and aligns with ours. We already have an agreement with another two."

"And if he doesn't?" I asked. Chase made it very clear he wanted no involvement with them.

"Then I will kill him," Cesar said, bluntly. I snarled in rage at him, but my mother stepped in between.

"Please, Esmore, listen," she said calmly. My fangs only hurt more as I bared them at my mother. How could she side with him over me? "It's the only way we can keep you safe. We need the numbers."

"I never asked for such treatment! I would rather be on my own with them, then locked within this coven, trying to find a way out!" I spat harshly. I stormed off, before I forced action upon them that I would regret. Tythian followed me silently.

"Is our agreement still in place?" I asked desperate to get Dillian and Julia away from this place safely. I needed to act soon. Time was running out. If I could have Tythian teleport us all out of here and near the human camp that we trafficked humans, then they might find a place they could be safe. It wasn't an ideal plan, but it was a starting point to get out. I needed to stop looking at the long haul of shifting movement and focus on my first task of Dillian and Chase. So much was constantly moving that I struggled to focus on one thing as I absorbed so much from this strange world.

"If you have found Whitney's brother's identity, then yes," he said, impartial.

"I did. I looked him dead in the eye without realizing it," I said, stopping and giving him the satisfaction to know he could have his revenge. His face twitched as I spoke the words. "When I found out his identity, I wanted to rip out his very throat. Whitney was not my familiar, but she never deserved such a death. He, Charlie, continues to practice on humans within that compound the same way. I saw it destroy a human within minutes in front of my very own eyes. You show us out, and I'll help you inside the walls to kill him. Yolo, of course, has nothing to do with this agreement."

Tythian crossed his arms, looking around to see if anyone else heard. Yolo would do anything he could to stop us if he found out about this bargain. Tythian had no real regard for it.

"Agreed. I still want my revenge on Fier," he said simply, alternating to his secondary agreement. For that, I still owed him after he teleported Chase and me out of the Vampire Council.

"And you will get it," I hissed. "I have a few things I need to handle right now as well. But I promise you, I want that vampire dead as much as you do. We *will* kill him together." And once we did, our agreements were done—all but one—to kill Thomas. In the span of days, I had signed away so much of myself in an attempt to protect the others. But if it weren't for Tythian, I'd be almost helpless each time. I hated giving my word and being so indebted to a vampire that I equally mistrust and hate.

With vampire speed, I swept through the tunnels and opened the doors to Cesar's room. The smell of freshly cooked meat hit my nose. I looked over to the dining table where Dillian, Julia, and Balzar sat. Balzar swirled and enjoyed a glass of blood. Dillian and Julia were uncomfortable as they ate a forkful, and yet they still sat at the one table, even though he had attacked them previously.

"Oh this," Balzar said light-heartedly as he pointed between them. "This is a peace offering and apology." I took two steps to the right, looking over at Yolo and Chase who were oddly positioned and twisted on the floor—only their hands and feet touched the odd colored mat.

"Oh, hey, honey," Chase said, with a grunt of effort. "Want to join us in a game of Twister? It's a bit before your time, but you'll learn quickly."

"Red!" Yolo laughed at Chase. Chase looked behind him at the furthest corner of the mat. Yolo was twisted beneath him. Chase arched his arm backward uncomfortably, his arm twisted until a definite snap was heard. He breathed threw it, placing his hand down.

"Hey!" Yolo yelled. "No breaking bones! That's cheating."

"No, it's not. I reached the spot, didn't I?" Chase mused. His leather jacket swept over Yolo's figure, his shirtless chest awkwardly thrust up.

"Eww, dude, that's so nasty. It's like sticking out grossly, look how it's healed back. I forfeit, that's nasty!" Yolo said. With vampire speed, Yolo created a small breeze in the room. He snatched the glass from Balzar's hand and took a sip. I stared at them wide-eyed. What had I just walked in on?

"Eww, you smell gross," Chase mused as he walked over to me, reconfiguring his arm. "You smell like men, like heaps of testosterone. What did you do, become their queen or something?" Chase teased.

"I think Sydney has the hots for her," Yolo teased as he poured his own glass of blood.

Chase arched an eyebrow. "Sydney," he prodded "Sounds like such a heroic name. Like ecstasy. I could only imagine his bulky arms and his—"

"Shut up," I said, slapping his bare chest. "And he does not, Yolo." I rubbed my temples, unsure of how I walked in on this odd gathering. I had the most perplexed and intense day, and this whole time, they were here, playing games? I knew they were stuck here, but this still wasn't what I'd been expecting. Chase was far too comfortable in the face of danger.

"Mmmm, Sydney." Chase laughed. "Seriously but, his smell is all over you. I'm going to have to scrub that beautiful body of yours and claim it as mine all over again."

Tythian and my mother walked into the room behind me.

"Are you ready to go?" Tythian asked Chase.

"I have a surprise for you." Chase smiled. "Since you came back and didn't break your vamp barrier, I thought I'd treat you," he mused, grabbing my nose and pinching it. He swept my legs out from beneath me and held me close to his chest.

"Where are we going? I'm not leaving without Dillian and Julia, and we have things we need to plan," I forced, trying to escape Chase's firm grip.

"They will be well looked after. This I can promise you. Esmore, we have a lifetime together of things to plan. We are allowed a few hours selfishly to ourselves." Chase kissed the top of my forehead.

"But I have to talk to my mother." I wiggled angrily. There was a barrage of things I had to plan, and I didn't like that he had made some sort of deal with Tythian, which I was learning came at a price. There was too much at stake here. "And—"

"Come on, my beautiful baby vamp. A few hours will flash by in a blink, and nobody makes good decisions while hungry and frustrated. We're going to teach you how to be a proper vampire." I looked up at Chase, confused and overwhelmed by the exhaustion that played on my body. As soon as I was in his arms, the day's work washed over me like a weight. And what did he mean about becoming a proper vampire?

Tythian's hand firmed around both of us. Again, I was swept into utter darkness before our next location was revealed.

CHAPTER 17

M Y MIND SWIRLED, and I attempted to press down the nauseous feeling that swelled up my throat. I focused on my bearings. Teleporting so often made me disorientated. Surely it took a toll on the body, or perhaps it hardly affected those who were beyond human. Chase had once told me it exhausted Tythian to an extent. A cool breeze of wind gushed past me. I squinted at the pillowing white before me, trying to see through it. Tythian vanished and left Chase and me alone in a swirl of snow. We stood on frozen water where large icebergs peaked. The temperature was freezing, it had to be, yet my skin didn't react. This had to be because of my vampire self, even my huntress form would've been cold in such temperature.

Chase still held me firmly to his chest, smiling. His leather coat flapped against the wind as his bare chest was unaffected by the freezing temperature. I brushed my finger over his hard nipple, which still seemed to respond.

"It's so nice to be out," he delighted. He began walking, still holding me in such a way, unbothered by my weight.

"Are you going to let me down and explain to me what's happening?" I asked with my arms delicately wrapped around his neck. It was pointless to argue with him. When Chase decided to do something even if irrational, he was determined to see it through no matter how inappropriately timed it was. I couldn't help but continuously think about Dillian and Julia's safety. Yet here we were, in the middle of the snow. My mother would've taken my position to protect them within the room, though that offered me no reassurance in our current situation. Although none of the coven had yet made a move, it was still plausible a rebellion could happen at any moment, and it wasn't a risk I wanted to take. Chase flicked my forehead. I rubbed it out of reflex.

"Stop thinking about it. You're lucky you don't age, and your skin doesn't sag, or you'd be a bag of wrinkly skin." He chuckled. I punched him in the chest.

"Why, are you saying you wouldn't care for me then?" I said, naturally being swayed into the atmosphere Chase created. I felt him hovering over my mind, calming me. I didn't think it was something he now consciously did, but as soon as we were together, this was the effect he had on me.

"Well, it'd just be troublesome, because I would still be ravishingly handsome. Don't you think people would question it?" He smiled, sliding his hand and grabbing a firm grasp on my ass.

"Coming from the vampire who is over four hundred years old and still acts like a child?" I taunted back with an arched eyebrow.

He offered me a devilish smile. "Still ravishingly handsome though." With vampire speed, he swept through the blizzard until we approached a rocky and frozen wall.

Chase looked at my chest, grabbing hold of the blue gemmed necklace he had given me so long ago, to claim me as his within the Vampire Council. It matched his singular earring of the same gem. "But, I would still keep you none the less. Maybe feed you soup every day. If you give me sass though, I'd starve you for a day at a time, maybe give you nothing but candy so you had a tummy ache," he teased. "But you will forever be mine." He stepped closer, his gray eyes pooling into me. It was overwhelming to feel this warmth and sensation, I could only feel this with a chosen few. And with Chase, it was heated passion and a possessiveness I never knew was contained within me. But there was softness. He was the only person I naturally stripped in front of, and showed my weakness that lay within.

"Why did you bring me here, Chase?" I asked. Chase, although eccentric, always had a reason and good judgment. If he made a deal with

Tythian to bring me to this place, I had to trust my familiar's actions. My eyes danced over his perfectly formed stomach that was exceptionally chiseled. I was surprised he hadn't made a joke about them cutting ice yet. A smile pulled up at his lips as he must've overheard the thought. "Get over yourself." He cupped the back of my neck, his tongue dominating mine. He pushed me against the cold icicle wall which left a burning sensation on my skin. Perhaps my skin did feel the cold. His tongue pushed deeper against mine as I dragged my nails down his stomach wanting more. It was immediate combustion as soon as he held me in such a way. I wanted his warmth to fill me entirely as his touch spread through my entirety.

He pulled away with a smile, a knowing smile, of what I wanted so much from him.

"Whoever scales the wall first wins! Whoever loses has to skinny dip in that freezing water. You might not feel it now, but when you jump into such extreme temperatures, oh yea, your body will get a shock," he teased. "When you get to the top, be quiet." I left my hand to linger on him, smiling at the challenge. I still didn't know what he was plotting, but even then I wasn't going to let him win, no matter how trivial the matter. He gave me one more passionate kiss before releasing me. "Cheer for me as I kick your ass, baby girl. Go!"

We both had firm holds on the wall, gripping into the slippery mess as we scaled. I used my thick nails to pinch at the top for extra measure. At vampire speed, we scaled up the elongated cliff edge and were at the top within the minute. Chase had beaten me by only a few seconds. He rested against the cave entrance, pretending he'd been waiting for a lifetime. He pressed his finger to his lips to remind me to be silent.

"There's an animal in here. We're not going to kill it. I'm going to teach you how to paralyze and drink from it, learning to stop in time," Chase said within my mind.

"Paralyze it? What kind of creature is it?" I asked. He grabbed my hand and slowly walked me into the dark cave entrance. Chase understood me better than I knew myself nowadays. He was doing this for me, so I could learn self-control, especially when locked in a room of temptation that was my own former hunters and best friend.

"It's rather ironic, actually. They were thought to be extinct, but when the world went into devastation and began freezing back over, they were one of the animals to survive. Not many sabers survive around these parts, the Antarctic, as they fall into

135

holes and get trapped beneath the frozen water's surface. This is a Polar Bear, they still hibernate during the colder time, which is ultimately always, but they've adjusted in their own measure," Chase said, as he led me toward a corner of the cave. In there was a giant creature with beautiful thick white fur. It was stunning. It slept, unsuspecting of our presence.

"All vampires can inject venom. It's used for two reasons. One, you can paralyze your victim. But it must be portioned, if you use too much then that's how you turn another into a vampire. If they were to die with that much venom in their system, then they'd come back as vampires. If that were to happen, there would be a very hard bond between them to break. Vampires who don't know how to control their venom are dangerous. If they're only a new vampire themselves and create another vampire, then that vampire would more than likely be reborn defective. I've seen it happen a few times. It caused such a yearning between the two, that when the defected vampire dies from either starving out or being killed by another vampire, it leaves an emotional blow on its maker. I've seen vampires commit suicide over this bond," Chase informed me.

"I didn't know vampires could do that," I said, digesting the information.

"There's a lot you don't know yet, which is why I'm going to teach you. Tythian spoke about this place a lot. Apparently, he often brought Whitney because she loved to watch the polar bear sleep and pat it. I asked Tythian to bring me here to train you." Chase still held my hand firmly, smiling at my disgruntled expression. *"He doesn't always ask for something in return, Esmore. Let your conscious be free of that. I owe him nothing for this. You seem to forget that Tythian and I have known one another for many lifetimes now."*

"Everything I ask of him, he has a price." I frowned. Was it because Tythian knew I was weak, that I couldn't achieve my own goals without him?

"That's because he can see you're in a position of power that will aid him. And you are, Esmore, you have a lot of power right now, even when you don't realize it. But, whatever he has asked of you, please tell me. If it puts you in danger, I want to know." I stared into his beautiful gray eyes, wanting to tell him everything. I no longer wanted to hide it from him. But those bargains we'd made, I had hidden from Chase on purpose. I couldn't tell him that we were aiming to take down his deceased mother's familiar, Fier, who was like a step-father to him. And that my mind still focused on my team members from my Hunter Guild. I couldn't let that part of me go no matter how much he hated hunters. I couldn't admit to him that I was willing to give Tythian the key to Whitney's brother and watch him as he slaughtered him. I don't think Chase would have minded that bargain, but there was a certain darkness that stirred within me, that would find relief and

wanted to join in on that motive; that was the part I was scared for Chase to see. Chase calmed me, restrained that darkness within me. What would he think of me if he knew I wanted at times to delve in that darker side and enjoy that blood thirsted nature?

"Show me how to paralyze it," I interjected, while I still hid all these thoughts from him. I could feel Chase scan over my mind, hoping for an inclination of what those thoughts might be. I had learned from Tythian, how I could block certain thoughts, specifically from Chase. His expression was saddened that I'd used it against him yet again. I didn't want Chase to see the evil that lay inside, the beast that cooed to me and thirsted for these bargains to be sought out. I didn't want him to see the ugly beast that lay within because I feared that it would claw through me and into him and devour him whole. He was my sanctuary, my calm, and the only thing that could seclude me from that darkness. I needed Chase's purity. I couldn't allow him to be a part of the darkness that I danced in.

"Come on," he whispered and led me closer to the Polar Bear. He crouched down in front of it, insisting I do the same. I watched it as it slept, almost majestically. This was a creature that had survived from all those years ago. Here, peacefully sleeping. Knowing that it should hide in a cave, high up where no one should be able to find it.

Chase's fangs were far larger than mine, showing our age difference and experience. I wanted to reach out and touch them. It felt as if it'd been a long time since Chase and I had been like this, in our purest and very real form. My eyesight glazed over purple as my hunter's eyes and fangs over swept me with relief. Chase shuffled around silently, to dip me closer toward the Polar Bear's neck.

"You must be quick because it'll stir. We don't want to cause it stress. It'll come naturally to you. Just think of yourself injecting, instead of sucking. The effects are almost instant. But remember to control it, only a little bit. We want to affect its bloodstream, not over run it with our venom," Chase educated me. I nodded and held my golden blonde plait to the side. I hesitated for a moment, alarmed by how little I resisted what Chase instructed me to do. I was both confident in his teachings but also felt natural in what I was doing, which only scared me more. I was incrementally swimming into my vampire form.

I looked at the white fur of its neck. I'd never bitten through fur before. I wondered how the texture would feel on my tongue. I bit into the bear's neck, doing exactly as Chase instructed. The bear woke, but only for a moment. I released the venom Chase spoke of. It astounded me how natural the process came to me. Within two seconds, the bear was silent once again. Chase stroked the head of the bear. I pulled away from its neck and looked at my achievement, a small black liquid dripped from the bite I'd left. I wiped and rubbed it between my fingers. It was a sticky substance. The smell of my venom couldn't overpower the scent of its now open wound. My body throbbed to taste this fresh blood.

"Go ahead, Esmore, this is what it's used for. You must be starving by now," Chase said, still patting its head. I looked between him and the bear uncertain. I craved for it, but feared if I had a taste, I wouldn't be able to stop. I'd tried to control myself for so long now. "It's okay."

Trusting Chase, I delved into the bear's neck savagely, enjoying the hot stream that flowed into my mouth. The metallic taste of its blood filled me and pooled into my bloodstream like I so thirsted for. My stomach felt hot and heavy. The food that I ate could not nourish me, this is what my body needed. My grip tightened around the creature as I hungered for more. I needed more. It wasn't quenching my thirst.

"Esmore," Chase whispered and pushed back a piece of my fringe. "If you don't stop, you'll kill this creature." I continued draining it. His words were incoherent to me. I was not full.

"Esmore," Chase said again. "I'll not stop you. This will be a consequence if you have no control. Do you really want to kill this creature you thought to be so peaceful and majestic?" I felt his fingers faintly roll over the back of my neck. I wanted more, but I could hear him clearly. My conscience faded in and out. I felt my eyes pinning as if they narrowed further down on my prey, an instinct to continue drinking. But Chase was right, I didn't want to kill this creature. I pulled away and scampered to the other corner of the cave, so I wouldn't be as tempted by the close proximity. The smell still swarmed me, and I wasn't sure if I could resist much longer. I looked at Chase, my fangs still revealed and my tongue panting for more. Parched, I felt even thirstier.

"Esmore, I'm proud of you," Chase said with a smile. He bit into his wrist and nuzzled it against the bear's lips. "This will make sure it recovers properly. It'll appear as if your damage was never done. Come here, Esmore." Chase stood and opened his arms wide for me to walk into them. But the beast and thirst within me were in a frenzy. I continued to look behind him, to see that my prey was still there. I could smell Chase, his scent, his natural endorphins, his testosterone. My body reacted, I wanted to either drain that bear entirely or fill my needs by pleasing Chase. In one clean sweep, I slammed Chase into the corner of the cave. My nails dug into his back as I forced my lips to his taking his breath. Between Chase's hot breath and smile, he stripped my shirt away in one clean tear, discarding it to the wind that howled outside the cave. His flame reacted to mine immediately. He split my leather pants, revealing my naked self. He looked over me hungrily, sweeping his hand over my stomach and brushing past my sensitive nipples. My nails dragged down his stomach, leaving scratch marks as I fumbled for his belt.

I could feel him beneath the thin material that came between us. I ripped them apart, no longer wanting to toy with them. His hard self rubbed up against me, forcing a moan to escape because I knew what was to come. I could feel how hard he was for me, which only made me more desperate to have my fill. His hard chest cooed to me as I bit into it, thirsting for his taste. He was like euphoria to me. Filling me and creating a blurred vision which only focused on him.

Chase lifted me and wrapped my legs around him. With one hand free, he jumped through the cave entrance and scaled the wall with efficiency. He came to a stop on the wall, entering and impaling me with such impact as he stopped from the drop. My eyes lit up with shock. I could feel myself gushing over him, devouring his size and moaning in the beautiful pain it was. I continued to bite down on his neck, delving in his taste. This was my claim.

Chase lifted me from him, venturing at vampire speed across the blizzard. The wind seemed to pass over me, my skin tingled at the sensation. Suddenly, Chase threw me into ice-cold water, the sensation hit me like fire. There was blackness to this water as I swam to the top and gasped in shock. I could *feel* this ice-cold water.

"You lost remember," Chase said with a smile. A ragged breath escaped my lips as I tried to focus on what he'd just done. Chase jumped in as well, leather jacket and all. I tried to crawl out, unhappy, and with all libido gone, but he pulled me back toward him. His wet long black hair stuck to his face.

"This is fucking freezing." I shook.

"When you're a vampire for so long, Esmore, you find this refreshing to be able to feel," he cooed as he swam closer toward me. "And to still be able to do this." He grabbed me by my inner thigh and pulled me closer toward him. I could feel that he was still hard, even at this temperature. "I told you. I wouldn't have you like that. It's hard for me to say no. But I want it to be you. I want you to crave me as well, not just your body," he said. He rested the tip of his shaft near my heat. I wrapped my hand around his neck and pulled him in for a kiss. He pressed me against the ice of the surface where I had previously tried to escape.

"I get scared of it. When I can't control it," I whispered through ragged breaths.

"I know," Chase purred. "Which is why I stopped you. It doesn't mean the experience won't be the same," he said, shoving himself hard into me. I gasped with satisfaction and surprise. A smile pulled at my lips. He returned the smile and enclosed me against the ice and slammed into me. The suction of the icy water offered a twisted and heated sensation. I kissed his neck, moaning as he thrust into me with vampire speed. I was unable to control my urge to scream loudly in such a barren place. Chase lifted me out of the water and rested my back on the freezing ground that burnt at my skin.

He began to impale me again as he bit into my supple breasts. His bite forced me to arch my body into him with a loud moan. The flowing sensation of being his, and marked by him, consumed me. I wrapped my legs around him and threw him to the side and onto his back as I drove him deep into myself, enjoying his size. I rode him, the tops of my feet burnt against the cold water that they tipped in. I pressed my hand down on Chase's chest, reminding myself that we didn't have all the time in the world, although I would have loved to live in this dream for years. Chase tried to get up, but I slammed him back into the ice, where the ice beneath him began to crack. I continued riding him faster and harder, almost peaking at my climax.

Chase shifted and overpowered me. He slammed me back onto the scorching cold ice. His hand toyed with my hard nipples as he leaned in. He kissed me and delved against my tongue as his speed pounded into me. Crack by crack, I could hear the ice shatter beneath us. But I wanted more, I needed more. I was almost there. I was almost there with Chase. My back arched as I screamed out my final prayers. Chase arched into me. He too, had succumbed to that urge. He leaned in and kissed my lips and cheekbone softly. A decisive crack moaned beneath us, and the ice shattered and plunged us into the water. The frozen water woke me from all sense that wanted to now slumber.

We both surfaced from the water with loud gasps, shocked. Chase smiled cockily. "Well, I think we should be thankful there are no ice glaciers nearby," he laughed. He bled from a deep gash on his forehead, where a piece of the ice must have cut him.

"Come here, you cut yourself," I said. I swam toward him to rub my thumb over it. I was no longer a ghastly creature that only wanted to delve into his wound. This was the side of me that only Chase could find. My nurturing self, which even I could not bring out. Within seconds it was healed. "I don't think I'll ever get used to this," I admitted.

Chase grabbed my hand and kissed it. He looked into my eyes and pressed his forehead to mine. "We'll go at whatever pace is comfortable for you. I'll forever be by your side—mostly to annoy you." He smiled. "But sometimes I might have my good qualities."

"Sometimes," I growled with a smile, and gave him a kiss.

"Now, let's get the fuck out of this freezing cold water." Chase laughed. "I don't know why on earth I followed you in here. You make me do terrible things," he taunted. The smile pulled at my lips. Even without a heart, I could have this moment of happiness with Chase. "Put this on," he said. He flicked his leather jacket off and wrapped it around me. I looked to the direction of the caves in thought of our scrapped clothes. We didn't think that far ahead, I suppose. Chase laid down naked against the ice. This wasn't at all a surprising image from Chase. He was well known for running through the Council naked, countless times. "A lady can't be seen naked so carelessly," he teased. He opened out his arm, so I could snuggle into him. It was freezing, but a coldness I learned to enjoy. We looked into the blizzard where there was no sight of the sun. It was peaceful here. It felt as if it were the calm before the storm.

"Tythian wants to kill Fier, doesn't he," Chase said. It wasn't a question, it was an assumption. He toyed with my hand that laid on his chest as he looked into the sky.

"Yes," I said quietly. Chase wasn't clueless. He was highly intelligent, and I questioned how long he'd probably known. "How did you know?"

"Because if he had killed my familiar, I would act the exact same way. Why didn't you tell me?" Chase asked, curiously. "You know I can help you."

"I know. I just, I know Fier was like a step-father to you," I said pathetically. "I didn't want to make you choose." Chase laughed at me.

"Esmore, you are the only family I have now. He was a part of my life because he was my mother's familiar, not mine. I respected him until he began to lose his mind to power. The day he tried to kill us was the day I lost all connection with him. I protect you now. If you see Fier as an enemy, then I do too. But, I don't want you getting involved with this fight. Leave it to me. I know what Fier is capable of, he has the same gifts that my mother did. He's not a weak enemy, Esmore. I believe in you more than anything else in this world. But I won't let you challenge him. Not if I can take your place. Would you like to tell me what else is going up in that brain of yours?" he deliberated. I propped myself onto my elbow, so I could look at him.

"How are you so calm about everything? With everything that's happening including your life being threatened, you still stay so calm like no action is required."

"Because you're my only concern. I'll become active when I need to be, Esmore. But, this is a war, and they can last lifetimes. You need only to take one day at a time, or you'll lose focus of what you need to do today," he said, pinching my cheek and stretching it childishly. I nestled back into his chest, enjoying his warmth that filled me.

"Cesar wants you to claim your coven and force an alliance between his, your coven, and others. He threatened your life if you resisted," I said as I drew circles on his chest with my finger.

"I thought it would be something like that. If it aids in protecting you, I can push aside my arrogance and do that for you, if you wish me to," he answered.

"But I know you're not doing it because you're arrogant. You shouldn't be forced into joining the coven which destroyed your childhood," I said angrily, surprised by my sudden surge of aggression toward the topic.

"It's okay, Esmore," Chase said, patting down my hair against my cheek. "This was something I had to deal with eventually. But I still think your father is an ass. I like Yolo though." Chase smiled. "He reminds me of a younger brother I never had. I think the others will protect you no matter what as well, so I have respect for them too. What will you do about the Human Compound, now that you've found out Dillian and Julia can't go there?"

I was unsure as to what truths I should tell him. I was tired of hiding everything from him. Being a Token Huntress was a part of me, and I couldn't neglect my sense of duty to my previous hunters who fought by my side those many times even in life and death situations.

"Kora and Kasey are in there," I exasperated no longer wanting to keep up with the lies. Here we were alone, and I didn't have to concern myself with who might be listening in. "They've been genetically modified into half saber-like creatures. I want to rescue them. I've made contact with Teary and Tori again. They'll help me in this." I held my breath, waiting to see how he'd react. Chase blew out a gush of air.

"You've really been busy while I've been stuck in a room throwing a rubber ball against the wall, haven't you?" Chase said, digesting the information. A noise in the distance grabbed our attention, and we both perked up. We listened for a little longer, unsure of what we were listening to. Chase nodded at me, thinking the same.

We both ran toward the noise with vampire speed, curious as to what made the noise. We stopped behind a pile of thick snow, looking over the tip of it. There was a largely built civilization, where a wooden piled fence enclosed the outskirts of some sort of human camp. A man with six dogs and a sled opened the wooden gates himself. There were a few huts outside, and the few remains of where dirt had been dug up. It seemed more than likely an experimental area for crops that I doubted would survive in such weather. He continued to the back of the area. He was thickly clothed in furs and a mask that covered his face from the blizzard. A cave opening that had been blocked off by wood opened, and the man slid in. The aroma of about one hundred dirty humans, which hadn't showered in weeks, consumed my nose. Amongst it I could smell four hunters and the scent of foliage and meat being cooked inside. The gates closed and I looked at Chase with wide eyes.

"They're humans," Chase said. "Who would've known some would survive in this temperature."

"I could smell hunters in there," I said. Chase had smelt the same. After my feed and feeling restored once again, my senses were further heightened. I could now distinguish the difference between human and hunter. I wondered what I smelt like to others?

"You smell like a human," Chase answered. "In your normal form. We should go back for now, Tythian might be waiting."

"Chase, if the human camp near my old Guild is overrun by the hunters and under Campture's command, this might be a place for Dillian and Julia to find purpose and refuge safely. Even Teary and Tori could safely be here. Even my mother if she permitted it." Chase took an exasperated sigh and studied the human camp for a moment longer.

"We'll inspect the first human camp. If that doesn't work, we'll bring them here," Chase said and pushed back my fringe. "I hope we can find them somewhere safe soon. I know how much relief this will bring to you. But, Esmore, have you thought about where and what you would like to do once you find them a safe place to go?" His question struck me into shock. I hadn't even the time to think about after, or about what would happen to me or even Chase by extension. I guess I would have to focus on the complexity of my heart and what it entailed to have such a poisonous gift that would lead to destruction. But without it, I felt entirely empty. I furrowed my eyebrows, surprised by the mixture of thoughts. What would I do?

"There you two are!" Tythian said, appearing amidst the blizzard. "My fine shirt is being destroyed in this blizzard." Tythian looked Chase up and down. I tightened Chase's jacket around me, so none of my skin was exposed. Chase gave Tythian a very proud and male smile. "Did your clothes get ripped away in the blizzard?" Tythian asked, rolling his eyes. "I swear every time I see you, Chase Bourne, you are naked." Tythian grabbed onto both of us. We would now return to what felt like our prison. But it allowed me to escape the reality of having no idea what I was to pursue, after those who I wanted to protect, were safe.

CHAPTER 18

I RESISTED THE urge to vomit when Tythian dropped us into Cesar's quarters. I felt like I'd been plucked and thrown against a parallel wall and spat out on the other end. All the teleportation was taking an exhausting toll on my body. I missed the days when I ran freely, where my destination and arrival time was within my control. My legs ran as quickly as I desired. I missed that understanding of my personal limitations. Only my mother, Dillian, and Julia were in the room. I sensed that Yolo, Balzar, and Connor were positioned on guard outside.

I straightened my wobbly legs. "Is there a reason why all three are guarding the door right now?" I asked Tythian as I hurried to put some appropriate attire on. Chase begrudgingly did the same after I gave him a stern glance. He would much rather be naked all the time.

Over the last few days, they'd guarded in rotation, but they didn't all heavily guard the door at once. They probably found it trivial defending their natural enemies, hunters of all guests, but it was under Cesar's order of which they had to obey. Something must've changed. I'd been so preoccupied with all the side missions that I didn't have the chance to investigate the coven further or study some of those, who might be an immediate threat, if not all of them. This temptation of hunter blood was too great for the coven to ignore. I wondered how powerful Cesar's firm word would intimidate them before they started devising their own ideas if they hadn't already.

"Just precautionary. However, between you and me, I'd be alarmed that Thomas is still alive. If an attack does happen, I could only imagine he instigated it from the shadows. Trust me when I say, the sooner he's dead the better," Tythian said as he looked between Chase and me.

"It feels so good being included in the master plan," Chase giddily joked. By Tythian saying it so openly and loudly, I imagined it was not only for Chase's ears and awareness but also for the other brothers. It meant that figures within the coven were becoming restless.

"Meet Yolo at the same time tomorrow. I'm going back to Fier's Council, so will be gone for a few hours. I'll come back to teleport you both to the outskirts of the Human Compound when it is time," Tythian concluded. He dismissed himself and left the room. He continued to walk with Yolo, and I could sense that Connor and Balzar stayed guard at the closed door. Because they were within hearing range, I grabbed a pen and paper from a small draw in the desk. I wrote a message on the paper that I could show the others. I was almost hesitant to show my mother, and the gesture didn't go unnoticed.

"What is it, Esmore?" she asked me inscrutably. I trusted my mother, but her lack of presence hadn't gone unnoticed. Sometimes she was here and sometimes she wasn't. Before I shared my plans and findings with her, I had to assure myself so completely that she was aligned with us and not Cesar and his coven.

"Where have you been?" I asked my mother. Her fluorescent orange eyes narrowed on my suspicion. My tone had come out accusingly like it would when I questioned any members of my team.

"It's as if you've forgotten who you're speaking with," my mother replied in a warning tone. Dillian and Julia shrunk back into the shadows. Chase simply watched on.

"I haven't seen you around much lately, and even when I do, we can't speak," I said, undeterred from her petulant tone.

"And how much do you think we can discuss in a setting such as this?" she replied evenly. "In a place where vampires surround us?" She folded her arms over her chest. We stared at one another.

"I don't think this is a time we should start tearing each other apart," Dillian intervened. "Esmore, your mother's been within here, making sure we're okay and guarding us while you're out there finding solutions."

It panged me when he compared us, not being able to be here physically to protect them. "These circumstances don't suit any of us," he reminded me. Dillian and Julia were most vulnerable within here not having any form of escape or weapons of defense. My mother had slight pardon within here being of the value she was to Cesar as his familiar.

My mother sighed heavily, relinquishing her hard exterior. I looked at Chase who nudged his head toward me, gesturing I should do the same. *Don't be a naughty child,* he telepathically joked to me.

"I've been working with Cesar, if you must know," my mother said, "on a plan that will keep you and your heart safe." Dillian gave me a perplexed expression. I tried to push the imploding whirlwind of thoughts aside when she spoke about my heart as a foreign matter. It still pained me to find a way to come to full terms with what had happened.

"It's a long story, trust me," I said to Dillian.

"And though I know you might not have complete trust in me right now, which you have every right to, I want you to know that I'm entirely focused on your safety, all of your safety," she said pointedly to Dillian and Julia.

What about little old me? Chase said, sulking in the back of my mind. I flashed him an effective glare which made him smile.

"I want to have a proper discussion with you as well, my daughter," my mother said. "But a place like this, where the walls have ears, isn't the right time for it. My inner workings in every way are to support you. And I'm not the only one here who has their own plans going abroad. Though you might be a former Token, you are still my daughter. Who do you think taught you to have such a calculating and cunning mind?" she asked rhetorically. Her orange eyes were gentle, and her face was as warm as a huntress mother could be showing her child love.

"It's just hard," I admitted, surprising myself. "That we haven't been able to talk since… well everything." My mother pressed her finger to her lips and directed her gaze toward the door. She was gesturing that this wasn't the place to speak so openly when our plan could go astray if listened in on.

"I'm sorry," I replied, scorned from not trusting my mother for a fleeting moment. I was alive because of her and yet I still felt so violated because of what she had taken from me. I could understand why it was necessary, but it still left an abyss in its wake.

"I'm sorry too," she replied with a heavy sigh. Though we still had a long way to go and would have to find time where we could speak freely, I had trust in her plans that would benefit us, and I would continue with my own.

I unfurled the piece of paper I had written on in my hands and showed my mother, Dillian, and Julia of the discovery of the human camp at Antarctica. Also, the things the Human Compound had done to Kasey and Kora and my desire to free them. The compound was completely ruled out for Dillian and Julia, not that I ever thought it would be a safe place to start with in the beginning. Then there was my meeting with Teary and Tori, and I was transparent about my agreement with Tythian, when he would have his vengeance on Whitney's brother who experimented on her. He would allow us to investigate the old human camp near our Guild. I didn't even delve into the possible repercussions Tythian might face from Cesar in consequence of freeing us. But this was his terms, and I didn't care about what happened to him either.

"I'm getting restless in here, Esmore," Dillian grumbled. The black rings under his pink eyes conveyed his tiredness. I doubted he'd slept at all since we'd been taken in. He'd pinned back his long black hair, so the bars in his ears were more exposed. "I've never felt so useless and defenseless in my life."

"I will get you both out," I promised to Julia and him. I looked at my mother, who watched us. "What do you plan on doing, mother?"

Her beautiful orange eyes expressed such sadness. Her golden blonde hair, same as mine, uncombed for weeks, yet still perfectly positioned. I hadn't meant to sound so harsh toward her, but it was more an inquiry as to whether her plans would rally alongside my own, or if it would be contradictory. "I will follow you, Esmore. Whatever you choose to do, I will do so as well. As long as it will keep you all safe. Let me see what I can organize with Cesar."

The thought infuriated me, though my mother might have sway with him, I doubted he'd let us out so freely after he'd locked us in here. I loved my mother and trusted her though I couldn't quench the infuriation that crept up quickly. Especially now that I had lives on the line, as well as my familiar's.

"Odd, since you would side with him on the idea of killing my familiar," I said. There was no venom in my words, only fact. My mother looked at Chase expecting a response, but there was none. He calmly leaned against the wall.

"I never sided with him. But, I would agree that if your familiar did claim the right to his coven, that you will be further protected. If he is their leader and you his familiar, you will be treated and protected as a priority. I am sure this has already crossed Chase's mind."

"I don't need protecting. Remember, you made me practically immortal," I said indifferently.

"And you know the reasons behind that, so we keep it that way," my mother said in a harsh tone that trumped my own. I felt defeated. I was unnecessarily building angst between us.

I looked at everyone that was within this circle. We would've never been here if it weren't for my gift arising on my eighteenth birthday, everything after that had been a ripple effect. My gift was a curse. How was I to control or suppress that weapon, when I had no idea what it even felt like within my body? My mother took it too soon for me to even taste, to see whether it was a gift I might be able to control. Now all she focused on was keeping my heart safe, and I wanted no association with it, because it would be fully admitting to the monster I was and the inability to save myself from it.

"My priority is getting Dillian and Julia to a safe place. I'll inform Teary and Tori of this tomorrow when I leave the Human Compound," I said indefinitely.

"I think for now, you need some rest," Chase interrupted. I had been aware he was hovering over my mind the entire time. "We all do. If tomorrow night goes to plan, Tythian will take us to the human camp near your old Guild. We need to prepare for the worst, and that's there are already hunters who know our faces and want us dead." We all agreed we had to prepare for that. I wondered how many of the hunters survived from the ambush of sabers. Did most of them stay together, or like Teary and Tori, Kasey and Kora, did they all separate? It was a risk to take Dillian and Julia, but I couldn't deny Dillian his right to protect himself anymore, it was because of me that he was now trapped below ground.

Jenn and I hardly spoke after Tythian teleported us to the outskirts of the border to the Human Compound. We walked in comfortable silence. I assisted Jenn in a few rounds of sedating the vampires. They made the rounds different and irregular, so vampires wouldn't get used to the one person or smell. As it currently was, I would consider Lincon as the only threat in there. This also gave Yolo an opportunity to assess the new vampires who went in, to make sure none were a part of his own coven. He'd planned his rounds and purpose within the Human Compound perfectly.

Jenn carried her suitcase and board with the cell numbers of the five vampires she had to sedate. She sedated the first sabers which looked as glazed as the last one she had shown me the day before. I looked into that saber's cell, noticing it was now empty. A few scratch marks remained on the floor as if it had been dragged out of the room. I examined the glass still surprised that this was all that came between the monsters and the humans who kept them. If Lincon wanted to escape, I was certain he'd find a way.

A woman entered the room behind us before Jenn could administer the second saber.

"Miss. Cadolwadt," the woman interrupted. "The fourth power grid is down. Mr. Richard wishes you to attend to it straight away," she said with upmost respect.

"Of course," Jenn responded and looked over the board again. "Do you think you are capable of doing this, Ellie?" she asked politely. Jenn was all service and protocol. I accepted them without hesitation. "You'll do great, now don't do anything I wouldn't," Jenn said and flicked the tip of my nose. I kept my gaze neutral, but I could see the humor in her eyes. Yolo was enjoying that I was following him around, pretending to be his assistant.

"Of course," I said with a smile that didn't reach my eyes. Jenn giggled at me before following the woman and taking their leave. At their departure, the irritating sound of Lincon's whistling began. I ignored it as best I could and injected the next two vampires. It was a menial task, but even I felt uneasy about drugging them. Just kill them. It was filthy to stand so close to the creatures I despised. I even stared at their chest cavities longingly, I could end their existence in mere seconds. But then that would give me away. So I would inject them instead, not at all sorry by how rough I might've been. Eventually the next cell I had to pass was Lincon's. I prepared for the mental attack that he might ambush me with.

"Do you hate me or something, why are you ignoring me?" he whined, with his face pressed up against the glass, his nose was smushed and flaring.

"Don't talk to me," I mumbled at him as if it were beneath me to even associate with him. I still tried to avoid him.

"I could be of some help, you know. With whatever you have planned." He smiled smugly as he stroked his goatee.

I sighed, annoyed, and pressed the clipboard against my waist. He might be crazy, delirious, and irritating, but if he so much as whispered to any of the humans what I might actually be, it could cause issues. "What makes you think I have something planned?"

He smiled knowingly, I fell for the bait. And yet the strategic side of me, a never ending tick in the back of my mind, acknowledged his gift and the numerous ways it could be implanted in raids and attacks. But that was the old huntress in me.

"Because a creature like you, a rare thing, always has a plan. You wouldn't be wasting your time in a Human Compound unless you had something spectacular coming up." He pressed himself up further to the glass giddily. "And on top of that, I can smell all different scents over you. Coven, humans, hunters, and you appear to be all of those things. You smell like a delightful human to thirst on. But when your true form emerges, you are both vampire and hunter. I can't smell any bi-product on or in you. The one's they experiment on in here, they all reek of deformity. Not you. You're organically crafted as a disastrous mutation. And me," he pointed to himself as if I'd asked him in way of introduction, "I'm a vampire with no purpose," he mused, as he scratched his white see-through shirt absentmindedly. "I get bored easily and follow no one. I simply go where there are food and games. But you, you smell interesting to me. It looks as if…it will be fun."

"I don't do fun," I said in a bland tone, indicating I was already bored of this conversation.

"No, darling, you don't. But what follows you smells like fun and havoc. I heard two scientists discussing hunters who had been modified within here. I wondered if that might have had something to do with it. I mean, you do have hunter's eyes after all. Maybe you are here to break them out." Lincon smiled. The area around me swirled and changed. Across the cell from me was Kora and Kasey, unaffected, their saber-like physical status gone.

"Please, Ellie, help us," Kora begged. I didn't run to them. This was a trick. Lincon stood in the corner and seemed impressed. The two girls vanished, and the illusion was gone. Within seconds it appeared and then vanished.

"You responded none the less," Lincon admitted. "I could help you know."

"What's in it for you, and what makes you think I need help?" I said harshly. My grip firmed around the suitcase with sedation in it. I felt like a fool for even entertaining the idea. I had enough on my plate and different plans to execute so why would I consider a new element with a ticking time bomb crazy vampire. When had I lowered myself to negotiating and making conversation with vampires? Months ago, I'd been under the impression of shoot first, ask questions later.

"Well, it's simple, love. I already told you. I want to follow you. I don't want power or gifts or gain. I am content with mine and mine alone. I just want something fun to do," he said as he sat down in the corner of his cell. "You know, I had a familiar once too. He was so handsome, and I was only about, I don't know, it was probably late 600's. Ah, that's right, I was 628 years old when he came in and swept me off my feet. I knew he was my familiar instantly. You just know these things. I was nothing then, I didn't even know 'gifts' existed. This was in the early 2100's mind you, so a few years ago," he said devilishly. "And he just couldn't say no to my beautiful supple skin. I was rather proud of my conquest." Lincon was entertaining himself. "He showed me his illusions, his worlds he could fabricate and told me he had such magical powers after draining a hunter completely dry. After we commemorated and became proper familiars and lovers—I put a dagger in his chest and watched him rot into a corpse. And ta-da, somehow, his gift became mine." He waited for my shocked expression with a smile. "You see, love, I'll only follow what I think is fun. I knew I'd be tied down to him the longer I dared be mesmerized by him. It was my first line of defense."

"Why are you telling me that disgusting story?" I asked. I could never think or had met anyone who would be willing to kill their own familiar. I didn't even think it was possible. He could not be sane, surely.

"Because of exactly that, you asked why you need me. Sometimes, little huntress, you need someone who can do the dirty work when you can't. I can smell a familiar all over you. I question, what kind of influence he has on a new baby vampire like you. I mean, you've walked in here, full of control, and haven't thirsted on anyone. It made me question." He frowned to himself. "Perhaps your familiar is suppressing those urges, no new vampire can do it themselves. And, I very much doubt you have friends who could press such an underlying impression of 'oh no don't eat that human.'" He began laughing as his mock tone of a squeaky voice. My instincts reacted at the mockery of Chase, and my fangs shot through my gums with a growl. It made him laugh only harder. "What I'm trying to say is you need someone in the shadows who is willing to do your dirty work. You don't have to tell me your secrets. In fact, I don't care. But I have lived well over eight hundred years. If you, little mixed breed, can create some fun for me, then consider me yours for the time," he said with a dashing smile. "Gift and all."

I studied him momentarily. He was a ticking time bomb, but hadn't that been the same description the others used against me? Usually, I wouldn't consider such an outsider's offer. But much had changed in recent days, it was continuously evolving, and if I were to trump those who were confiding me or following me, I had to equip my arsenal. I didn't have to accept his offer, the mere thought of it revolted me, but perhaps with such a gift at my disposal, I could effectively break Kora and Kasey out without asking Jenn for help, nor needing Teary and Tori to come close to this place.

"You're locked in a cell, where there are silver darts and high security down the hallway. How do you dare think you can escape?" I coolly asked. He was so mad that I considered he'd be able to pull it off, and if he didn't, I wouldn't be sad to see him rot.

"My, dear, I'm an illusionist, and in being so, I do not give away my tricks freely. Whatever you ask of me, I can do it," he said, with a smug expression. "Whenever you want."

I studied him for a moment longer. I couldn't trust him, he was a vampire of all things. But I weighed the outcome of asking Jenn for assistance which I doubted she'd agree to because it might jeopardize her own works of locking Kora and Kasey in. If I asked Tythian, he would want another bargain or outright say no. I couldn't get the two out of here alive on my own, I didn't know the security well enough, and I couldn't risk having them in here much longer. They'd experimented and mutated them to such an extent in only days, if I left it much longer, they might fully turn into sabers. The worst that could happen is Lincon would fail and die, or at best, he could pull it off and free them, then I would deal with him afterward. It might create some commotion in the meantime, but no one would know it was me who ordered it. And even if he told others I had instructed him to do so they wouldn't listen, they'd only focus on bringing him down.

"The two hunters who are being experimented on are in heavier security than you. Do you think you could break them out?" I blatantly asked. His smile stretched thin.

"I thought you'd never ask. But, if you could be so kind as to point me into the direction of their cell, then I'll have no problem locating them. But, you do understand that the person who doesn't sedate me last, might lose their life over this," he said twistedly. "You know, consequence and all."

"You said I needed someone to do the dirty work for me. So make it happen," I promptly said. I wouldn't allow him to try and manipulate me into guilt. I once dedicated my life to the survival of humans, and I recently came to the realization that maybe they were never deserving. My best friend Dillian might have kindness and love for them, but I could no longer share the same feelings toward them. I had saved them from duty, and when my own kind turned on me, I'd been set free.

They went beyond measures to twist and manipulate their own kind; I was no worse a person than them. "You don't *need* to kill anyone. Their own kind will deal with that individual with their beliefs and punishment, no doubt in a similar cell like yours." He smiled at that as if I had shown him something wicked that brought him much glee. "I can show you where to go, but you have to open your mind to me, you're not the only one with a particular gift." I scanned over his mind. Within seconds, he was entirely open to me as if he were opening his hands wide for a smothering hug. His mind was twisted and sick, it made me want to vomit, yet he was sane at the same time. I ignored the things that popped up, and he openly wanted to share with me. The murders and pain he'd caused in the past. This was one of the most twisted vampires I'd ever met.

"Yea, my friends say I'm a bit crazy," he mused to himself. He stopped suddenly, serious. "Actually, I don't believe I have any friends. How pathetic." Lincon was very receptive to my mind. Considering that his gift was mixing with one's mind, it seemed to make our gifts connect swimmingly. "I knew you had a gift with your mind, I sensed it the day you walked in, I just couldn't figure it out."

I conveyed to him images and the direction he could go to reach the secret room that Kora and Kasey were imprisoned. I showed him the only exits I knew and how he might be able to leave the compound with them. "Very detailed," he mused. "When will I know it's showtime?" I sent a huge surge of motivation to him. Instantly he responded by standing. He looked at me with surprise and then smiled. He began lightly tapping his temple. "Well, I can say that no one has ever made me feel like that before," he mused. "Consider it done. Call on me when you need me. I'll linger around closely afterward so you can find me with your little friends. But don't take too long or I will kill them."

"If you cross me," I warned, domineeringly.

"Little vampire, if you think I'll take your threat seriously, you are sadly mistaken in the difference of you and I. You are not the superior one here. It just so happens that I like you and want to follow these games you might have in stall for me," he charmed. He continued to chat with me, but I walked off. I focused on sedating the next vampire, who looked as if she'd been experimented on recently. Her face also had begun to look as if it were melting. What were they doing to these vampires?

After sedating the last one, I left the room and the whistling Lincon behind, of whom I felt as if I had made a deal with the son of all darkness.

CHAPTER 19

I RETURNED THE suitcase with emptied syringes and signed off on it. I had every intention to desert Lincon once his goal was achieved. I had no desire to associate with a creature who had the most wicked of minds to figuratively stand by my side. Though I would be pleased if he could assist in the escape of Kora and Kasey. Asking for help wasn't a particularly strong suit for any hunter. But in this case, to protect and not to risk those I cared about, I had no issue using a vampire that I had no attachment to. If he dies failing to do the task, then he dies, I didn't care. And if he could break Kora and Kasey out safely, then I didn't have to involve Yolo, ask for his assistance, or complicate the matter further when he'd show resistance. He'd already showcased his hatred for them because they were hunters. I could now focus on Charlie, and how I would provide Tythian access to take his revenge. Would I lead Charlie out or would I bring Tythian in? Either way, Yolo would know it was me. But that was the risk I had to take so my friends and I could escape.

I could use Lincon as a distraction if I tied the two together at the same time. Amongst the chaos and confusion and attention Lincon draws to himself, I could summon Tythian into the Human Compound. It would go unsuspected, and when others found Charlie's body ripped apart, they would assume it was the vampires who had escaped.

I wouldn't have to involve Teary and Tori, and create a third plan that included risking them to assist me. If I pulled this off, then I could focus on securely finding everyone a camp where they could rest and be safe.

I walked toward the residential area, I wanted to inspect its placement and resources. The more I knew about the Human Compound, the greater my knowledge if I ever had to use it against them, or use it to my advantage. When I exited the glass tube and into the residential area, my gaze fixated on the broad man in front of me. Sydney was crouched on one knee, talking to a young girl. He blocked the open space on the dirt path that allowed me to inspect past him. He'd notice me immediately if I tried to walk around him so instead, I pretended approaching him was my sole purpose. The girl nodded to Sydney, and looked up at me with caution.

"Ah, Ellie," Sydney said, waving me over. I assessed the size of the small child which had delicately tanned skin, midnight black hair, and brown eyes. She appeared to be the age of six, at most.

"Titan, this is Ellie. Ellie is new on my team," Sydney said to the girl. "Ellie, this is my daughter, Titan." I looked at her again, somewhat interested that he had a daughter. Military soldiers didn't often have children. Dedication to the cause was usually the focal point and was selfishly demanding. Though my mother had me, her focus had to remain within her team and the Guild's overall ambition. The child began to stare at me. "Titan, don't be rude."

"Her eyes are like Mommy's," the child whispered to him, but I could hear. Sydney looked at her and at my eyes for a moment, as if he too had just realized something. Gray eyes were a rarity and had taken me some time to get used to after my purple haze vanished. I wondered if the mother was still alive.

"Why don't you go play for a little while, I have to go outside and do a few things, okay?" he said. Sydney's demeanor changed, he seemed fully exposed around this child. The hard exterior I had known only yesterday, vanished when he was with his daughter. Titan hugged him and ran toward the residential area.

"Sorry about that. Her mother died two years ago. She's been a bit funny around women since," Sydney said as he stood up and watched his daughter safely return to a group of boys her age. "She seems to be growing into a bit of a tomboy," he mused. He looked at my indifferent expression as if reminding himself who he was talking to. "Right, well, I didn't think you'd make it today. Jenn usually comes and goes as she pleases. I'm about to check some of the netting we have around the place. Want to come for a round? You'll need to get used to the traps surrounding the compound, we race in and out, often. It would be an issue if one of our members got caught in them."

"Have you hooked yourself a few times?" I mused.

"Good to see a knock to your head didn't take away your sense of humor," Sydney retorted.

"Or perhaps you have a delicate ego," I counteracted. He clenched his jaw as if to say something, but he said nothing. We collected extra weapons, which included the bow and arrows that were already strapped to my back. I grabbed another two knives. Sydney and I exited through the front wall, where Jenn and I always entered. The sun wasn't as strong today, which left me at ease. It was only another issue I'd have to be concerned with. Today, I felt far more relieved and not tempted by Sydney's sweet smell to drain him entirely. After my feast yesterday, I was content. I hadn't even known I was so hungry, but Chase knew. When would I be able to measure my hunger and cravings?

We began to walk through the thick mist that billowed around our ankles. For some reason it was heaviest at the Human Compound walls, its thickness like miasma smelt unbearable to my sensitive nose.

"You don't wear a mask or anything?" I asked Sydney.

"Shit, I should have asked if you wanted one, sorry," he said. "No, I don't, other members do. I don't rely on them. My body needs to adjust to what the world is. Everyone keeps talking about it reverting to the days before any of our time. I don't believe in that. If the animals around us adjust, then so can we humans."

I considered this, which led me to my next question. "So, what do you think of all the testing and test subjects?" His expression snapped like wildfire on me. He looked away ashamed by his expression and continued leading me through the forest.

"I hate them. I'm fully against it," he said, pushing back a dead branch that was at his eye level. The branch made a clean snap.

"So why do you capture them and bring them back?" I asked, curious as to why someone would help the very project they were against.

"Because something has to change. Our resources and survival aren't guaranteed. Fighting is the only thing I'm good at. I'd have no other role in the compound, and I need to guarantee Titan's safety. So even if I'm going against my beliefs, as long as she is safe, I'll continue doing so until the day I die. We can't live on the outside, I'm not so narrow-minded to think I'm all mighty and powerful. I'm basically a piece of meat in the world full of beasts. She's safest behind those walls." I had never considered how powerful the connection between parent and child was, and the things they might do for their own. I thought of my mother. I had a disassociation in understanding what she had done. She removed my heart without my permission and abandoned me in hopes of hiding it. She was the informant to tell me that my gift would erode and kill anyone within my presence, which could damn any kind of species without my control.

I tried to put myself into her matter of perception. *If I were her would have I done the same?* She had always said she'd never violate me with her gift unless given permission, but was this similar to what Sydney spoke of? Even though she didn't believe in what she was doing and it went against her beliefs, she did it to protect me. She went against the Guild, and her own kind, facing the harshness of the outer world where most wouldn't survive on their own, all in hopes of keeping me safe—in keeping my gift a secret.

I was so harsh toward her, despite loving her and trying my hardest to understand her motives. Deep down, what I was most disgusted and angry about was myself. I was angry that I was the problem, though her love affair with Cesar was the reason for my creation. But I couldn't even fault her on that, now being a familiar to a vampire myself. This world of ours had a deplorable form of amusement that geared us all into a war we might've not necessarily chosen for ourselves.

Although I might've felt out of the loop of my mother's purpose and ambitions now, I knew that my safety was on the forefront of her mind. I didn't necessarily require her protection, but there was warmth to it that I didn't entirely understand. My mother and Chase would do anything for me, and I would do the same for them in return. Perhaps that was the same sentiment that Sydney felt toward his daughter.

I followed Sydney as he led me further away from the wall. "The scar that's on your neck, was that from a vampire?" I asked. He remained silent for a moment and hesitated to answer.

"I've been attacked by a lot of vampires and sabers. But this one, no. This one was by my father. He had an illness in his mind, which no one realized until it was too late. He was in charge of the military force like I am now. One night I checked up on him. He thought I was a vampire, and so he attacked and cut me from my jawline down. I was lucky to survive."

A high-pitched squeal broke our conversation. I strung back an arrow on my bow into the direction it came from. Sydney held his two swords comfortably by his side as he walked slowly toward it.

"It's okay, we've snagged one," he said, reassuring me to lower my weapon. I followed him closely to where the saber squealed. It was high in the treetops, where it had stepped into a trap. I could smell its suffering and burning from here.

"Silver?" I said impartially. Of course the netting would be silver. I remembered its effects on my own skin as I tried to free Chase from it. It burned at my skin, which is why I actively avoided it within the compound. That saber would have felt as if it were roasting alive.

"Good eye," he said with a smile. "Silver drains the vampires, it's the only weakness they have. We'll leave it here overnight. The sun will exhaust it as well. It's probably been trapped here since last night, sabers rarely come out during the day. Hopefully, its screams will draw the attention of more, and they'll be caught as well."

A flash of speed flew between us. Sydney was thrown back against one of the trees and knocked out instantly. I could smell the blood oozing out of his head. I raised my bow and arrow toward the vampire that lined him up, tempted by the wound. The smell of Sydney's blood called to me. I froze on the spot, fighting back the urge to jump him and be tempted by the nagging pull that called to me. I would not allow myself to attack a human, no matter how little I thought of them. I would not attack Sydney, I was stronger than this temptation. I reminded myself I was revitalized from the feast I had the day before, I didn't need Sydney's blood. I was better than this.

"Don't go near him," I said, still pretending to be human. I couldn't take much damage if I continued the pretense of being human, but even if I were attacked, I was immortal. The vampire teased and took another step toward Sydney. I shot an arrow, barely missing him.

"You're very strong for only a young human girl," another voice cooed out of the trees. There were now two vampires. Slowly, I circled them, so I could stand in front of Sydney. The second vampire did the same and walked toward the other. The vampire, who had first attacked, seemed to have a hunchback, his neck continued to click, and his eye twitched. He continued to walk with his arms forward, and his hands crunched over. His physical posture looked to be deformed. But he was definitely vampire.

The woman he walked toward held her head high. Her long black hair cascaded to her knees. Her face was gaunt and ghostly white, against her dark brown, almost black eyes. I couldn't sense any other vampires around me. I searched further out and tried to scan for other creatures. I searched for two in particular, and as we discussed, they stayed close by waiting for my next order. I found them, Teary and Tori, whose mind patterns were so similar to their personalities. I slammed the sensation and urgency for them to run north toward the Human Compound wall. I knew they'd find me, they were both fast, and all I had to do was stall for time. Teary could take them both on without me breaking my fake identity.

The deformed male vampire clicked his tongue. "Not yet, Spungee," the woman purred to him. "You can't eat them yet."

"Who are you?" I demanded. I could sense that Teary and Tori were on their way. I was relieved Teary made a rounded assumption that the sudden mind-altering beacon would be from me. Upon seeing me in my circumstance, they'd summarize the situation and attack these vampires who caught us off guard. Who more specifically caught me off guard, I'd been too preoccupied thinking of my mother and Chase that I didn't even notice their presence creep up on me.

"You're very daring for a weak little girl, aren't you? Don't you fear vampires, child?" She began to laugh. "Of course not. I can smell your familiar all over you. That vampire certainly has his way with you, doesn't he? I wonder if he's ever hurt you while he forces you to please him."

I shot an arrow at her, being the only way I could release my anger. I held in my other instincts, the ones that urged me to kill her. The ones that savored in the thought of ripping her head from her body. How did she know about Chase? What was her connection to my familiar?

"I've come to collect you. Do you know how long it's been since we first started hunting for our leader? He's very good at hiding. It was much to our surprise, when we smelt his scent amongst the assassination of Tracey's Council and then, poof, that scent suddenly vanished."

Tythian had mentioned he'd encountered Chase's coven that day. So they were there, close by, and now here one of the members stood, having tracked Chase's scent on me.

"You're Chase's coven?" I asked for confirmation, drawing this conversation out. Killing them wouldn't aid me right now. I had to keep my cool. If anyone within the Human Compound saw me change into my huntress or vampire form, I'd blow everything I was depending on.

"Ahh, she's cluey too," she said and clasped her frail hands together. "Did you see that, Spungee? Clever. So, you can only imagine our surprise when our coven leader's scent continued to pop up here, on the outskirts of this Human Compound. And just like magic his scent disappears, what a greater treasure to know that it's you, instead. I'm sure we can use you as bait, very nicely. We'll be taking you now as bait, child. He *will* face what he abandoned those many years ago."

"What do you want with him?" I asked, bored with her theatrics. Vampires always acted in a way of superiority, as if they were toying with their prey. This had always happened to me after my eighteenth birthday, and my hunter's eyes vanished. It was an insult knowing I had the strength to kill them but was mocked in a sing-song way. I found it harder to act weak and restrain myself from proving her wrong.

"That's not for us to discuss. Spungee, grab her," she said and clicked her fingers. The timing of Teary and Tori's arrival was exceptional. Flames swept between the two vampires and me. I grabbed Sydney's body, fed up with my fake façade of being human.

"Are ye still playing that game Esmore, of being human?" she said between the crackles of the flames. The two vampires, who had spoken so confidently, vanished within the mist. They must have only been weak vampires, to have fled so quickly. Tori came and grabbed Sydney with no strain. He was a bulky and heavy man, but his weight was nothing for us hunters.

"Thank you for coming. I've organized an escape plan for Kora and Kasey. I don't trust the vampire that's breaking them out so might have to redesign the plan as we go."

"Vampire?" Teary asked dubiously.

"It's a long story, but he might be one of the few who is capable of singlehandedly getting them out. Make sure you're on the lookout for their escape. Tonight Dillian, Julia, my mother, and I will be investigating the human camp near our old Guild. I need to find somewhere safe for them. If not, I'm considering breaking out of our location and bringing them to you. I think in numbers we'll be safe, even if exposed out in the open."

Teary's expression had gone blank. "Ye mother?" she repeated. "I thought I was hallucinating when I saw her for a fleeting moment back at the Guild." Though we didn't show much emotion toward one another, I recalled securely that my mother and Teary were associated within the Guild. I supposed it could've been considered as close of a friendship as it was comradery. And then it suddenly dawned on me. My mother had once explicitly told me she had alliances within the Guild, and some had sworn to her they would watch over me if anything were to happen to her.

"You—" I moistened my mouth. "You were one of the ones who looked out for me?"

Teary offered an uncharacteristic smile, where two teeth were missing. "Ye mother saved me life in me earlier years on a mission. Looking after her wee one was the least I could do for her."

It dawned on me then why she was one of the few hunters, alongside Pac who decided to remain on my team when I was announced Token after Drue had been killed. A warmth filled me. My mother had been living a life in precaution, in case the day would come that my vampire self might show itself. And even after she fled, there were those who remained in the shadows and watched over me. And I had been none the wiser.

"This plan though," Teary said in consideration. It was a lot for Teary and Tori to take in. I could tell Teary had questions running around the forefront of her mind. Teary did what she was commanded to doing, she focused on the objective and would ask questions later when we had more time.

"And that?" Teary asked in her thick accent and pointed to where the vampires of Chase's coven once stood.

"That's Chase's coven. My familiar. He left on bad terms, and it would appear they're trying to take me in thinking I'm human and use me as bait to lure him out. I need to keep up this pretense of being human until this role serves me no further purpose."

"Ye got a lot happening don't ye, Esmore," Teary said and put her hands on her hips.

"If I'm entirely honest with you, Teary, this is the least of it right now," I said. I looked at Tori who held Sydney and back at Teary expectantly. "Do you think you can carry me and take me back to the border wall? Just don't get caught." I had to fake human and pretend to have been rescued by the hunters, which would also act as a convenient story. A human woman my size would struggle to drag Sydney back to the compound and then I'd have to explain how I was able to avoid being ambushed myself and deterred two vampires from killing us both.

Teary's eyebrows rose. Tori began to snicker under his breath. "Would ye like to get on my back, for a piggyback, little miss?" Teary teased.

I walked up to her doing so, with an expression of amusement in my eyes. I jumped onto her back swiftly, avoiding the large, tight bun of red hair. "Ye gained a bit of weight, Esmore."

I slapped her back, most comfortable in the warmth of her. It was nice to feel connected with my former huntress life. Though months ago, I never thought I'd have asked my comrade to do this for me. As I commanded, they quickly dropped us off at the wall. Guards saw, but I distracted them by screaming out help for Sydney. I told them that two vampires had attacked and the hunters who chased and killed them, brought us back to safety. I acted as surprised as they did when I informed them. A small part of me found amusement in the situation because if Chase had been watching my performance, I imagined he'd be laughing at me the entire time with a scorecard. Teary knew better than to come closer now. And Teary and Tori were careful not to get snagged in the traps that surrounded the compound like the unsuspecting Kora and Kasey had. The humans would have scouts in search for them. They'd want to experiment on them like they had the twins.

Jenn was less than impressed by my very well performed dramatics. By the time I had left the Human Compound, Sydney still had not woken up from his head injury. Jenn was fuming on the walk home, skeptical of my involvement with the hunters.

CHAPTER 20

T YTHIAN WAITED IMPATIENTLY for us, apparently, we were a few minutes late. He seemed slightly on edge. I was suspicious that he could sense the remains or still relevant presence of Chase's coven. I couldn't feel any within our range, but I was limited in my natural form. I continued my façade of being a weak, pathetic human. Tythian teleported us back into the underground tunnels of the coven. It felt like another punch to my stomach as we drifted from one space to another within seconds.

Jenn reformed into the shirtless Yolo. He brushed through his long blond hair with relief. The smell of blood consumed us all. It came from the direction of Cesar's room, where the others rested. I ran at vampire speed. I could hear through the tunnels that Cesar and my mother followed not far behind me.

I stopped, unsure of what I was witnessing. Twelve vampires gasped on their knees. They clutched their heads as blood oozed from their noses and ears. Connor stood in front of the open door. Balzar and Chase stood behind him, unalarmed. Connor's outstretched hand, somehow, had a connection to these vampires that screamed for mercy. Connor's gift was destructively powerful and had no restraint on working individually.

"You dare defy the direct order of Cesar?" he queried. "The penalty is death."

"Please, Connor." One of the vampires gasped as they choked on their own blood. "It's not right to have them here. But we won't try again. We swear." Cesar and my mother now stood behind us and watched Connor's face contort into a fierce rage.

"You're a traitor and a monster. You have no right to live!" Connor raged. He scrunched his hand together, enforcing a deafening scream from each of the vampires. A pop noise simultaneously echoed out of them. The burst of their heart seeped through their chest and all twelve vampires decomposed onto the ground. Their bodies darkened as they sagged further as a corpse. Connor stared at their corpses for a while in disgust before looking up at us, with his usual indifferent gaze.

"You didn't wait for my order, son?" Cesar said, bearing witness to the death of twelve of his coven members. Though, he didn't object to it when he saw the intent in Connor's eyes.

"It was by your commandment that if they were to attack, I was to kill them. How foolish of them to think they'd get past me because they had a bulk number, I'm ashamed to have had any association with them, really," Connor said with little emotion. Cesar wasn't upset with him and only nodded in gratitude.

"Those were my words, son, thank you for obeying," Cesar admitted. "Balzar, please clean this mess." My mother looked from the corpses to Connor. Like me, she was assessing the new threat if he ever turned on us. What was Connor's gift? Not that I needed to know the specifics to understand how deadly it was. To be able to take out twelve vampires without moving himself was an intimidating gift. I knew of Tythian's and Yolo's gifts, but for Connor to kill so many vampires in one swift movement, meant I had to be wary of him. When we left of our own accord without Cesar's permission, would Connor enforce the same strike against us?

"That's why Connor is our first line of defense. Most don't make it past him," Yolo jollily said, clasping an unwelcome hand on Connor's shoulder. He walked past him, to help Balzar discard of the bodies. Lydia ran up to us in a panic and assessed the corpses.

Without looking at her, Tythian spoke. "Thomas is not here. I wonder if he had a part to play in this, and used them as puppets."

A sigh of relief escaped Lydia. I turned savage at the thought and accusation. Thomas could have been behind this, he told me himself, that he'd come after them. He threatened them, he had to be behind this. If Connor hadn't been here then it would've been a lot messier, and maybe just maybe one might've gotten through the door. Maybe my familiar might've been hurt. Perhaps Dillian might not have been able to defend Julia in time.

I sped past Tythian, I was now on the hunt for Thomas. Tythian was instigating, knowing I'd react to the thought of Thomas being involved. Whether he felt like he was playing me or not, it now became my personal ambition to gain answers from Thomas and even further kill him for his meddling. Until I could remove those I cared about out of this coven, I'd have to silence any immediate threats within these tunnels.

I focused my sensitive hearing into the direction of the tunnels and searched for his voice. There were many vampires talking, some fed and laughed, others moaning and making love. I heard his distinct voice in a large room, which made cluttering noises with what I assumed to be weapons. He was amongst other voices I recognized. It was the elite team I had only a few days ago led for the assassination of Tracey's Council.

I hadn't yet explored these tunnels, so I let Thomas' voice lead me in his direction. I had come to a dead end twice before pursuing the correct path. He tried to kill those who I vowed to protect. I would kill him. My eyes hazed with their purple and my fangs slipped out fiercely. It was a darkly lit room, but I didn't need the light, because I saw perfectly fine.

I ignored the other vampires and leaped for Thomas. I wrapped my hands around his neck. He'd already caught my hands and flung me toward the wall. He patted over his shoulder as if I were dirty to him.

"Did you set an ambush up against my friends?" I hissed. The other vampires around us were unsure of what to do. Which leader were they to follow, their old or their new? They circled us, letting us fight between ourselves.

"I don't know what you're talking about." Thomas smiled wickedly. I surveyed my surroundings. There were weapons on my left that I could pick up. The only noise I heard was the vampires around us as they lightly stepped toward the walls, so they would not get in our way. I only focused on Thomas. I felt my eyes pinning on him—he was my prey. Thomas toyed with the sword in his hand, egging me to attack.

I snatched the razor-like sword from the vampire beside me. Thomas leaped for me with glee. His blade smashed into mine as we challenged one another's barbaric strength. He head-butted me. I took a step back from the blow and scraped my blade against his sword, and flicked it away. I elbowed him in the ribs as I spun to his side. He twisted his blade toward my stomach, but I dodged using my own blade to stop him.

The swords scraped against one another again, in domineering strength. Cracks appeared in the metal of my sword, and it shattered from his might. I discarded the broken weapon and threw the handle away. He swung for my neck, but I lowered to the ground. The crunch of the metal beneath my feet was very distinct. I hit precisely two points in his arm with my fingers, which forced it to freeze for a moment. I knocked his blade out of his hand and smashed my palm into his jaw. He flipped backward into the air. He was already prepared for me as I jumped on him. In one clean, swift movement, he circled me and kicked me in the back and against the weapons stand. The items made a clanging noise as I crashed to the floor, embarrassing myself.

Vampires hissed as Chase walked in, watching us as we fought. He would not intervene, not when he knew I could win this.

"Stop!" Cesar roared. My mother, Tythian, and Lydia walked in behind him. I snarled at Thomas again. I would not. I raised my fists and shuffled on my feet lightly. I would beat the truth out of him. Thomas smiled wickedly. He grabbed a dart from his inner jacket and threw it toward Chase's chest. Chase raised his hand to catch it, but Lydia had intervened. The jagged edges of the dagger sliced her hand. She stared at her brother with fury. Her blood encompassed the smell of the room. With Thomas caught off guard, I punched him in the stomach. With my other fist, I'd intended to snap his neck, but he'd already grabbed it and spun me in the air.

I landed on my feet and hissed at him as I looked up. He was fast and strong. Four of the vampires within the room grabbed at him from behind. Thomas flung two of them against the wall. Sharon grabbed him from behind, her tiny form hardly seen. Another three vampires from the group caught hold of him.

"Are you fucking kidding me? You're turning on me for her?!" Thomas snapped angrily.

"I've had enough!" Cesar bellowed. I looked at Chase who injected his thoughts into my own.

"Calm," he said, with that ever soothing effect he so easily glittered me with. *"Let Cesar deal with him now. This is a coven matter. No harm has come to Dillian or Julia."*

The other vampires from the elite team now stood by my side. Was this their show of support? Could they so quickly change the person whom they took command from and was led by? Cesar approached Thomas and stood in front of him, looking down at him with disgrace. Or was this the power of Cesar's words? Were these vampires so dedicated to Cesar and this coven that they'd cut all bonds and ties with a former friend and leader if required of them?

The vampires were unsettled by Chase and my mother now being in the room, but none looked in their direction. Only a few drops of blood from Lydia's hand had reached the ground before it had healed.

"Please, Cesar. He didn't harm Esmore's familiar. I'll make him apologize formerly," Lydia begged on behalf of her brother.

"Enough!" Cesar snapped. "I told you, Thomas, I gave you one chance," Cesar began.

"She attacked me, how am I to defend myself. If I hadn't, I would already be dead!" Thomas snapped.

Balzar interrupted as he walked into the room. "Perhaps when you convince thirteen vampires to attack the very room Cesar forbade anyone to go toward, or the very guests he housed and protected, you should make sure all are loyal to that endeavor." Balzar crossed the room and stood beside Cesar. "The death count after Connor killed them within seconds was twelve. The last one reported your treachery before it even went into motion."

"It's a lie!" Thomas snarled. I hovered my mind over his and wanted to confirm his treachery for myself. His eyes went into a frenzy as he snapped and snarled at me. "Get the fuck out of my head!"

Cesar took a step closer to Thomas. "Some men develop into leaders, and they gain respect and power. Others are consumed by it and become greedy. They sacrifice their men for their own gain and tower over the weakest of the coven. You are no leader if you would misuse your soldiers in such a way," Cesar said, angrily. "I will not have you as a part of this coven any longer."

"Tythian set me up!" Thomas roared, desperately. Lydia watched between everyone, uncertain.

"But I was not here, Thomas," Tythian purred with satisfaction. "A desperate man turns sloppy in his endeavors. What did you really think would happen? You have, for so many years stood by my father's side. Faithfully you were one of the best and a great leader. I wonder if your sanity is finally coming undone. Am I to guess you are slowly disintegrating into a saber?"

"That's bullshit, you slimy dog!" Thomas bellowed. "Cesar, look at this coven. You are destroying it! Every form of abomination is in this room. Having another coven's leader as a guest makes me sick." Thomas spat toward Chase's feet. Cesar looked down, unfazed by it. "You loved my sister once, Cesar! And then you trade her in for a huntress?!" Thomas snarled. Lydia diverted her gaze to the ground. Cesar and Lydia were…Cesar grabbed Thomas by the throat and lifted him so that his feet couldn't touch the ground. All other vampires stepped away. "You have an abomination for a daughter!" Thomas continued. "And hunters to be protected, you are the one who is losing your sanity!" Thomas spat on Cesar's leather jacket.

Cesar looked at the spit on his jacket. His eyes were stone cold when he looked back at Thomas. It was like watching a beast ensnare small prey. I had never seen Cesar like this, his look was deadly. This was a side I'd never seen of him, and now understood why everyone followed his command without question. He was an old, powerful, and lethal vampire.

"I'll enjoy watching you be torn to shreds," Cesar said slowly in his thick accent with a sneering smile. With vampire speed, he breezed through the tunnels. Everyone followed. Cesar stopped at the entrance of the tunnels. The sabers which began to wake on the brink of night were moving. "We've fought for many years. But you have been the maker of your own death."

Thomas began snarling incoherent threats. Cesar threw Thomas through the crack. The sabers reacted, their snarls and pace slammed into a pile toward Thomas. Lydia ran past me, but Cesar grabbed her wrist before she passed through the barrier.

"You don't have to watch. And you don't have to die because of your brother's actions," Cesar said, calmly as he continued to watch on. Lydia looked up at him wide-eyed and at her brother, who was being mounted by a pack of sabers. He was fighting them off, but for every saber he killed, another two jumped on him.

Lydia looked at me, unable to process what she'd done. She probably thought she contributed to the decision of his death, by catching the dagger that was thrown at Chase. Her eyes blurred with tears. I'd never seen a vampire cry before. But this was her brother. How many lifetimes had they lived together? She pushed past all the vampires who acknowledged her pain, but let her pass by, and back into the tunnels with vampire speed in silence.

Cesar turned to all of us. He looked at the team who he considered to be his elite. He'd just damned and killed their leader. Chase held my hand and rubbed his thumb over my knuckles. He wasn't meant to be outside the room, and was at risk right now for being here. For following me when I put myself in danger once again. He always made sure to stand by as a safety net just in case I stepped over my bounds, even when it put himself at risk.

"Let this be a lesson to the lot of you and make sure the message passes through," Cesar announced. I looked past Cesar to where I could see the drag marks of blood and still hear a loud commotion. I could sense that Thomas was still fighting, he was an old vampire after all. Cesar turned his back and walked past all of us, my mother not far behind him. My mother slipped a note into my hand. Only Chase and Tythian had seemed to notice the exchange. I too followed them and continued through the tunnels, so I could check on Dillian and Julia myself, and to thank Connor for what he had done and his efforts to protect them.

"I didn't do it for you or your friends," he said. "It was my orders, as simple as that." And then he stiffened at the door once again, like the good soldier he was.

Chase held my hand firmly, to help me conceal the note that my mother had given me. I heard whispers amongst the tunnels, as word already began to spread into the coven of vampires. Everything began to stir. This was the awakening of a rebellion.

TEMPTATION

I have a lover, friends, and family who stand by my side.
They support me, and endure me at my ugliest of times.
They ensure I always gaze at eye level with head raised high.
I do not grovel, and I will not let my knee hit the ground.
But I cannot speak so loudly as to what my sacrifices have already been.
This darkness claws at me, and I love its sensation.
I don't want to be the monster they try to keep me from.
But, its temptation beckons me and feels so good.
I love you. But, I cannot confirm that it's enough to keep this disaster at bay.
This monster is not resting in peace, and I want to be within the claws of its inner turmoil.
This darkness consumes me with a twisted smile.
And we come hand in hand.

CHAPTER 21

ONNOR AND BALZAR continued to guard the door. The mess had already been cleaned, but the stench of twelve decomposing vampires still lingered in the air like the offensive smell of human feces. Connor was now a threat as much as he was a barrier from other vampires entering. He was certainly a brother I couldn't let my eyes off for a moment. Balzar stood beside him, much like the soldier he was himself, and I realized how very different the brothers were. Cesar had found qualities within all of them that were unique. Tythian had a strategic demeanor and ability to motion things unsuspectingly to those around him within the coven; Connor's silence, obedience to order, structure, and ability to discard of any betrayal, his gift—the first wave of defense against enemies. Yolo's ability to adapt to his surroundings, role-play, and implanting himself into unsuspecting enemy groups; and Balzar, the youngest, who doesn't yet have a gift but has the strength and knowledge of a human soldier, from after the change of the new world. He was permitted to act boldly against threats within the coven, and was also well equipped for fights outside with a strategic mind on the line of battle.

"Are you okay?" I asked Dillian and Julia who sat at the chairs around the wooden table.

"I can't keep doing this, Esmore, we need to leave," Dillian said, his passive nature now receding. And I couldn't blame him. I wouldn't have been able to control myself within these walls as a sitting meal either. Even if they'd inspected the tunnel where the running water drifted through they would've encountered issues. This coven was built in such a way that no one could escape unless permitted. It was the perfect level of protection and hiding, but also the worst form of imprisonment.

"I know. I'm working on it. I just need one more day to align a few more things. But everything's in motion," I said. "I'm sorry, Dillian, I truly am."

"Sorry isn't good enough," Dillian snapped angrily. It was the first I'd seen him so angry, and Julia flinched under his tone. "I'm sorry," he said to her, all his strength diminished. He hadn't slept at all since we arrived. Though they were offered food, I could see physically it was taking a toll on him. I had thought anywhere would be better for them then within the Guild when sabers ambushed, and buildings began to explode with firearms. But a coven wasn't what I expected, and I'd failed them in that regard. "Please, Esmore, we're so powerless here."

"I know," I said, stepping closer toward him. "And I'm sorry. You've been my only friend, and I promise you I am doing everything within my power to get you and Julia out of here safely. I promise you."

His iridescent pink eyes lingered on me for a moment longer until his demeanor changed entirely and his shoulders sagged. He stroked a hand through his black hair and looked up at Chase. "I know, it's just frustrating." Dillian was in a worst position then me to be in the presence of vampires. I could understand his overwhelming frustration. Julia grabbed hold of his hand and offered him a warm smile.

"We have each other. We'll be okay," she said, acting as a pillar for him. Her inner strength or optimism reminded me much of Whitney. I looked away disgruntled by the memory. Dillian leaned down and left a tender kiss on her lips.

I opened my mother's note. *Be ready*. I scrunched up the very simple and elusive piece of paper. Be ready for what? Tythian walked in, dusting his shoulder as if our very presence dirtied him. He combed over his blond hair, his blue eyes rounding the room in one quick inspection.

"I've made a deal with your mother, Esmore, however I still would like for you to offer me the information I asked for," he said, indicating he still wanted Whitney's brother, Charlie.

"What did my mother make a deal with you about? I'm surprised you could speak freely with her, without Cesar hearing," I retorted.

"Oh no, he was in the room. He knows of our bargain. It's nothing that affects you for now, however. So, do not be alarmed by it," he said, holding out his hands. Balzar walked in with a handful of weapons.

"These are for the others," he said and offered them to Dillian, who jumped on the weapons in glee. I would have suffered within the coven if I hadn't earned the leniency of being allowed out. I couldn't imagine what it was like for Dillian. Not even being able to feel the sweet sensation of a blade slicing through air, at the very least. I looked at my sword and Barnett crossbow, which leaned beside the doorframe of the bathing chamber.

"Where are we going?" I asked. I didn't want the details of the bargain my mother and Tythian made. If he were going to tell me, he would have already. All I needed to know was why he was presenting Dillian and Julia with weapons. I needed to use my bargaining chip of Charlie to get Dillian and Julia out. I felt powerless to Tythian in a way as if he were the gatekeeper of getting in and out of this place. Everyone was conspiring with him and creating deals for their own satisfaction and way of survival. I wondered how many coven members had something worthy enough to offer him so they could escape if only for a moment.

"I'm taking you four to investigate the human camp near your old Guild. You'll have to send me a visual of the location," he said.

"My mother bargained this with you?" I asked, not expecting her to intervene in such a way, though I trusted her best intentions, I also understood the pull to conspire and side with one's familiar. If she had organized this I wondered if Cesar knew. I thought Charlie had been my only way to provide this opportunity for the others. Dillian and Julia's eyes danced with hope. It offered me peace, that if for any reason, even if the human camp was overrun by the hunters from our old Guild; I could use my information of Charlie as a new form of bargain, to take them to and inspect the area within Antarctica. My mother's intervention had crafted a secondary option. I hoped that I didn't need to resort to that back-up plan. I wanted the first encounter within this human camp to go well. To give Dillian and Julia purpose once again as hunters.

I could show Tythian an image, an area that was close to the camp. He opened his mind to me, allowing me to transfer the image of the place I had in mind. It was upon a hill, where it looked down on the human camp. There were only a few spots where we could watch from, without being noticed by the humans themselves.

Chase had grabbed my weapons and slipped my sheath over my

shoulders. I adjusted it and grabbed my crossbow. Chase grabbed a sword for himself, musing at it with a smile almost trivially. He didn't have much use for weapons but took one anyway. Dillian equipped himself so heavily it was as if he thought he'd never have the excitement of holding a weapon again. Although he wanted to protect Julia more than anything, I imagined that my old training partner missed the thrill of the fight. In here, he was imprisoned and unable to make any moves of his own without exposing Julia or himself. If I'd known we'd be taken to a place like this, perhaps I wouldn't have wanted to go with Tythian so freely. I trapped us all, within the mercy of what either Tythian or Cesar allowed to happen. If my mother had made this deal in front of Cesar, then that meant he knew we would be leaving. I wondered what bargain she made to convince Cesar to allow that freedom.

Julia held a knife to her chest, but I knew she was our main parcel that we would protect at all costs. She could fight in defense, but was not as well trained as Dillian or me. She wasn't built for this expertise within the Guild. We needed to prepare and encourage ourselves, that we may be walking into a trap. If the others were there and spotted us, we might become victim to an ambush. But, this was a risk we'd have to be willing to take, in hopes that Dillian and Julia and even the others had a place they could reside in and find normality within their lives once again.

Chase and I grabbed Tythian's hand, the nauseous sweep of my stomach took flight. Out of the swirl of darkness, a breeze of dust blew into my face. Chase and I instantly crouched to the ground, to partially conceal our visibility. Only seconds after Dillian and Julia dropped to the ground beside us. Moments after, my mother was also teleported beside me. I hadn't accounted for her arrival. We watched over the human camp, from the hill in the dark night.

It seemed to have been unaffected. The sabers didn't find their whereabouts after the ambush of our Guild. The human camp was surrounded by water, only one frail bridge was the gateway in and out. We'd built it in such a way, so only a few at a time could enter. If too much weight was applied to the bridge then it would snap. But, the current that usually flowed underneath the bridge wasn't there. If a large pack of sabers ran on the bridge at once and collapsed into the water, then they would've been swept away. The water was still. Someone had created a wall to block the flow of water.

I continued to study the few humans I could see who were on patrol. They were doing their usual route. It alarmed me that I saw no hunters;

surely a few of them would've ventured back here after the Guild members split into separate directions. Or perhaps they hadn't abandoned the Guild like Kora and Kasey had mentioned. Had they attempted to rebuild or venture elsewhere? I couldn't imagine Campture staying within those walls after Fier's Council found their location. Maybe she was unsuspecting of that.

"I'll be back in an hours' time," Tythian said. "I must return to Fier's Council." Tythian vanished, and the mist around his feet pillowed towards us. I wondered if Tythian slept at all. He was constantly behind the scenes orchestrating his own mischief and Cesar's orders. The dark and haunted clouds almost entirely cloaked the moon. An hour wasn't enough time to do a proper evaluation. Something like this needed to be watched over for days, until it could be deemed as safe. But I wasn't going to argue with what little freedom we now had.

With no time to lose, I slid down the hill and into the foliage of dead trees. The mist was thick enough to conceal the lower half of my body. I stayed low as I crept closer to the human camp. The others followed me, silent as both hunters and vampires.

A stillness hit the air, it was too quiet. I raised my hand to alert everyone to stop. I couldn't sense anyone around, but I felt an unsettling twist within my stomach. Something here wasn't right. I flicked my fingers backward, in instruction that everyone steps back and climbs the hill once again. We shouldn't follow this path. I looked to Dillian, relying on him for his gift and his heightened foresight. Chase and I did the same. We searched into the distance in case one of us had missed something. I knew they could sense it too. Dillian's pink eyes scanned over the area, but he reported nothing suspicious. Still, I couldn't risk it; instinct was something I learned to rely on heavily in my earlier years.

Chase and I followed the others up on the hill, only footsteps away from one another. I heard a snap in the near distance and took a step toward it, ready for any attackers. I stepped onto something light that shifted under the rustle of dead foliage. With lightning speed, Chase pushed me to the side. A silver clamp ensnared him. One of the metal pieces had pierced through his hand and pinned awkwardly within it.

He'd pushed me into another trap, which instantly entrapped me. He had tried to guard me, but unintentionally pushed me into one close by. A small silver net encased me, burning every part of my skin with excruciating pain. I could feel my energy drain, as my body tried to fight off this foreign pain.

"Fuck," Chase snapped. "I tried to push you out the way. What are the odds of throwing you into another one by accident?" He tried to joke to pull my attention away from the excruciating pain. He always tried to convey humor when he was uncertain in serious situations. Chase dropped to his knees, his hand still pierced through by one of the silver pieces. Though he seemed okay, when I scraped over his mind, he was anything but calm. He was fighting off his urge to show any pain or fear in our situation. He only focused with a clear head on one thing—and that was me.

"Esmore!" Dillian went to run to my aid, but paused to evaluate the ground first. Julia grabbed his hand with a smile. She closed her eyes and focused for a moment. The ground shifted slightly, and foliage began to grow. This was Julia's gift, the ability to increase growth and prosperity amongst plants. This was why she was within the farming area of the Guild. Even the mist around her stayed clear. There was an absolute purity that surrounded her. But her gift was not an offensive one. She didn't make plants grow this quickly because it was too exhausting for her. The foliage thickened. One by one, metal traps that surrounded us began to trigger and snap shut. My mother waited patiently until all the traps had triggered. All of them were silver, a vampire's greatest weakness. These were new additions since the last time I'd come to the human camp. Julia opened her eyes and smiled. A few droplets of sweat had beaded on her face.

"I knew you'd come back," a familiar voice swept through the trees. I unhinged the focus of my pain and cringed at the last voice in the world I ever wanted to hear again. James crept from the shadows of the dead trees, the mist billowing around him. He hadn't changed since I'd last seen him. He was still cleanly shaven and his green fluorescent eyes locked on me intently. "I knew you'd survive and come back to me, so I can make you better." He convinced himself. So many acid-like feelings crept up my throat, he made me want to vomit. James, my ex-boyfriend, who believed in the hunter's code and desired for me to be his property. He believed that I needed to be saved and that he could make me better as if I were some disease. His controlling nature turned into a much more violent monster all of its own twisted and obsessive desire.

My purple hazed eyes distorted his image. I snapped my fangs at him in warning to stay back. But, the silver that enclosed me only seemed to react more as I moved. I hissed in pain, not having known the true effects of silver before. They must have stayed out of sight until we were trapped, which meant that Campture was close too. She must've been reading our thoughts the whole time we were here. Chase hadn't yet distorted all of our minds. The only two she couldn't read were mine and Chase's, and with all we knew, it had to stay that way. "I created these traps with you in mind. I knew it wouldn't be long until you came to inspect the human camp. Knowing you like I do, Esmore, I knew you'd choose this positioning as well. You always did prefer on top."

Chase snarled at him feverishly, trying to break out of his imprisonment. "A mercy fuck goes a long way, ey?" He spat at James. An arrow from behind James shot into Chase's shoulder. We had no room in these cages, we couldn't dodge any attacks.

"You're the very creature that made her sick. I'll enjoy killing you," James sneered with a twisted satisfaction. My mother stood in front of us with a smug expression. Before her suspicious death, she was one of the greatest huntresses within our Guild. Her expression mirrored what I imagined my own to be when challenged; it was a very superior demeanor. But, against another hunter, and from within our own Guild, was not a battle we'd ever anticipated for. Her forward challenge confirmed that my mother now viewed them as the enemy and they as her prey.

Dillian stayed close to Julia and rounded her toward us. Another ten hunters crept from the shadows, this had once been a part of my Guild and so easily would they turn on me. I snarled again as if to make a point, but whimpered at the silver that sapped my energy so quickly.

"Give Julia time," Dillian whispered to my mother. Julia closed her eyes and began to concentrate. Dillian stayed close to her and intervened with the few arrows that were shot at her. He flicked them away effortlessly with his sword.

James and my mother ran at one another, a heavy impact blew the mist around them as their swords collided. My mother's flexibility and strength were renowned. She flicked his sword away, pivoting in a circle and kicked James to the ground with such force that he plummeted into a tree. Already his body had changed into metal, which was impossible to penetrate.

Another four hunters surrounded my mother. One by one, she dodged and diverted their blades with effortless precision. I could feel another huntress approach us. I recognized the presence and the smell of her filth, Campture. Kelf followed her, as was always his role. Dillian fought off other hunters and protected Julia. She concentrated with her eyes closed, completely entrusting her life in Dillian's hands. She dropped to her knees in exhaustion though she didn't stop focusing. I'd never seen her gift be used as an offense. Small vine-like tentacles grew from the ground and began to wrap themselves around the metal of both Chase's and my trap. The longer I stayed within the trap, the more sluggish I became. I could feel my vampire self attempting to renew and overcome the draining properties of the silver. I was useless in here and unable to pry it open myself. I was too weak. Chase tried, his hand still bled as he tried to open it with one hand. I could smell the burning of his flesh as he held tightly onto the silver. The vines continued to grow, and slowly their strength began to pry the bars of the trap open.

"Get to her!" I heard Campture's voice echo through the woodland. I was ashamed of my weakness as I watched Chase continue to do his best to pry the trap open himself. Chase had more experience with the effect and withdrawal of silver. I still had so much to learn and was useless in this form. The purple haze of my eyes vanished. I no longer had the strength to keep my fangs exposed or threatening. My mouth was so parched, and I was thirsty, so thirsty for blood. I had used this technique so many times on vampires. I had used silver against them and only now did I truly understand its effects.

The hunters turned their intentions onto me. They tried to avoid my mother who danced amongst them so beautifully with her swordsmanship. They attempted to run around her, but her egotistic smile announced otherwise. She couldn't be so easily avoided.

The small vinery like plants continued to strain under their might. Dillian was now fighting off three hunters who came close to Julia. I knew there were only a few within the Guild who could match his strength and skill, especially when he was protecting her.

Panting harshly, I watched as James stalked my way, his iridescent green eyes still visible through his metal form. I offered a pathetic state of a snarl at him. How had my strength dispersed so quickly? How could I be affected so dramatically? James watched me for a moment and placed his hand through the metal to touch me, to stroke my cheek. I pressed myself further against the claws of the silver to resist the touch. The burning from the silver only worsened.

Chase's bars snapped as he pried them open desperately, with the aid of Julia's vines. He shredded his hand into two, and leaped on top of my cage, snarling protectively over me. His blade sliced over James' throat, but broke in two instantly. Chase's leather boots dropped dirt onto my face. I could see the glisten of his large fangs from my vantage point. He was old and strong, even after being affected by the same silver as me. I was only young, a baby vampire as they formerly teased me. I was confronted with my one weakness as a vampire, even with my huntress self and blood—that remark had never felt so real until now. In this moment, I understood where I really was in my life and world. I was weak as a vampire, and only time could strengthen that. I depended on my strengths, but now, ultimately, my vampire self was my obvious weakness.

Chase wasn't as fast or strong as he usually was. He was exhausted from being in the silver trap; I was surprised he could still bare his fangs. My mother and I had freed him once before, from Campture's silver chains. He could hardly stand then. James' speed came at Chase at a rapid pace, but with me inside the cage, he didn't move. James stabbed Chase in the stomach. He didn't flinch from the puncture. He took the wound as a decoy so he could grab James' shoulders and fling him through the air. He took the moment, where James was propelling freely in the air to grab my trap's silver bars, prying them open. Blood from his hands dripped onto my face as the silver burnt him.

"I've got you," he said calmly within my mind. His voice seemed almost incoherent to me. Finally, they opened. He scooped me up within seconds and held me close to his chest. I could tell he wanted to flee, in such a weakened state we were easy targets. But, he respected I'd never abandon the others. His fangs were so large compared to mine, showcasing the age difference between us in vampire years.

Julia panted heavily, having exhausted her strength. I never knew she was capable of growth to this magnitude. She was at her limit. This wasn't the purpose of her gift. Chase placed me down beside her and prepared himself for the tackle James lined up as he ran toward him. Chase punched him in the stomach, with little effect against the metal. James punched Chase's jaw with a stifling crack.

My mother jumped on James' back and flung his weight over her shoulder and into the distance. All they could do was throw him away, there was no penetrating his metal skin or harming him. I tried to stand, but my legs didn't respond. I felt entirely useless. I had so quickly fallen to my knees.

One of the hunters tried to scathe Chase with his sword. Chase dodged it and delved into his neck savagely and ripped at the artery. The hunter gasped and choked. Chase dropped him in front of me. He could control himself enough to offer the meal he required, and instead give it to me. I looked at the hunter that fell into my lap. Chase provided me with what I needed. There was a glimmer of hesitation as I looked the hunter in the eyes who was once a part of my Guild. But the urge to survive and restore my strength was too great. They had attacked *us*. They were willing to kill Dillian and Julia simply by association with me. These were not my people any longer, nor did I believe in their values.

I hunched over him, my tongue rolled over the already open wound. The blood which poured tasted so sweet in my mouth. He tasted exceptional, better than any blood I had savored before. I wanted more, needed more. So this was the taste of a hunter. I viciously tore into him further and enjoyed every drop. My memory became hazy as I caught glimpses of his life, of his gift. One that I didn't want.

I wanted to pull myself away, but I couldn't, he was my prey. I clung to him tightly as if someone were going to take him away. My senses were acutely aware of my surroundings now. I didn't feel so parched. I wasn't at my full strength, but now I would be able to stand.

Before I finished my meal, a hunter ran for me from behind. I didn't want to put my meal down, but I had no choice. I grabbed Julia and pulled her away from where the sword came down. Julia looked at me, mortified. Blood dripped down my neck and chest. I had been a savage. It wasn't enough to restore me, but I had more than Chase. If they hadn't attacked Julia, I don't know if I would've snapped out of my haze entirely.

Chase and James took blow for blow. They punched into one another pointlessly as both of them seemed impenetrable. My mother danced amongst the other hunters, and sliced them when they gave her an opening. Dillian too, fought his best, conscious of where Julia and I were at all times. I searched for the person I wanted to find most. The one who had orchestrated such chaos. I could see the outline of her in the distance—Campture stood behind her hunters.

The hunter behind me swung their sword at my back. I dodged it and pushed the limp Julia back. She was extremely weak and panted heavily. The hunter swung again. I unsheathed my sword and dodged their attack. I glided my sword up their stomach. My eyes started to pin on the oozing blood. I wanted and thirsted for more. This deadly wound was my announcement of rebellion. I was not a part of this Guild any more. My mother danced amongst them in the same way. I too, would follow her footsteps of the unknown and fight those who raised and taught me to be everything that I was today. I would not hold back.

I grabbed my Barnett crossbow from the ground. Dillian was only deflecting the weapons. He hesitated to cut down the two hunters that attacked him. Three times, the opening was there to kill them. I aimed for one of their calves and shot him. I then shot the other's shoulder. Dillian hadn't yet made such a decision to turn his back on the Guild, and I wouldn't force him to. I'd be the one to do the dirty work for him. Just because I was in this darkness, it didn't mean he had to convert with me. He looked back at me, surprised.

"Take Julia now, we'll hold them off. I'll find you," I promised. It wasn't safe here. We had to fight until Tythian could take them back. If we ran on foot, they'd only follow. But, I wouldn't leave this battle unfinished; I would kill both Campture and James.

James sat on top of Chase, beating his face in. I aimed my arrow at him, shot two to distract him. He looked up at me as I lunged for him like a savage, and rolled over the foliage with him. Chase was weak, and this wasn't a fair fight. I punched into James' face like I had watched him do to Chase. With such force against the metal of James' face that my hand broke. I pulled away in a glimmer of pain. James curled his hands around me, forcefully, as he began to crush my spine. I gasped in the pain of my breath being knocked out of me. I was fighting sloppily, I needed my full strength to return. I resisted him and tried to press my own arms out to escape, but it was of no use.

"Stop, I need her conscious!" Campture demanded, from the shadows. She stepped down with a smug expression. "You might not open your thoughts to me willingly. But, I'll steal them and learn of the location of your heart, Esmore." I resisted and pulled away, but James' iron grip pinned me. I had always wondered how much Campture knew about my heart. That during my mother's panic as she removed it, how much she might've accidentally slipped and the knowledge Campture might've gained. But now, I realized as she stretched her elongated fingers out greedily toward me, she probably knew more than we had hoped. Perhaps, she knew everything about what my heart and gift could entail and how if she used me as a weapon, and controlled me, I might be able to kill off the vampires as a living plague myself.

Campture stepped back as my mother's long legs swung for her face.

"I won't let you touch my daughter!" my mother snapped. "Do you really think between you and me, that you can win?" My hand awkwardly healed itself, the crunch of bones returning into their rightful position. I felt the release of James' hands as Chase towered over me, prying off his grip. I slid from it when it loosened. I crawled out from beneath and guarded Chase's back. I shot two hunters in the chest as they attacked him from behind. James kicked Chase, plowing him through the air. The ground began to sink as one of the hunters used their gift against us. I grabbed Chase by the collar of his leather jacket before he touched the ground. I knew this gift, the earth would've consumed him. My mother jumped back and away from the sinkhole. I looked over the hunters that we'd already killed. They were all only apprentices. None of them would have been old enough to activate their gift. I snarled at Campture and her disgusting tricks.

The first line of attack was a weak one, but I felt more hunters draw to our location. These would be the hunters who had gifts. Some tracked Dillian and Julia.

"Fall back," my mother warned. We continued to jump back and dodge the sinking ground. I held Chase over my shoulders. He was weaker than I had anticipated, we all were. I couldn't even feel the strength or the last resort of the Descendant. Was I that weak from the silver?

I followed my mother's orders. We were outnumbered and exhausted. I had to find Dillian and Julia before the others got to them. With vampire speed, which wasn't as heightened as I would've liked, we tracked Julia and Dillian's footsteps. I still held on to Chase, worried that he couldn't run the distance by himself in his state. I took aim over my shoulder with my crossbow and aimed for their legs and shot them down. Only a few were taken down, others used their gifts and swords to deflect them.

I heard Campture's voice in the distance, crooning with displeasure to capture us all. Suddenly, Tythian ran beside us. Had it already been one hour? How long had we been fighting, it felt like mere minutes went by.

"I left for one hour, and you somehow manage to oppose a Hunter Guild. Look at you, Chase, you can hardly run," he said irritated. Tythian disappeared. I could feel his presence reappear beside the enemies behind us. Tythian knocked their feet out from beneath them. He grabbed one of their hearts and threw it to the ground. I pulled away from the urge and temptation that the wafting smell of blood had on me. Tythian reappeared by my mother's side.

"Go ahead and get the others first," my mother commanded. I shot another three arrows, missing two. Tythian had returned. Dillian and Julia were no longer running ahead of us. They had been safely teleported back to the coven. Tythian grabbed my mother first and then came back for us. I looked behind me, the last image I saw was James who had his hand outstretched to catch the tips of my hair, crooning my name angrily between a sob and utter rage.

CHAPTER 22

M Y VISION SWAM in and out. Chase and I dropped to our knees. I was angry at myself for being so inexcusably weak. Chase coughed into the cement of Cesar's room, with a smile on his face.

"Why are you smiling?" I interjected into his mind angrily.

"It's thrilling is it not, to be so weak and outnumbered, yet still survive? We are an A team," he mused and outstretched his fist to me for a fist bump. *"And plus, I look like such a badass boyfriend."*

"That's not a good thing, you idiot, we almost died," I said. He only smiled and looked down at his posed fist.

"Don't leave me hanging," he teased. I growled in anger and bumped it. He wouldn't have given up. A sense of relief washed over him, and he sagged further to the floor.

"I let you out for one hour, and you come back like this!" Yolo retorted. He walked in with bottles of blood to help us replenish. He squatted near Chase and offered him one. It was obvious the two had created some sort of bond. He then offered me one. I snatched it, parched and thirsting for my full strength back. The bottled blood was distasteful in comparison to the hot pooling essence of that hunter I feasted from.

"Trinity!" Dillian shouted. My mother ran over to Dillian. Julia panted heavily on the bed. "She exerted herself, her gift shouldn't be used like that. It helps stimulate growth, not excel at that rate."

I got to my feet but held myself there. I looked at the fragile Julia with thirst. I wanted to take a step closer to help, but I couldn't. I knew if I were any closer to the very pulse that pumped through her veins, I was too tempted. But I wanted to help, I had to be there to make sure she was okay. Chase grabbed my hand, still crouched to the ground.

"Your mother can handle this, Esmore, we should leave," Chase said. Yolo watched me skeptically. I pricked the tip of my finger on my ejected fang. I hadn't even realized. My mother checked over Julia's temperature and rested her hand on her chest. She would be able to use her gift to help replenish Julia's strength. Dillian looked at my frozen status, openly disheartened. A rip divided me, and I felt anguished to see such a betrayed expression on Dillian. He had every right to be angry, in such a state, I was praying on his lover—because it was out of my control. I was out of control. He looked back to Julia in comfort. He pushed back her hair and spoke to her lovingly.

"Come along, Esmore," Chase said and pulled me out of the room. Connor and Balzar still stood frozen, guarding the door. Connor looked at my bloody chest and face in a quick summary. I'd forgotten about it and began to wipe vigorously. I must've looked like a monster. Chase, still exhausted, pulled me down to sit beside him. He threw back the blood in a bottle, finishing it within seconds. I continued to wipe, ashamed of how I looked. Tythian walked out of the room and offered his handkerchief to me. His once well-groomed shirt now had sprays of blood across it.

I hesitated to take it. It was Tythian, would he ask for something in return? Chase took it instead and began to wipe at my face for me.

"Never be ashamed of this, Esmore, this is who we are," Chase said with a soft voice.

"It gets better and easier with time," Balzar admitted, he looked down as if contemplating his own memories.

"I massacred hundreds within my first year of being turned. I was unable to control myself," Yolo admitted as he walked out from the room and closed the door behind him. "If I didn't have my gift now, I think I would still be the same."

"I still have no remorse for the lives I take," Connor said. "It's harder to have the strength to resist, you're doing better than I am after all these years." But I understood that Connor was comfortable with that.

"Do you understand now, Esmore, your position?" Tythian asked. "We all have our battles. But you couldn't start your own until you realized what it was you were fighting against. You used your vampirism for power, and now you understand the difficulties of what it actually means to be a fresh vampire."

I looked between the four who claimed to be my brothers. In a twisted way, I knew they were comforting me. I never required comfort, but somehow I felt oddly exposed to their words.

"I'll help you through every step," Chase said, still wiping at my bottom lip. I felt as if they were talking down to me like I was admittingly sick.

"I was so weak," I said to him. I could only admit it to him.

"Esmore, it shows strength to be able to admit you lost a battle. It was different for you when you were within the Guild. You could control the outcome of most things. It's a different world you now dabble in. You need to learn from these experiences."

I looked down at the bottle of blood. I began to drink it and allowed time for their words to sink in. It was different, and I was no longer in control. I resisted accepting it. I tried to control the situation and every outcome since leaving the Guild. A weight lifted from my shoulders as I digested and understood. I still had the weight of responsibility and urgency to help my Guild members, who were still loyal to me. I had to help Kora and Kasey, even if they turned on me. I had to, so I would be able to close that part of me that I would inevitably have to let go of entirely. I was continuously fighting myself.

I wanted Teary and Tori close by if they would still have me. It was a selfish act and thought, as I was a threat to them all. I now understood that no matter how much effort I put in, I might not be able to control myself. No, I couldn't accept that. I couldn't have everyone force me to believe that was my only option. If it were, what would I then believe in? I knew nothing of this new world. The lines I once painted for myself in boundary were no longer there.

"No," I said loudly. "I can control myself, and I won't allow myself to harm them. I'm only part vampire, I won't let it affect me." I didn't feel moved or any sense of emotion. But, I understood this was called, a glimmer of hope. If I claimed myself to be a vampire, then the world I knew would be utterly changed. I had no place to go, and no purpose I could think of. Being hunter was the only way I could still manage and pursue purpose, without having something to fight for, I had nothing. The others said nothing, whether they thought I was in some self-denial, I didn't care. It was a decision of mine to either continue fighting this thing that I was raised to hate—vampirism; or to be consumed by it and allow myself to use it as an excuse for my ill actions. I couldn't be that darkness. Even though it toyed and loved the power, I also felt it could kill those closest to me. Without that, I was nothing.

I emptied my bottle, still not fully quenched. My mother walked out of the room, filthy and bloodied. It was peculiar to see the sons of Cesar straighten before her. They hated hunters, we were mutual enemies, and yet those lines were blurred with my mother—the familiar of their leader and father.

"They're both fine and resting," she said with a sigh of relief. "I think we all need rest. Has Cesar not yet returned?"

"No Ma'am," Balzar responded. "He's still inspecting, with the elite group. Tythian is due to collect them in a few hours."

"Inspecting?" I asked. Tythian responded.

"The next group Cesar wants us to confront. He's inspecting them personally, in case Oppollo is within range. If he is, we're not to make contact under any circumstance. However, if it's just a small group, then we'll confront them to send a message. We are the children of Cesar. Sending us out with the risk to our own lives definitely suggests his confidence within the war. Oppollo is not an enemy that we can face. But we can take down his men, blow by brutal blow. Depending on the size of those who march toward the Council meeting first, we may all have shared leadership in the elite group. But of course, there are other matters to be attended to first."

"I don't want you coming to the Human Compound with me," Yolo said. "Just for a few days, anyway. You've lost a lot of strength, your body will thirst to recharge, and the only way to do that is…" He gestured down at the empty bottle of blood in my hand.

"No. I want to go, I need to go," I responded. I had to get Kora and Kasey out of there before I focused my mind on this war that I'd been dragged into. I hadn't even the time to properly digest and think about the demand Campture wanted of me—to find out where my heart was. I had to focus on that later. I needed to free them first, and then I could move on and consider my next step.

"I agree with Yolo," Chase said grimly. He finished his bottle of blood. "It's too risky. I've told you before, you're only new as a vampire, Esmore. I believe in you more than anyone, but in this regard, you're out of your depth and control. I always told you I would never tell you what to do, but, in this matter, I hope you would heed my advice." Having my familiar so against something I needed to do broke me. I didn't want to disagree with him on anything. But we were two fine warriors of our own accord who respected one another's sometimes unorthodox actions. I cupped his strong jawline besotted with his beautiful eyes.

"I'm fine. I can suppress it. It's only a part of me. It's not my entirety. Tythian?" I questioned. I looked at him for support, in the hopes that he could persuade them. He was my only way out of this underground coven.

"Unless it profits me, I won't take you," he said dully.

"It does benefit you," I snapped. Everyone looked at me as interested as he did. He knew what I meant. I was ready to give him the identity and location of Charlie. Tomorrow, I was due to go on a mission with Sydney and the other members. I wouldn't be within the compound to be blamed or be made suspicious of. If Lincon could keep his promise to free Kasey and Kora, then Tythian would have his revenge, and I could bargain to take Dillian and Julia to the Antarctic human camp. I could even manage to negotiate Teary and Tori's teleportation there. I knew how desperately Tythian wanted his revenge. I could only offer Kora and Kasey freedom. I wasn't sure how they would proceed afterward because of the manipulation done to them, no human or hunter camp would accept them.

"Sister…" Yolo began. "Why do you want to be there so much now?" He snapped on me. "It's not safe for your hunter friends, or is it because you want to break out those hunter twins that I'm trying to conceal in?" I snarled in response. Chase put a hand on my shoulder to keep me rested against the wall.

"You should not be concerned with my affairs, unless Cesar instructs it," I snapped.

"If it affects my affairs, then you bet your sorry ass it has everything to do with me," Yolo retaliated. His usual calm, collected, and bouncy self, was gone. Connor pressed his hand against Yolo's chest to make him aware to stay back.

"Go," Connor simply said. Yolo looked between the brothers and then to my mother. He put his head down in agitation, breaking through them and walking into the tunnels.

"You must use very fragile footing around Yolo and his concern for the Human Compound," Balzar said. "He's worked very hard on that project, and it is benefiting us. He'll always put this coven first. Don't dishonor him by messing it up."

Chase, too, was silent. My mother said nothing and returned to the room. After an eeriness of silence, Chase led me through the room and into the separate one, which Dillian and Julia usually rested in. There was a hammock and a small shelf of his favorite bobblehead dolls that we'd taken from his room in Fier's Council.

"Where did you find this?" I asked, surprised. He closed the door behind us, so no one could intrude.

"Tythian grabbed the hammock for me. I used to sway in it all the time if I were tense about a situation. And well, my bobblehead dolls seem to ground me, make me feel nostalgic about an easier day and time." He tapped one of them, and its head bobbled. *Considering I lost the bag of my favorite ones when we were ambushed at your Guild,* he internally grumbled.

He sat on the edge of the hammock and invited me to sit next to him. He held out his hand to me. His leather jacket opened wide to show his shirtless chest and stomach underneath.

"Sway with me for a little while. Before we clean you up and send you off again to the Human Compound." I leaned into him. We laid in the hammock, and Chase began to push against the wall lightly, so we would sway.

"I hate not being around when you put yourself in danger. I believe in your strength, Esmore. But, I know how out of depth you are in dealing with your vampire self. I want to stop you," he admitted.

"I know," I whispered. I looked up at his beautiful gray eyes, consumed by them. I needed this moment of rest, just so my next steps wouldn't consume my thoughts. "But I have to keep stepping forward, I can't be frozen. Everything else is moving around me. If I stop stepping into the hurricane of things that are happening right now, I'll be stuck in the eeriness of its silence. Thank you for believing in me." I pooled myself into him and kissed up his neck, which had dry blood on it. Chase accepted my flaws, and I accepted his. I kissed the corner of his lip as he tried to be stubborn against me. Finally, he gave in, flushing his hot breath into my own and twisting his tongue with mine. He held my jaw softly as he continued to kiss me passionately rough.

"I hate that you have a way with words and can win me over every time," he smiled. He kissed my forehead and guided my head back down on his chest. "Just please never stop listening to my advice. You are my familiar. Everything I say and do will always be in your best interest and safety." Chase kissed the top of my head and held me closer. I hugged him tightly, embracing the warmth he offered me. *I know.*

CHAPTER 23

WITHOUT SLEEP, MY endurance and stamina were still highly alert due to my vampire self. But even then, I still needed it. Like Chase had explained, we could go weeks without it. But like any normal body's response or action, that part very deep within us that was human needed a moment to stop and just rest. Without rest, the likelihood of turning into a saber increased significantly. A new foreign and ambiguous threat to my survival.

I woke in Chase's arms and was comforted by his low snore. I felt more tired than I had my entire life. I still wasn't at my full strength. It was the first sleep I'd had since being here.

I bathed and clothed myself in fresh leather. I kissed the slumbering Chase goodbye who felt so comfortable and safe that he didn't wake with my movement or sound. That was something he'd done even before I admitted my attraction to him. He'd even done the same back in the Vampire Council when we were enemies, and I was a threat, he still slept directly across from me without a care in a world. A smile lingered on my lips, or perhaps my familiar was ever so cocky that I'd fall for him.

I united with Yolo and Tythian at the usual meeting place. The vampires within the coven that I scarcely saw whispered amongst themselves as I walked past them. They remained in the shadows as if to look directly at me would summon their own death. Rumor had already spread about Thomas' outcast and demise.

"I'm sorry about last night," Yolo said sheepishly as he scratched the back of his blond hair. He began to fidget with the large wooden cross on his bare chest not meeting my gaze. I couldn't blame him for his anger toward me, because he was correct in suspecting me to have ulterior motives. He shifted and reformed into Jenn, who smiled at me charmingly as if everything had been said and forgiven. It was peculiar to know that it was still Yolo, but when he transformed it was like a different personality entirely.

Tythian watched me intensely. I had promised him his revenge. He couldn't openly ask me about it in front of Yolo, but I nodded at him in the way of confirmation that I would pull through on my end of the bargain. He grabbed my hand and teleported me to an open field with cracked ground and deserted land. The sun was harshest here. I placed my hand above my eyes in irritation. This sun was the worst. No mist was here, and this land just felt dead. The sensation of pins ran up my body as I tried to defy the agitation of its heat.

"It's a desert; still the ice has not yet glazed over its heat. I give it another three hundred years maybe," Tythian said. "I figured you would want to discuss the bargain we had in place prior to your new day within the Human Compound."

I hoped that with time, I could feel as casual or become unaffected by the sun as everyone else seemed to be. I had the impression that came with age and experience.

"I have a plan in motion which will happen today, there will be a lot of commotion made. I won't be within the Compound at the time so you must be visual, a lot of traps are within the Human Compound. If you linger around the border, I should be able to reach your mind and find you while this happens. I'll let you know when the time is right, as long as you leave your mind exposed to me. You must hastily be in and then out," I sharply said. I still had my hand raised above my eyes to try and block the sun's rays. Of all the places he could've brought me, of course it would be the one I was most uncomfortable in. This was a simple show of power as Tythian much preferred. Although I was now doing him a favor, I should be grateful for his services and that I could be of use to him. That was the impression I had of Tythian's bargains.

"Show me," he said, while he licked his lips. Charlie was the one who'd experimented on Tythian's human familiar, Whitney. When I first met her, I thought she was dying of an old disease in the human world, called cancer. However, it had been a lie in an attempt to put her at ease. It was the aftermath and defects from injections and experimentation she was forced to endure at her brother's hand. Because of it, Tythian couldn't turn her. He fed her blood to slow down the effects, but still her time came to an end. She didn't die from old age or a natural death. Fier took her life as he slit her throat after she'd protected Chase and me. A part of me would always be in debt to her. I could never return the favor, but maybe this would bring her familiar some sense of peace.

After Tythian executed his revenge on Charlie, he would then focus on Fier. I could see the thirst in his eyes and the darkness of despair. His familiar was gone, and no amount of revenge could ever bring her back. But this was Tythian's way, like my own, of stepping forward into the hurricane of our new world.

"Firstly, if I make this agreement, I want you to guarantee me and my hunter companions passage to inspect a human camp in the Antarctic. I may need a few days, and this might extend to more than Dillian and Julia, I may have a few others too. Hopefully, the human camp is secure, and they can live amongst them." My skin scorched under the sun's ray. An ugly bird circled above us, preying on me as if I might collapse any second. I was intrigued by some of the animals that had survived from the technology era.

"You could always counter my other offer. Instead of trying to protect and save others, you could ask to have no involvement with my take down of Fier, of which you've already promised me," Tythian said, adjusting the collar of his salmon shirt. As he said the words, I doubted it was his genuine offer. It was yet again another test to see if I would shy away from our previous agreement. Though I didn't think I was smarter than Tythian, I'd begun to understand a few of his basic traps. Contracts and verbal agreements were something he'd execute in blood if they weren't served. And I wasn't going to fall for such an easy trap.

"That's not what I'm bargaining. Do you agree?" I pushed my hand out for him to shake. The agreement between Tythian and me, and taking down Fier stayed. Plus, I had my personal grudges against the Council Leader. He killed Whitney in front of me, someone I was unable to protect. It was because she took the blame for my impulsive actions that led to her demise. I wanted to avenge her death, also in an attempt to scrub her blood from my hands.

Tythian shook my hand. With his mind opened to me, I showed him an image of Charlie. The memory of him stirred anger in me as well. I gave him a brief on my journey through the Human Compound, and where the laboratory was that he spent most of his time in. It wasn't guaranteed that he'd be there, but the likelihood was high. I tried to converse my sense of smell to Tythian, so he knew the scent of Charlie. I struggled to create the sensation in my own mind, to remind myself of his distinct smell. Eventually, I clumsily conveyed it and tried to imprint it on Tythian. He raised his eyebrows. "You've learned a great deal on that gift, Esmore." I removed my hand from his, relieved to have successfully accomplished it. I found confidence in being able to expand my gift and learn more about it.

"You aren't concerned about Yolo's reaction to this if he finds out you were involved?" I asked skeptically.

"Esmore, my dear, even though we are brothers, we all have our demons and tasks to bear in the attempt to find closure—especially, when it comes to the rarity of a familiar and losing her. Yolo in the past was no exception to this." Before I could question him more about Yolo's familiar, Tythian grabbed me and pulled me into his teleportation.

Jenn tapped her foot impatiently as we re-emerged. My stomach churned. "Are you kidding me? Did you remember you left someone behind?" She snorted. Tythian grabbed hold of her hand and teleported us to the border. He nodded at me and disappeared. I knew he would stay close by to the Human Compound hidden within the forestry for today.

"Damn secret meetings." Jenn kicked a rock underneath her small heel as she began to walk toward the border. "I give up on asking what it's about. I guess I already have a rough idea."

"Apologies, Jenn, I mean no offense. But I have a task of my own to achieve as well," Tythian said, straightening the cuffs of his shirt. It settled me to know that Tythian felt the same and had no concern for doing so. Every man had his battle to conquer.

I scanned over the many minds within the Human Compound and detected the one I was searching for—Lincon. He was highly active and alert, obviously doing as he said he would, and keeping off the drugs so he'd be ready when I needed him. It was a lot of trust to invest in him with such an important task, and I wasn't entirely sure if he could pull it off. But, he'd also cause the perfect distraction for Tythian to sneak in and take his revenge and be the reason why I could free Kora and Kasey, without being a suspect. Though I had no doubt Yolo would know full well who was behind the assault.

Jenn and I walked throughout the glass tunnels. The dome overhead was still closed. I hadn't seen it open since the first time I arrived, which was a relief for my very easily irritated skin. We walked around the founder's statue, where Sydney and his daughter, Titan, walked toward us. I focused myself. It had been difficult to control myself around the guards and the women in the booth before our daily scan. The others had warned me, not being at my full strength, I would be tempted...and I was. My vampire self was on edge, predatory-like to every human within sight, Sydney and his daughter being no exclusion. I took a large inhale and reminded myself that I was a huntress, not a vampire, as if the repetitive thought would rein in my hot desire to pounce. I had to rely on my huntress skill set. I only drank blood if I required, from a bottle. That was what I reminded myself of. They weren't food.

Titan gave me a cautious glare as she walked with her father. Sydney had a patch over his head from the wound he'd acquired only yesterday.

"What happened yesterday?" he demanded from across the domed glass hallway, rather angrily. "Others told me what happened, but I need to confirm with you. Attacked by vampires and then saved by hunters, you can't be serious?" He crossed his arms over his chest. He waited for my response, impatiently.

"I keep going over it in my head too. But yea, that's what happened," I lied. "Why do you have weapons on you? I thought you'd be excused from the mission today, after such a knock to the head?" Titan tugged on her father's skintight shirt that emphasized his broad chest and arms.

"No, I'm still going. I don't care what the doctors said. Yes, Titan, why don't you go play?" I could smell his wound slowly healing, it left a lingering metallic and parched taste in my mouth. It was harder when confronted by a wounded person, they were easy for the taking.

"Ellie," Jenn said. She snapped me out of my fixation. I looked at her, unaware I had zoned in on Sydney's head wound. She looked at me unsettled, as if knowing.

"But, the Endoor brothers haven't come out of their room yet," Titan moaned in displeasure.

"Well, why don't you go play with Sarah?" Sydney said, crouching to his daughter's eye level. She dressed similarly to her father, with a long white shirt and small light cotton pants. I'd seen a few female children within the compound now, most wore at least something 'girlie,' a concept I had no idea of really. Titan, however, dressed similarly to the boys.

"I don't want to play with the girls. Ellie plays with the boys too, and she's strong." She looked up at me from under her thick eyelashes, as if asking for my help in the matter and to side with her. I looked between Sydney and her, unsure of what to say. I had never had a child put me on the spot like that.

"Ah," I choked. "I have Jenn as a friend." Who was actually a man, I thought sarcastically within myself.

"But you don't all the time. You're strong. I want to be strong too, but all the girls only want to cook. I want to fight the monsters outside." Sydney sighed with a smile. He looked to his feet in defeat. I measured the young girl's size, a little higher than my hip bone. She was six, yet toyed with her father's emotions, saying that she wanted to be the exact thing he tried to shelter her from. I wondered if she'd ever seen these monsters before. I never thought I would hear a human child say they wanted to fight against the monsters. Not that I'd had much to do with human children. Nor had I ever seen a child be capable of manipulating a full-grown man before.

Hunter children did not act like this. We were firm, trained, and honest. Sex didn't matter on our equal tasks, it was survival of the fittest. Whereas within these walls the matter seemed relevant. I supposed it had to do with their limitations in strength and the human men were somewhat superior in that regard.

"I agree with Titan," I said with thought of my own childhood and the companionship I found with Dillian, who was a boy. This was the only way I could relate in any way. Dillian and I always pushed and challenged one another. Until I was older and found James to be a good duel partner—the thought of him leaving a shudder up my spine. "If you feel you'll become stronger by playing with the boys, then I think it's a good plan. You can always do things by yourself, don't be dependent on just your friends."

Jenn raised her eyebrows at me and was surprised by Titan's smile that had two teeth missing. "Okay," she simply said, gave Sydney a kiss on the cheek, and ran in the other direction and back toward the residential sector.

"Wow," Jenn said. "I was just about to tell you, that was the worst pep talk I'd ever heard someone give a child, and that you're terrible with children." I could sense Yolo's tone in this. "But alas, you two are kindred."

"Well, at least that'll keep her entertained for half the day. In whatever she went to do." Sydney frowned, questioning what it was his daughter was now doing. "Come on. We have to grab the crew. Today's your first day out, isn't it? It's only a small team and mission today so you'll be all right. Not much pressure. C'mon."

Before I could follow Sydney further down the hall, Jenn grabbed my wrist. She gave me a stern look of warning. I knew what she was warning me of—to not lose control. I pulled my wrist away from her grasp. I could do this. I was in control, I convinced myself. I had to stay focused on executing my plans. And when I was further away from the Human Compound walls, I would initiate those schemes.

Sydney and I walked through the doors and outside onto the field, where many of the younger members trained. Like he'd previously ordered, there was double the amount of guards who patrolled the wall. A team of eight waited for us, six men and two women. They looked at me with little interest and waited for Sydney to speak. I continued to wear the same crossbow that I took from the facility on the first day. I couldn't bring in my prized weapons that I felt so comfortable with, in case others questioned where I might've obtained such quality weapons. I was supposed to be a patient with amnesia, the fewer questions, the better.

"Today, we have a team of ten," Sydney announced. "The objective is to forage for outside animals we can use and breed as livestock, and return with at least two vampires. The traps haven't been as sturdy lately, and we've been catching less. Mr. Richard wants us to find more. So, we'll see if we can locate sabers that are in slumber further out from our border. We're not to approach a group that has any more than three. All detail is to come to me first before any action is taken, understood?" Everyone nodded, their backs straight. "Right, everyone make sure you have your weapons and are strapped tightly. Angela, you're to carry the medical bag and kit." A lady ran off to do so. The rest dispersed and grabbed various weapons. Some I noted had guns, a weapon that existed before my time.

"Let me guess, you don't know how to use one," Sydney teased. "The all-knowing, Ellie, doesn't know."

"You shouldn't tease a person with amnesia," I said, seriously. I was insulted because I didn't know how to use them. I hadn't seen many guns in my lifetime. "I think I would've been more of a traditional weaponry person, anyway."

I searched over the array of swords cautious not to touch the silver tips of the blade. It would be the same from now on, the same with my arrows. The weapons from both my Guild and within the Human Compound had been forged and tipped in silver to be used against vampires. They were just as dangerous toward me now as well.

I toyed with a few finding one that better suited my grip and size. I made sure to find something light and durable for a human with my supposed strength. I strapped the sheath and sword to my back and made sure that it was underneath the bow and arrows.

"That's all the weapons you want to take, not even a dagger?" Sydney asked as he strapped himself down with more daggers concealing some even in his boots, around his arms, and hips. I needed weapons that I could control, such as a sword and arrows. If I grabbed daggers, I didn't know to what force I would throw them. It was easier to control weapons I was already used to using now, with human force. I placed a garter with a few daggers for show value not that I had any intention of using them.

"I'll be fine," I said. "Just worry about not getting yourself killed. The monsters might get you." I clicked my tongue in a teasing manner. He reminded me so much of the relationship I had with my previous Token Hunter, Drue. He'd always teased me about not being enough, not yet strong enough to match him, and so I did more to prove him wrong. With all those lessons, I became one of the strongest huntress's of my generation. I hadn't the chance to have a final battle with him to gauge myself on his spectrum.

Sydney smiled at me. He rounded up the other team members before we headed toward the wall. I stayed to the back due to the overwhelming smell of Sydney's wound that teased me to bite. I didn't want to acknowledge this side of me. It was not a part of me, especially while I pretended to be human. A gnawing feeling nagged at me as we approached our mission.

CHAPTER 24

THE SUN BORE down on me again. It was an overcast day, yet I could feel it tingle on my skin like tiny droplets of fire. Mist clung to our every step as we walked through the dead trees. I scanned the area to keep tabs on Tythian who still lingered around the border, and Lincon who still remained within the Human Compound.

The team I was led by had their guns raised the entire time in case a vampire came for us. I couldn't sense one close by. In the far distance, I could sense Teary and Tori's presence hovering around the border. I would keep tabs on them to make sure they didn't come any closer. It exhausted me slowly to outstretch my mind for such a long period keeping everyone in check. But, I needed to make sure everyone was impeccably positioned until the perfect time to execute my plan. I was surprised that Tythian held any form of restraint as he waited for my go-ahead, instead of pouncing at the chance immediately. To some degree, he must've respected Yolo's hard work and commitment to his project. I wanted to give the command when the group stopped moving, where I could concentrate on the individuals that would be acting on my behalf. I needed to know what the results were, especially if Lincon could break Kora and Kasey out.

We continued to walk for another hour before Sydney suggested everyone take a break. We were now on the border. Past here, they were no longer protected by their traps. It had only been two hours that they had walked on foot, but already they showed signs of fatigue and required a break. I sat down furthest away from them and leaned against a tree. My hunter team used to run for full days with minimal breaks. How peculiar, that we derived from humans and still held the same physical form, yet the difference in survival and strength was so evident.

Half of the members carried heavy back-packs. They began to share around bottles of water. I focused my mind on Lincon. His mind wasn't attentive, but it was alert and open, he was waiting. Now was the time.

I compressed my thoughts and sensation of motivation, just as I had practiced with him. I felt his mind go into overload for a moment and then he was blocked off from me, he shut me out, so he could concentrate on his task. I didn't know how he would manage to break through all the security, but he thought so highly of himself, that I hoped he could pull it off. I located Tythian, his mind was calm and collected, but impatient. I sent him a strong urge of motivation, as well. His mind vanished entirely from the borders of the Human Compound. Within seconds I located him inside the compound. He also had closed his mind off to me. Now I waited.

"Water, Ellie?" Sydney offered me a bottle of water. My hand twitched oddly as I had the overwhelming sensation of darkness. I was inevitably tired from using my gift for so long, and in the sun at that. I fell back from my body's temptation and straightened my thoughts.

"No, thank you," I said. I looked away, hoping that when I did, the smell of him would wash away. My senses were acutely aware of his every movement. I continued to ignore the urges that screamed at me. My blood cells felt as if they were on fire and my inner vampire thrust within me, not wanting to feel the thirst of what I had suffered last night. It was like trying to tame something wild within me, there was no reasoning. I couldn't convince the instinct I would be fine, that another day will not hurt or exhaust me, and that I would never allow myself to thirst in that way again. It was the instinct of survival and excessive drinking.

"Are you okay, Ellie?" Sydney asked. His movement shuffled closer to me, and my body froze. The dual sides of me rolled over one another in dominancy. This was the line of control I was battling. I continued to ignore him as I tried to push the vampire part of me down. I would not lose my control, not now after I'd worked so hard toward everything. I thought of Dillian, my dear friend, and Teary and Tori who were relying on me. I could control this.

"We have four rodents!" one of the men screamed. Sydney walked away from me in a hurry, and the relief washed over me.

"Move out!" Sydney demanded. In groups of twos and threes, they swarmed. In the near distance, I could hear the wobbly steps of the rodents who ran toward us.

"Come on, Ellie, we'll circle them from behind," Sydney instructed. He grabbed the back of my leather shirt as if to lift me. The touch ignited flames on my skin as I buried further into myself to contain my thirst that set my body aflame. I followed him, trying to focus only on the sounds of the rodent's footsteps, which we ran past and circled from behind as the others took the force at the front.

Sydney stopped. He was listening out for something. "Can you hear that?" he asked, arching his neck. Gunshots fired and screeching noises followed. The smell of blood filled the air. "I think a vampire might be close."

I noticed the vision of my purple eyes fading in and out as my own warning signal. I tried to focus on the sound that he heard. It was another vampire, I could sense it. It was what threw me over the edge, to know that another hunter was within the woods preying on my victim—on my feast. I couldn't deprive myself of the thirst any longer. My fangs slipped out elegantly. I wanted to pull away, but that small part of me was silenced. I wanted to feast, I thirsted for it. I was a superior race. They were only human, what was wrong with just a taste?

Sydney turned around to me and waited for a response. I stood there, my arms inward to my body. I couldn't resist it anymore. "I'm sorry," I whispered. I jumped on him and delved into his neck. I bit into him, excreting my venom, so his yelling would stop. I covered his mouth until I could sense the paralysis working. His blood oozed into me, filling me and releasing all tension I had within my body. I continued to drink from him, feeling enlightened as I did.

This wasn't darkness, this was purity. It made me feel good, it made me feel strong. I continued to drink. I needed more as if it were my last feed. I couldn't let myself starve as much as I had yesterday, never again could I leave myself so vulnerable and exposed. I felt Sydney's memories flood into me, I wanted to see more of his story, more of his world.

"Esmore." A hand grabbed my shoulder, and I snapped in response. I looked over my shoulder and snarled at the vampire who dared interrupt my feast and my prey. Chase's gray eyes pooled into me, they were blank as if a mirror of my own. Why was Chase here? I blinked and retracted my fangs. I came to the realization of what I had done. I looked down at Sydney's heavy body that I held limp in my arms. "No, no, no," I slapped his face, but his pale skin didn't show any life. His blue eyes continued to stare toward the sky. "No, no, no."

Chase crouched beside me and wiped at the bite mark I had left behind. He evaluated my venom as he rubbed it between his fingers. "This is a lot of venom, Esmore." He rubbed his leather sleeve over my mouth and wiped away the blood. "I was worried you were too weak to be here today. I thought this might happen." He collected Sydney's oversized limp body.

"I didn't mean to. I didn't want to," I said, embarrassed by my own weakness. I'd given in to temptation, and I could no longer hear the pulse of Sydney's beating heart. Chase must've been on the borders with Tythian today. I didn't sense him, because I was so focused on Tythian and Lincon.

"Wipe your lips a little more," Chase said, soothingly. I could feel him excreting his calmness over me like he always did. "I'll take him back with me. We'll see what happens from there." My eyes opened wide. Chase said I had injected too much venom, could he mean that he might now turn vampire?

"Over here!" Someone yelled. The members began circling Chase.

"Raaawrr, I am the evil vampire!" Chase said in a robotic voice. "I eat human. Nom Nom. Rawwwwrrr," he antagonized. The members began to shoot their bullets at him. Chase easily dodged them, enjoying the game.

"I love human, nommy," he repeated with a mischievous smile, taunting them. With vampire speed, he stopped behind one of the humans. "Nip," he said and laughed as he swirled in circles, effortlessly carrying Sydney in his arms with vampire speed. His back was too us now. He looked over his shoulder dramatically, his abs sticking out of his open leather jacket as if he were posing. "Bye now," he charmed with a smile, before vanishing into the foliage.

"Are you okay, Ellie?" one of the men asked. He lifted me by my arm. "She seems unhurt. But she has blood on her," he told the others. "We need to pull back now!"

That two-hour run back to the Human Compound was the most unnerving dash I'd ever experienced. I felt numb, conscious of what I'd done, but there was a part of me that felt so relieved and overcome with joy to be fully quenched. I was unable to decide on which side I wanted to highlight the most. It was easier to listen to the darkness that murmured it was okay and only natural. That I am the hunter and everyone else is my prey.

We climbed up the ladders of the back wall, the atmosphere still and eerie. I didn't want to risk losing control again. I didn't dare use my gift to see where Tythian and Lincon might be or if they were successful in case it would slump me into a stupor again and antagonize me to lose control once more. One of the guards confronted us, addressing the new leader of the team with a somber expression. He looked around in search of Sydney.

The man, who now led us, shook his head with a saddened expression. The guard's voice came out distant. "Sydney too?" The temporary leader looked up at him for a moment and questioned what he meant. "There was an incident here while you were gone. A break out of a vampire and two hunters, I didn't even know we had two hunters within the compound. But these one's looked different, I thought they were sabers. Well, the glimmer I had of their image before they jumped over the wall and fled. And then Charlie…" His eyes bulged, mortified.

"I wish I never saw anything like that," the guard said recoiling. "His eyes had been gouged out, and his chest has been stripped with claw marks. The inside of his stomach had been clawed out and he'd been choked by his own intestines," the guard began crazily speaking and went a ghostly pale. Atop of the wall, I searched through the forestry below us, the mist rising against the wall. I wanted to picture anything, but that. So, both Lincon and Tythian had succeeded. "And eight guards and two nurses were killed."

I showed no movement or inclination to listen, but I was angry to hear that another ten were killed, after I instructed Lincon not to hurt any humans. I knew Tythian wouldn't have wasted his time on anyone other than Charlie. The others scaled down the wall and into the training grounds, dejected. They rested their weaponry on the ground and looked at one another, lost.

"I think we should go back to our families for today," the temporary leader said. He had oddly shaven tracks in the side of his hair. "I'll report the news to Mr. Richard."

"Wait, Cole," one of the women grabbed him before he left. "Titan?" The rest of the group sagged in depression. The reality of my actions seeped further in. I had taken that child's father away from her, the man in her life she idolized and adored so much. I could no longer handle being amidst this chaos, pretending like I was a victim. I had done this.

"Either Mr. Richard or I will find her," Cole said. "I'll see you all here first thing in the morning. Let us have some time to pay our respects." Everyone dispersed. At first, I didn't know where to go. I had no family here. I had Jenn, but I was too ashamed of what I'd done to meet Yolo's gaze. Yet, my footsteps followed the path of where she might be. By the time I reached her, I imagined this unsettling dejection would pass, and I'd be back to my righteous form. This had to be done. I found myself standing in front of the two attendants that permitted people to go into the science lab. By myself I couldn't go in and had to wait for Jenn.

"What are you doing?" Jenn asked from behind me. She walked toward me and smiled politely at the attendants. Without answering, I followed her. I wanted to slam a huge sensation of panic into her. Like I was supposed to if I felt like I was losing control. Jenn grabbed my hand and held it firm. She didn't look at me. I could see Jenn's beautiful face and frame, but in this moment, I felt the overpowering sense of Yolo reaching out to me.

"You succeeded," Jenn whispered angrily. We reached the end of the steps, and the smell of blood encircled my nose. The human whom it belonged to, was now dead. Charlie was now dead. Within the first laboratory room and cell where Charlie must have once sat, blood was sprayed everywhere. Blood was smeared along the glass, rolled over the bed, and affected the white shelving that held tubes of blood.

"I hope you both find some form of peace after this," Jenn quietly accused. She released my hand and attended to the furthest room and spoke to someone there. I continued to stare at the blood, replaying the guard's words who informed us of the painful manner Charlie had died. I thought of Sydney, sending him out a prayer. I prayed that after Chase took him back to the coven, he was alive and that Chase could save him. If not, I didn't know how I felt if he turned vampire. It could take up to days for him to turn.

I considered the very thing Chase now watched out for. Was it possible for Sydney to turn into a vampire? Could I still return Titan to her father? Would Sydney ever allow it, now being the monster he hated so much? The monsters that I hated so much. Did I hope for him to have been turned, magically somehow, without realizing it? What did I consider worse for him, to be dead or to turn him into the very thing both of us hated? But what I despised most right now, above all other monsters, was myself.

CHAPTER 25

I FOLLOWED JENN silently for the rest of the day. I ignored all those around me as if only Jenn and I walked through the halls. I knew this was a situation where I should find guilt. But without either Chase or my mother, I felt nothing. But I was conscious, what I had done had wronged others. It consumed me to have this emptiness, I wanted to feel regret, sympathy, and guilt. But those emotions didn't come. I was a monster.

The Human Compound went into silent lockdown. Most stayed within their homes and soldiers guarded the area heavily. A few were regrouping to go on the hunt for Lincon, Kora and Kasey, of which I still had no idea how he'd done it. He was an illusionist and advised he wouldn't tell me his tricks. It made me question to what extent his illusions could form into. Mr. Richard was furious and demanded his property was to be returned to him. He told Jenn that she was not to leave the Human Compound tonight. She was completely against it. She smiled as charmingly as ever and told him sternly, she would still return to her own lodgings.

Our walk to the border was silent, Jenn asked no questions about the day's event. Tythian waited for us, he was neatly groomed and cleaned up. I imagined it would've been hours of scrubbing for him to look so cleansed. There was an emptiness to his gaze. He had acquired revenge, the one thing he wanted most, and yet it was apparent it had brought him no peace. It only validated how insignificant Charlie's life was. He was a significant part and memory of Whitney's world, and just like that, he could be killed. Tythian and I didn't appear to be that different at all.

The nauseous sensation of being teleported by Tythian grabbed hold of my stomach. The dusty smell of the coven underground hit me. It felt as if it were a burst of life. I was back now. Back in the shadows of where I felt I now belonged. Chase had taken Sydney. Was he alive or had I… a sickness swirled in my stomach as I sniffed for Chase's scent.

"Wait, Esmore, you must brace yourself first," Tythian said somberly. "It's not the easiest to face."

Jenn's beautiful body formed into Yolo, who looked between us skeptically. "What isn't?" Yolo challenged me to tell him the truth. I suspected that a part of him already knew. I could smell Sydney's blood all over me, the small particles that were left on my skin that hadn't washed off. Yolo would be able to detect that too.

With vampire speed, I dashed through the tunnels to where I could smell Chase. Before I opened the door my hand froze. There was an aroma in there that smelt like *me*. But I could also distinguish it was Sydney. My blood froze in suspense. What would I find behind this door I resisted opening? An overwhelming surge of grief, disappointment, pain, and suffering rolled over me. I clenched my stomach, unable to control this affliction. What were all these feelings, where had they come from?

Tythian and Yolo stood beside me, both of them studying me. "I thought it might be like this," Tythian said. "You're only a new vampire, Esmore. Those who turn another vampire are emotionally connected. These are not your own feelings. For someone who cannot feel, it must be overwhelming."

Tythian reached for the door handle, and I panicked. I didn't want to see it. Why didn't I want to see it? I could sense something was wrong. My stomach churned. But Sydney is vampire, he's alive. A slight relief washed over me. But it was fake relief, I knew something disturbingly sinister waited on the other side of this door. I heard a cry as if a newborn child had screamed for its mother. Uncontrollably, I barged Tythian out of the way and opened the door. What was this pull of attachment and maternal instinct?

Chase studied me when I entered the room. My jaw dropped. Sydney's broad back was turned to me. He sat in the corner of the room. Every step I took toward him, created heaviness in my stomach. I thought that soon my legs would collapse. But he was calling out to me, I couldn't resist him. I couldn't reject him, this child of mine.

Sydney gave out a stifling scream, and he charged his shoulder into the wall, with such force I heard it crunch.

"Don't do that," I said worriedly. I ran over to his side, able to take those final steps. I pulled him away from the wall, wanting to see his face. I pushed aside his hair, and he began to make a cooing noise. "Sydney, look at me," I whimpered. Already my tears had spilled. I couldn't sense the man that I had teased only today. I scanned over his mind. Only small pulses of thought came from him, tiny and insignificant.

Sydney looked at me, rubbing his cheek into my hand. His neck clicked awkwardly as he did. I gasped in shock, yet, I'd sensed that this was already there.

"He's a defect vampire," Chase said, studying my reaction from the edge of the room. I choked on my own words. Tears blurred my sight. What was this? I held Sydney's face to my chest. His large frame cowered toward me. I couldn't let any harm come to him. I had to protect him, I had to look after him.

"Ah." I jarred back and pushed Sydney away from me. "He bit me." A small part of my chest had been ripped away, skin and all.

"He can't feed properly, Esmore..." Chase began.

"No!" I snapped. "You cannot hurt him. You cannot take him away from me." I stroked his sandy brown hair protectively, and began to snarl at the others who felt as if they were towering over us.

Tythian and Chase exchanged a look. Yolo watched the exchange between Sydney and me, with little interest—he was only disgusted.

Chase leaped across the room. "You can't hurt him!" I said savagely. I stood up and slammed my hands hard against Chase's chest. Chase overpowered me and slammed me against the wall. We struggled in dominancy. I kneed him in the stomach three times. I had to get to Sydney. I had to protect Sydney. Sydney. Sydney. Chase blocked my knee on the fourth. He held me with only one hand, before firmly punching me hard in the stomach, winding me for a second. But that second was all that he required.

With no mercy in his eyes, he leaned over Sydney.

"No, Chase, No!" I screamed. I ran for him. Chase plunged his hand into Sydney's chest and pulled out his heart. I gasped in disbelief as Tythian caught me. I had my outstretched hand over his shoulder, gasping to get to my baby. *My Sydney.* The room around us swirled into darkness. Tythian teleported us back to the hot day of the desert. I dropped to my knees in shock. I stared at the desert ground. Tears escaped my eyes as I snarled, and pledged my revenge against Chase.

"Esmore," Tythian said, calmly. "Have you come to your senses yet?" I snapped my fangs at him. I realized how pathetic I looked but was almost incoherent. It took me minutes to attempt to dig out of my foggy haze that kicked and screamed at my inability to protect him.

I sat on the dry ground with Tythian watching over me. I looked around and reevaluated my surroundings. The tears I shed became dry. I took shallow breaths. The upheaving pains in my chest and the panic attack that I endured, lessening.

I looked to Tythian for some form of explanation, my overwhelming sensation of pain and suffering began to deplete. A maternal instinct that had swept over me disappeared.

"Chase had to do it. You would've destroyed yourself in the process. We weren't sure if you would be overwhelmed by the emotional connection, due to you having none without your heart. Sydney was defective. Without being spoon-fed every day, he would've died. You wouldn't act like your normal self. You too would have been led down such a path," Tythian explained.

I sat on the ground, processing all that had happened. I didn't want Sydney to die, but the remains of that man no longer existed. He was taken from this world because of me.

"Chase would have killed him in front of you so you would hate him, instead of hating and blaming yourself for what had happened," Tythian said, honestly.

"I killed Sydney," I said with a parched mouth after all my screaming. That was something Chase would do for me. He would risk a world where I could possibly hate him, so I didn't hate myself. How did he know I would revert to my old self if he killed Sydney? He had once explained to me that he knew vampires who had committed suicide once they lost the vampire they created and were connected to. How did he know I would revert, or was it just a gamble? He couldn't have known, he just didn't want me to blame myself.

"You did kill him." This was Tythian, he didn't hold back. I was dangerous and a monster. I was delusional if I thought I could protect Dillian and Julia when I was the threat. I understood that now. I had to break away from my hunter life completely before I attacked them next.

"Tythian, can you please take me to the border of the Human Compound. There's someone I must meet. I'd be grateful if you could give me an hour? They might be the companions I wish to take to the human camp in the Antarctic, as well as Dillian and Julia." I was a predator and a threat to them all. What if I had attacked one of them instead of Sydney? What if it was Dillian? I had to accept this undying thirst that could easily control me. I now admitted that I had been wrong. No matter how much I struggled against the thought of being vampire, it was an overwhelming part that was encased inside of me. I couldn't control it, so I had to let those I might endanger, be free. This was the only parting gift I could offer.

CHAPTER 26

I SCANNED OVER the border of the Human Compound, searching for Tori and Teary's minds. When I pinpointed their location, I swept through, not at vampire speed, but at my huntress speed. I could feel the wind cascading over my face. I couldn't feel its coolness, but I still found it to be refreshing. When I approached them, both were on guard. They lowered their weapons when they realized it was me. They sat on top of a large rock.

There wasn't much room for hiding within these woods, the trees were mostly thin and dead. But the fog mounted as good cover. From their position, they could search outward, but could also be pinned easily by others. I wondered how long they'd stayed within this position, awaiting my order because I'd selfishly asked them to stay close by.

"Eh, Esmore, I was wondering when ye'd get back," Teary said. Tori walked up to me with a gleam of respect in his eye. Even though so much had happened and they'd seen the ugliness of me upon the night Campture tried to kill Chase and me, they stayed loyal to my command. "How have ye gone with the plan?"

"They both escaped. I had a vampire from within, break them out. However, I haven't seen or sensed them since." They were no longer in the area. "The girls were highly mutilated. I fear that their mindset might not be the same. With the physical defects, they were evidently saber as well. I did as much to give them their freedom, and now I'm offering yours."

"What do you mean, Esmore?" Tori asked, confused. "We want to follow you."

"I've found a human camp within the Antarctic. Originally, I was to take Dillian and Julia there to inspect it and see if they can be incorporated into the camp. I'd like to offer you two the same. I have no guarantee of it working. But it's a start, and if it doesn't work out, then at least you have built your numbers and strength."

"Ye won't be joining us, Esmore?" Teary said, skeptically.

"But I'll go where you do, Esmore," Tori said with certainty.

"I wanted that as well," I admitted. But, I couldn't risk their lives. "But I can't do that. I killed someone today. I drained him completely dry." I pointed to my chest, trying to convey the words I needed to express myself. "I cannot control this side of me any longer. It appears the more days that rollover, the larger it grows within me. There are a lot of things I don't understand about myself, and a lot of enemies I now have to face because of this thing I've become. This isn't something I can do as a Token Huntress. I won't be able to fight clearly if I'm worried about the lives of those who follow me, and whether I'll be tempted to attack them or not. If I stay amongst vampires right now, I won't be so compelled. I don't want to hurt any of you."

A silence swept between us. This was as honest as I could be. I was only a risk to them and the others. At least this way I could regroup them, even if I couldn't lead them.

"Esmore, ye've let it go to ye head," Teary said. She pointed her sword into the ground and drove it in hard. "We ourselves are tainted with blood on our hands. Ye do what ye have to do. I'd like to join Dillian and Julia. But when ye are ready for battle, and ye need warriors, ye know ye can trust. Ye'll find us again, yea?"

I stood there with little sensation. I should've felt relief in this, or something…any emotion. I felt the insecurity of pulling away from duty and walking away from my comrades. Teary and I searched our surroundings. The presence of numerous vampires surrounded us. I recalled the stench of two. It was Chase's coven members, all of them consistent with a similar smell. Just as Cesar's coven was the same. Because of our reaction, Tori also prepared his weapons.

I considered fighting. I could have fun dancing amongst them to relieve me of this darkness for some time. But, then what if I turned on Teary and Tori? I now understood how thin my line of control was. This was an excellent opportunity to be taken, they wanted me as bait. Though it was a bit rushed and not how my familiar might've intended, he had admitted he was now prepared to confront his fears. He'd helped me by taking the initiative and killing Sydney, to relieve me of that pain. I, too, could do the same for him by forcing him to accept his past, and confront this coven that he'd been running away from for so long. It was time for us to take claim into the darkness that was formidable and beckoning our attention. If we were to become stronger, we needed to face our demons together.

"You two run. They have less on that side." I pointed to a fracture in their circle. They'd be able to fight their way through there. And besides, I knew who they were after. Teary and Tori were hesitant. "Go! I'll be fine. I plan to become a hostage. After all, they still consider me as human."

"Are ye bonkers?" Teary asked. Tori was hesitant to lower his weapons.

"Trust me. I'll find you both and bring you together with Dillian and Julia. I'll find you all a safe place instead of being exposed in the open. Now go." With much hesitation, they both ran at hunter speed. I smelt flames and screams in the distance as Teary and Tori fought through the few vampires that blocked their escape. But, this coven was not focused on the hunters. They were here for me. They pooled from the trees. Some looked over me as if savoring the taste. The thought of Chase's theatrics came to my mind. If I had a sense of humor, I might have said something like, 'Oh, please don't get me, the weak human.' But it didn't amuse me, it only reminded me of something Chase might do.

"It seems your hunter friends abandoned you when they're outnumbered," the woman with long black hair and pale skin mused. "I never thought much of the whole hunters protecting human thing." The same defective vampire, Spungee, followed her. About thirty vampires surrounded. I was curious as to whether this was the extent of the coven's entire force. Cesar had a large coven. But in comparison to this group, Cesar's was far cleaner and organized. Half of these vampires looked as if they were on the verge of becoming sabers. I held back my annoyance and boredom with her superior tone. Between Teary, Tori, and me, this fight would've only lasted minutes. I looked at the size of some of the vampires' fangs, and was surprised that several had some age to them. Perhaps, it wouldn't have been as quick as I first assumed. "Will you come with us now, human girl? I doubt it'll be long until your familiar comes out of hiding to save you. On the contrary, he might be a coward in that regard too."

Her voice left an irritating humming in my ears. Her words came in and out as I had no interest in listening to her. Two vampires came beside me and grabbed me forcefully. I held back my natural instinct to fight them off. I was still pretending to be human. I looked around and gave a pathetic gasp as if to fear them and show I was scared. The woman smiled in pleasure. "Dylan will be so pleased we finally caught you."

They dragged me away at vampire speed for three hours. Their hideout was further than I'd thought, considering they continued keeping tabs on where I was. They ran along a shoreline. Sand flicked up at their speed, and shallow waves seeped in and out. I looked out to the ocean's vastness and then on the opposite side where dead trees concealed it. I could hear growls and savage vampires in the distance. I heard the whimpers of a human girl before she was silenced and her throat ripped apart. I suppressed my heightened senses. I couldn't focus on the smell of her and give away my fake identity by trying to fight over the girl's bloody corpse. If they knew I was vampire, then that would change this situation and my element of surprise. It was better they underestimated me until I knew how Chase wanted to deal with them. If he thought them worthless, then I would aid him in slaughtering them.

In the distance there was an opening, where the vampires danced around a blazing fire. There were hundreds of them. The enormity of their coven took me by surprise. Their numbers could even compare to Cesar's. How had they managed to stay so large in size, when they were in the open like this? A large cage was hanging by a high metal pole that was impaled into the ground. It was beside the fire. I wondered if that was supposed to be for me. A bit dramatic, I thought. I had no doubt in my mind that when Tythian came to find me hours ago, he would've reported to Chase.

Chase would find me. I'd even considered dropping pieces of my clothes, so he could follow the path of my scent easier. But it was no use, the vampires would've seen me doing such a thing as they surrounded me when they ran. They wanted Chase to track me, but I wanted him to do it in his own way. A way where he could enter by element of surprise.

The rowdy vampires silenced. Whispers began to pool around me as they fawned over me. They inhaled my scent, indulgently. I heard voices murmur, 'it's his familiar.'

"Clarissa, you finally caught the teeny tiny human," a heavy accent purred from the crowd of vampires. Vampires separated away for him to walk through. A very pale and dirty vampire emerged. I could sense he was strong just by the way he walked and the power that emitted from him. The vampire with long black hair, Clarissa, brightened red in the cheeks. The praise embarrassed her. She flicked her long black hair away from her shoulders. Her defect vampire began to tug on her dress.

"Not now, Spungee." She kicked him away from her. The vampire dragged across the ground and lowered itself as it crawled back toward her. "I'm sorry, Mommy didn't mean it." She opened her arms for it to come back quickly. I frowned at the relationship between them. Could that have been Sydney and me? Is this what Chase had saved me from?

"I apologize for the delay Dylan," Clarissa said. The man stroked his pointy beard.

"Us French are not patient, you understand that, no?" he said arrogantly. "But, you're lucky your results came through in the end. I will show lenience this once." The man had a strong build on him, with lightly tanned skin. His dark eyes consumed me hungrily. When he spoke, I looked for the size of his fangs, trying to gage his age, but he hadn't yet ejected them. "Well, lock her up in the cage. I like the theatrics of it. If Chase doesn't arrive in twenty-four hours, we shall eat her."

The vampires cheered as they dragged me toward the cage, rambling in sing-song ways. I accepted it without much fear. It'd be exceptionally hard for me to break away from these vampires if Chase didn't make it in time. The notion didn't bother me, I knew he'd find me.

The man named Dylan blocked my path. "Why do you not smell of fear?" he queried with his foreign accent I'd never heard before. His dirty fingers grazed against my cheekbone. "You're very beautiful, aren't you? It's such a shame he hasn't turned you vampire. Maybe I won't kill you. Maybe I'll chain you and treat myself to you, over and over again."

I smiled. "I can't wait until Chase comes and kicks your ass," I said, with a gleam of confidence. Chase wouldn't lose to such a vampire. This vampire who now obviously led this coven was no match for my familiar. Although he'd run away from that duty since even his human years, Chase was their technical leader. Against those who now wanted to challenge and kill him for leadership, I knew he would not lose. Dylan stroked his beard. "Interesting. You're as fragile as a butterfly but have the heart of a lion."

The vampires continued to drag me toward the cage. One of them threw me over his shoulder and scaled the pole with efficiency. He threw me into the cage, which I was blessed to find was copper and not silver. The cage swung with my impact from being thrown. I looked up at the chain from which it hung. It didn't seem to be very strong. He clamped down a lock over the door and jumped from the cage. It continued to sway. I looked into the glimmer of night which cascaded with clouds.

The vampires below me continued to dance and chat. It was a very uncivilized coven when I compared it to Cesar's. I found no real structure nor strength behind it. But they had the numbers, and they had members with age and experience. I sat uncomfortably in the cage and watched their every movement. I absorbed details of their members. Often, my gaze would trail off and follow Spungee, the defect vampire, and his master, Clarissa attentively. I continued to watch them interact more than I would have liked to.

CHAPTER 27

I WAITED WITH boredom being my only true companion. I continuously scanned the surrounding trees in search of Chase. The night passed over and the sun began to creep up. I felt like I'd soon be a cooked vampire if I had to hang in this cage directly under it for any longer. The other vampires began sighing and getting agitated, as well. A lot of them asked if they could return to the shadows of their coven. So, this open meeting place wasn't where they stayed. Dylan permitted no one to leave, and they grumbled their complaint. He wanted his numbers to remain impressive and strong. I closed my eyes still listening to the movement below me, considering rest even in a situation like this.

"Esmore," Chase's voice interjected in my mind. My eyes fluttered open. I could finally sense him around. *"Are you okay?"*

"They think I'm human," I mused to him. I knew he'd find humor in that. *"I'm unscathed. They have me in a cage. You'll see it when you get closer. The one in charge here, from what I can see, is Dylan. He has a presence about him, which suggests he's old and might be a slight challenge."*

It wasn't only Chase's presence I could feel, but Cesar's four sons and the members of his elite group were also positioned behind him. They stayed further back. I was surprised to see they'd all come for me, but this was more than likely Cesar's direct order. They stayed far back, so the other vampires couldn't detect them. If Chase did want to reclaim his coven, then bringing in another coven's force would only start a war.

The vampires began to snarl and run at Chase, but Dylan called them back. Slowly Chase crept out of the trees' mist and overlooked their numbers, his fangs already bared. His leather jacket flicked back in the breeze, as his shirtless chest was poised in a show of dominance.

"Welcome, finally. After four hundred and sixteen years, we finally meet, Chase. No more running away," Dylan snapped as he walked amongst the vampires who parted for him, and toward Chase. It'd been that long since Chase killed their past leader. I recalled the story he told me—he was still human then. He'd killed the previous coven leader to release his mother from his cruel and abusive grasp. He was unsuspecting of the consequence after that.

"I don't know you, but you pissed me off!" Chase snarled. "You dare take my familiar as some kind of bait?!" I'd never seen Chase so savage. It was a show between the two leaders, the rightful one and the temporary one.

"I only wanted to coax you out, so I can kill you and take my place. I fought alongside our leader, the one you killed in his sleep. How embarrassing for you to reside and have a weak human as a familiar," he laughed.

"I've come back to claim this coven," Chase announced, surprising me. I thought he'd rather kill them so he could face his demons and make peace with his past once they were wiped from the face of this earth. This coven had destroyed his mother's and his human life. "You'll either bow to me, Dylan, or I'll kill you. Your greatest mistake was ever thinking that the familiar to match me, was weak." Chase locked his beautiful gray eyes on me. "Esmore, dear, let's not toy with them anymore. Come down from there."

Dylan snarled savagely. The other vampires did the same, like a pack of sabers responding to one another.

"Well, it can't be helped then," I said. I stood and slammed my foot hard into the bottom of the cage, and snapped the chains that I suspended from, in half from the impact. I kicked out the door and jumped over the group of vampires. I flipped in the air and landed on my feet to crouch at Chase's side. Vampires dispersed from beneath the cage they once kept me in. The copper smashed to pieces against the ground, and fire flickered everywhere. I flicked my golden hair over my face and looked up at them through the purple haze of my hunter's eyes. I smiled, displaying my fangs.

"And you said you didn't like theatrics," Chase teased. I stood up as his equal beside him. 'Trickery,' 'abomination,' 'what is it?' the vampires whispered as they stared at me in bewilderment. Dylan looked around at his vampires who already began to come unbound. This army could be led, but only if they had the right leader. This Dylan was not a leader.

"I'm two hundred years older than you, boy!" Dylan snapped. He showcased his staunch self. "Don't make me laugh!"

"With that extra two hundred years, you've learned nothing about being a leader," Chase sneered. "I ask you again, you either die or you follow me. No others involved, after all, I don't want to kill my members," he said, taunting him. "Those who oppose me however, step forward now. I'll kill you too."

Dylan snorted and spat on the ground. "You're not taking this coven after all these years. This is nothing but protocol. I can't wait to behead you and take that pretty little familiar of yours."

Chase snarled and ran for Dylan. The two collided with vampire speed, slamming into one another. Neither used their weapons. I waited on the outskirts with anticipation. Though, I wouldn't let it show. I stared down the vampires who fidgeted or wanted to involve themselves with the fight. If they tried to intervene, I would be their opponent. This was Chase's fight. No matter how much I wanted to help him, I had done my part to lead him here. Dylan became sluggish. Chase was hitting him strong in the stomach, knocking the wind out of him. I hovered over Chase and Dylan's minds, realizing the effect that Chase was playing on him. While he fought Dylan, he was also overpowering his mind with a sense of drainage and sluggish behavior.

I was impressed by Chase's ability to concentrate on using his gift which was so consuming, as well as fighting at the same time. Chase knocked Dylan to the ground. Dylan rolled across the dirt, and other vampires snarled at him to get up. I could see already as I watched the covens' reaction, some of the members began to look at one another, uncertain of the outcome. A coven needed a strong leader, how they survived all these years, I didn't know, especially a group sized at this magnitude.

Tythian was suddenly by my side. "We have a problem," he said. The coven's vampires gasped and began yelling 'treachery.' "Oppollo's group isn't far from here. Fier's information was either wrong or misguiding." Cesar had only recently scoped out his group, had they made an advancement he hadn't accounted for? But, Cesar wanted this group taken out. "I've scanned over the numbers, and it appears Oppollo isn't amongst them. Cesar wants us to act now and counterattack them while they're on the move." Tythian dropped my Barnette crossbow and sword at my feet. A large black hole consumed him from beneath as he teleported. The brothers who remained still hid, waiting for Chase to complete his task and take ownership. They waited for this battle to be over, in case they required his new followers to join in on the fight before they started the next one. I wasn't sure how coven politics worked and if they would follow him so freely and unyielding immediately. But one thing I was certain of was Chase wouldn't fail.

Chase backhanded Dylan across the face. Dylan charged him with part of the copper from the cage. Other vampires began to get closer, to encircle Chase. I wouldn't move unless one of them advanced first. They steadily watched the fight and me, now perplexed with the understanding that I wasn't the weak human they thought they dragged here.

Dylan speared the pole toward Chase. He grabbed it and elbowed Dylan in the face, and knocked him off his feet. With one swift movement, Chase wrapped the pole around his fingers and caught it steadily. He plunged it directly into Dylan's chest. His shocked expression didn't wager as his form went brown and he began to decompose. Chase reefed the pole out and flicked the pole around his back and in front of him, in a matter of precaution if anyone else attacked. From the tips of the pole, blood spluttered across those who stood closest.

There was a stillness in the air. This was Chase's victory. We waited to see if any others opposed. The vampires looked at one another in silence. Slowly, Clarissa stepped forward and looked over Dylan's corpse. Chase was wary of her movement as he pointed the pole at her challengingly. She immediately dipped her knee and bowed to Chase, not wanting to endanger her own life. Slowly one by one, others did the same, until the hundreds of vampires in front of Chase pledged their allegiance to him within a matter of seconds.

"We've waited for you," Clarissa honored, still looking at the ground. I found irony in how they celebrated the thought of killing Chase only hours ago. How quickly their disdain and hatred for him vanished when they were threatened themselves. "If your strength can restore our coven, then we accept you. We've lost a considerable amount of members in recent years. I cannot say all are welcoming since you had abandoned us once," she confessed. She no longer diverted her gaze and looked at Chase with sincerity. Spungee, who bowed beside her looked between her and Chase, unable to stop fidgeting. "But we need that strength."

"So, you'll do as I say. And if I'm not here for any matter, for as long as I live and reign, you are to listen and to protect my familiar," Chase said loudly so all could hear.

"We apologize for the conduct and way we treated you," Clarissa said to me. Their attitude against both me and Chase had changed so quickly. So this was the power of a coven leader's word.

"Esmore!" Yolo whispered, not far behind me. The vampires could sense him, but none raised their heads to argue with the outsider's presence. I quickly strapped my sheath to my back. It was now time for my fight, with the brothers that I was considered equal to, and the elite team that followed under my command. Cesar wanted us to dispose of this group, and with the thrill and excitement of the fight, I wouldn't ignore the chance to prove myself, not as a huntress but my growth and strength as a vampire.

Chase came to my side. "I won't be long," he whispered and pushed back part of my fringe.

"I know. This is my fight now," I said and kissed him passionately on the lips. "I don't know why you changed your mind about your decision in leading this coven, but I support it. I won't be long. I, too, have a strong team behind me." Chase nipped my bottom lip and merged his tongue with mine. His hot breath pulled away as I began to run and follow Yolo. Chase had to confirm the obedience of his coven. He had to reinforce that power. I now had my own challenge ahead of me. I accepted the idea of letting myself go and allowing this darkness to consume me. I was a vampire and wanted to dance amongst my equals and what was claimed to be my brothers. The time of pretending to be anything other than vampire was behind me.

CHAPTER 28

I FOLLOWED YOLO. The others had already run ahead. I let the urge and atmosphere of battle sweep over me like I had the first time I was amongst this elite team of vampires and Balzar. Only now, I had another two members—Tythian and Yolo, who hadn't yet seen me fight. I had to prove to them that I wasn't a form of weakness in this group. My blood and ears pounded with every step I took on the hard and dead ground. My breathing was near non-existent. I was excited to accept this blood lust that so easily consumed me.

The foliage around us cleared, and we broke away from the trees. I watched the others run into the distance in front of me. I propelled myself to catch up, so I wouldn't miss out on the excitement. Within the large open space was a field of enemy vampires. Their numbers would have peaked at near eighty. The sun broke through the trees on the other side of the field. The color rose to a red, the same color to soon stain this battlefield. Some rode horses and were already alerted to the ambush as we swarmed over the hills. Balzar was first to reach them, but in good challenge, I couldn't let him have the first kill. I aimed my Barnett crossbow at the same vampire he targeted. I shot him directly in the chest before Balzar could slice his sword through him. With little hesitation, Balzar moved onto the next one. I could hear his irritated growl from here.

Connor stopped and projected his hands in front of him. Within seconds, twenty of the vampires in front of him dropped and began to scream. My group poured around Connor with lightning speed, slicing, and killing through the vampires that Connor controlled. I ran past Connor with a wicked smile. I unsheathed my sword, thrilled for the first vampire that attacked me. I slit my sword across their throat. She clutched at it in reflex. I pierced my sword into her calf to drop her completely. Balzar plunged his sword into her chest and claimed my kill with a smile. An eye for an eye.

He spun to intersect the vampire who attacked him from behind. He cut him across the chest who was unaffected by the pain, and clashed his own weapon against Balzar's. The sun's red rays amongst the trees in the distance began to flicker with shadows. More vampires crept out. Their numbers grew. We hadn't anticipated these numbers. It dawned on me instead of being the ambushers that we might've stepped into a trap. Fier might have purposefully misinformed Tythian. Still, the vampires of Cesar's coven expressed such glee. Even Tythian was enjoying himself.

I jumped over my comrade to intersect a vampire who was trying to sneak up from behind. I jumped on its shoulders and scraped my sword against his. I balanced on his shoulders for a moment, before I jumped and flicked his sword away. I shot my crossbow at his chest, but missed as he dodged it. He ripped the arrow out from his shoulder.

He snarled at me, his fangs dripping with saliva. He charged me and tried to cut across my stomach. I jumped back and shot another arrow that he dodged. Shaz approached him from behind, her smile wicked. I took the vampire's attention and lunged at him. I scraped my sword against him in a show of strength. I could share the kill with her. She aimed her blade for his chest from behind.

A large gust of wind blew between us, and my hair blocked my sight. Once my blonde hair cleared, I opened my eyes wide. Shaz stood there for a moment her mouth and eyes wide. Her stomach had been slit open, and her insides pooled out. The thick wind that tore between us held a tension. Suddenly, Shaz was lifted from the ground by something I couldn't see. Her heart was ripped out from her chest, and she immediately began to decompose into the ground. I flicked away the sword of the vampire I fought. There was an enemy lurking that I couldn't see. I pierced the vampire's chest in front of me in rage. I wanted to step closer toward the enemy who killed her. The vampire before me dropped and began to decompose. I could feel heaviness in the air. I could sense that I was being preyed on. Someone watched me greedily. I snarled in the direction.

"Retreat!" I heard Tythian bellow from the fight. I could feel the presence creep toward me. I cut my sword strong through the air and felt that it had made contact with that entity. But no wound appeared. There's someone there. A hand clutched around my throat and lifted my feet from the ground. I stabbed my sword into where I presumed to be their stomach. But again, my sword sliced through.

"Interesting, you can sense me," a man's rough voice purred. The light mist of a man's face and sturdy frame emerged. "So, you're Cesar's daughter?" He assessed me for a moment. I shot an arrow at him, which pierced straight through and into the distance. "I'll have fun killing you and all his sons today."

The presence of death followed his words. The name came to my thoughts as if instinctually. "Oppollo," I whispered. I could see the glimmer of a smile stretch wide. He was death. He was a Phantom. I felt the army of Chase's coven pour over the hill. That Balzar, Tythian, and Connor ran for me as I was held in mid-air. I was struck by one sudden realization and fear. He would kill us all. That fear sparked within me like an instant whirlpool of darkness. I wouldn't let Chase die. I called upon that darkness that presented itself. I could sense Oppollo's hand reach for my chest. None of them could die!

My back shifted uncomfortably. I was consumed by the overpowering surge of more power. Two blades pierced through my back, from the corner of my eye I could see they weren't blades. Two great wings emerged. I had called upon the Descendant. I swirled with my wings cocooning me in protection. I'd managed to flick him off and crouched to the ground. I still looked to the position where I thought Oppollo was. Perhaps my wings would act as a deterrent. Maybe he couldn't touch my wings, but I was willing to rely on that speculation.

"Ahh, the gift of the Descendant," he purred with a crisp voice. "I knew the huntress who originally had that gift. Her wings however were white. Have you tainted yourself so much with the thirst of darkness, that you're being consumed by power? You have one black and one white. It seems to be a reflection of your former huntress self and your now, vampire self," he said and began to chuckle. "What a tragic monstrosity," he said deadpan. I snarled at him, fully in control. I had to call upon this strength to protect the others. And even if it appeared monstrous or would eventually consume me, it was a risk I was willing to take to ensure they'd all make it out alive.

He countered physical attacks. I scanned over his mind but found nothing as if he was entirely non-existent. Chase's coven fought alongside Cesar's elite and hacked through Oppollo's vampires. But, those vampires were not the concern. Oppollo began to laugh.

Balzar ran in our direction and threw a dagger at where Oppollo stood. So Balzar could sense him as well. I could detect Oppollo's movements and made sure I was faster than his attack. I had to be faster. I lunged for Balzar before Oppollo could kill him, sweeping him into my arms protectively and enabling my wings to flex and offer their strength. We shot up from the ground and whistled into the clouds. I hadn't known these wings would be so powerful. *My wings.* The movement felt fluent as if I'd done this a lifetime before.

"Holy shit!" Balzar said and climbed up me awkwardly as he looked down.

"Get everyone out of here, including Chase's coven. I'll deal with Oppollo for a time," I said, trying to pinpoint his location again.

"You can't!" Balzar snapped.

"I can!" I growled at the sibling rivalry. "I'm the only one right now who can. Oppollo doesn't know I'm immortal. He can't kill me if he aims for my heart."

"But you can be beheaded!" he spat. I located Oppollo and plummeted to the ground. I lowered my wings to drop Balzar out of my grasp. He rolled against the ground until he skidded into a steady footing. I charged toward the location I sensed Oppollo. I swirled and allowed my feet to touch the ground, hoping that even the breeze from my powerful wings might affect him. But again, it went straight through him. How could I penetrate an enemy who couldn't be physically attacked?

Balzar called for everyone to retreat, respecting my wishes. Hesitantly, they scurried up the hills. Chase continued to break through the others, he was coming for me, but I couldn't let him face this enemy. I could, however, bait Oppollo. I skimmed the ground as my wings took flight again. I whooshed against the surface of the ground and aimed directly for Oppollo. I hoped he'd take the bait. He dove his hand straight into my chest. His fingers squirmed within me, searching aimlessly. I ignited all my strength into my wings and plunged for the sky. I felt the clouds around us disperse. I aimed with all my strength and might for the ocean.

I gasped at the pain and suffering I endured. Even without a heart, the pain was excruciating. Such a wound sapped me of all my strength.

"What is this trickery?" Oppollo snapped. He was still attached to my chest. The clouds below us concealed the ocean that was there. He pulled out his hand, no longer physically connected to me and inevitably dropped through the clouds. When the clouds parted with his presence vanishing between them, I caught a glimmer of the ocean that paled purple because of the redness from the sun. I listened out for the splash as he hit the water. It wouldn't be long until he resurfaced. My wings dipped weakly as the wound to my chest affected my strength and attempted to heal. I could sense Oppollo had plummeted into the sea. It'd only be a matter of time before he swam back to the surface and ran into our direction. I doubted I'd be able to use the same trick twice. I had to make sure everyone was okay. I dipped and staggered in the sky limply flying back as fast as I could to reach them in time.

I choked out blood, and my hands began to shake as I realized the implication of my chest wound. Though it might've made me immune to death, it certainly didn't prevent me from heavily being wounded. I focused on one thing. I had to find Chase. I used that as the propellant to reach them.

Finally, I could see the clearing. The vampires who we fought now dragged two behind them in silver nettings. My eyes opened wide as I realized they'd captured Tythian and Chase. My wings dipped again, and I could no longer hold my strength. The muscles in my wings locked. There was a moment of eerie silence as I suspended in the air and then I plummeted toward the ground, preparing for the impact. I whistled through the sky in the opposite direction to Chase who was being dragged away. I was unable to control my movement and listened to the flapping wind that cascaded through my wings as I fell. I desperately had to get to Chase. Wind plastered my skin as I dove for the ground that crept closer. I impacted hard into the earth. Black. Alone. Dark.

I swarmed in the darkness of peace. There were no thoughts or movements, simply being in my entirety and form. Who was I? What was my purpose? Who's name was revolving in my head?

"Esmore!" Lincon's voice reached me. My eyes slowly peeled open. I gasped shallowly. "Oh, darling, you're alive. I knew you'd be fun to follow, look at this epic battle. Although, you shattered your wings a bit." I willed to stand but couldn't move. Everything swarmed me like a suction of reality. I gasped as the memories overflowed me painfully. I'd landed face-first into the ground. I lifted my head, barely able to. I looked into the distance where I knew Chase and Tythian had been dragged. I squinted at the two figures that stood behind Lincon. Kora and Kasey. They cautiously looked around at the others who now encircled them and planned to attack.

"No," I parched. Connor, Balzar, and Yolo were trying to break in. Connor tried to use his gift against them, but with no effect through their shield. "Allies," I whispered. They were the only words I could produce. Kora and Kasey gave me a side glance before they dropped their shield. Without saying anything further, Connor swept me in his arms and snatched me from Lincon protectively. The army of Chase's coven stood behind them, their numbers depleted. Only six members of the Elite remained.

"We have to go now! We have no chance against Oppollo," Connor ordered. He heaped my broken wings. I hadn't the strength to call them back into my skin. I felt as if I were slowly and painfully dying. I had no energy and lacked concentration. I was fading in and out of consciousness.

"Chase and Tythian," I gasped, weakly. "Your brother." My mouth was parched. I desperately thirsted for blood to replenish. *My familiar. I had to reach him.*

"In good time, Esmore," Balzar said, crouching to my level. "This had Fier's involvement, as well. We'll get them back, but for now we must run. Look at the numbers around you, we cannot sacrifice them."

"This is only one battle of many," Yolo added, trying to convince and change my will. The others looked behind them.

"I can sense Oppollo in the distance," Connor announced. "Everyone run! We stay in numbers!"

"We don't listen to you!" Clarissa sneered, as she stepped in front of her coven. "You're an enemy coven to us. But," she interjected before she was attacked by Yolo and Balzar. Her gaze locked with mine. She snapped a small vile from her necklace. "The little miss, we listen to. Under the declaration of our Leader, we are at your disposal," she announced. She opened the vile which sent a shivering sweetness to my nose. It was only a small amount of blood, but I would take anything I could get right now.

She poured the small amount onto my lips, the taste of it hardly moistened my mouth. With the tiny amount of strength I now had, I summoned my wings back in. I was unable to escape the darkness that I began to doze back into. My wings created a scraping noise, as their shattered bones slowly merge into my back once again.

"Esmore, you've used too much strength and lost too much blood," Yolo began to explain. "You're going to go into a state of weakness and coma-like status. We'll restore you with blood, but for now, we must..." I outstretched my hand toward him. I felt the blood within my body begin to freeze, the voices of everyone around me silenced. The touch of Connor's chest and arms that held me, vanished.

I dropped into a space of darkness. It was an empty place, where no thought or form of life was visible. The acceptance and empowerment of my vampire self have caused me to freeze in weakness and isolation.

I am a vampire, and it seems to have changed my form and created a weakness. My last glimmering image and prayer were of Chase. I wanted to see him again, and alive. I wanted my familiar.

ABOUT THE AUTHOR

Kia grew up in the Darling Downs Region in Queensland, Australia. Graduating High School, she pursued a career in freelance journalism. In 2014, having always had a passion for writing fiction, she decided to follow her dream of becoming an accomplished author.

Now living on the Gold Coast, Australia and travelling every spare minute she gets, Kia is constantly searching for new inspiration for her writing and filling her heart with adventure, one country at a time.

OTHER BOOKS BY KIA CARRINGTON-RUSSELL

Mad Hatter Vampire Prince:

A PREQUEL NOVELLA TO THE TOKEN HUNTRESS SERIES.
CAN ALSO BE READ AS A STANDALONE.

Kyran Klaus is the prince of Grand Klaus, his reputation honoring him the title of the Mad Hatter Vampire Prince. Crazy, deadly, lustful, and utterly bored with life.

Sasha Pierce is one of a kind. Having been experimented on by her mother as a child, she's become a human weapon who's looking for answers beyond the walls where her kind aren't enslaved to vampires.

When the Mad Hatter Prince takes a sudden interest in Sasha and her work, she scarcely begins to cover her tracks and hide her secrets. What she doesn't anticipate is being a pawn in his most sinister performance yet.

Disturbingly Wicked! This novella is not for the fainthearted. Lust, Gore, Wit, and Malicious Humor. Prepare to be deliciously tainted.

Token Huntress

Being born a hunter, Esmore has been raised with one purpose, to hunt and kill the vampire race that destroyed the world as it was known. At eighteen, Esmore's a Token Huntress in her Guild, surpassing her mentor's expectations of her, despite having no magical ability, like all hunters before her.

During a raid in the once iconic San Fransisco, Esmore's team is ambushed, and a mysterious vampire that she is drawn to captures and takes her to the Vampire Council as a prisoner. Her captor- Chase, a lethal, immortal, sexy, and charming vampire who will stop at nothing to claim her as his familiar.

While in captivity, Esmore learns information that makes her question everything she's been taught.

Now in the year 2341, Esmore fights for her survival. But who exactly is she fighting against? The very people who nurtured her, or the evil she's supposed to hate?

The Shadow Minds Journal:

In this world, there are creatures lurking in the shadows. As a child, I once played with them. As a teenager, I began to fear them and became victim to their attacks. As an adult, I now realize that no matter how much I try to escape the grasp of this world, I was inevitably born into it.

Now reborn as a Guardian in the year of 2986, Vivian Lair must uphold the treaty between Angels and Demons on the human world and city of Shabeah. Contracted to seven demons who she can shift into while taking direct orders from the Underworld Lord, Haymen, it wasn't exactly her ideal rebirth. Involving herself with the Angel of War, Gabe is even worse.

Still fighting those who try to possess her during her sleep, Vivian must now record and try to hunt the Volv through the Shadow Minds Journal. Now stuck between the hatred and lust of two of the most powerful entities in all worlds, Vivian is involved inevitably in the upcoming conflict.

Blood. Lust. War. She must kill before being killed.

My Escort Collection:

A collection of the Best Selling contemporary series that includes: My Escort, My Exception and My Expectation. Clover is personal assistant to Debra Coorman, the merciless boss of Candice fashion magazine. The bright lights of New York are dim for Clover, who is tormented by a work schedule like no other. Debra is relentless in her determination to demean Clover. For once, Clover dares to play Debra's games, and intends to prove her wrong at the next glittering event. With mixed emotions, Clover contacts a male escort, Damon. If his velvet voice over the phone is anything to go by, Clover knows her money will be well spent. But when Damon appears at her door, something unexpected happens. The taunts and the games begin. Who is truly going to win at this game?

Aroused: Taming Himself

"Remember my name because you will be begging me for more. This is my promise to you."

Meet Hayden Zilch: entrepreneur, sports manager, investor. Cocky, tantalizing, and an utter womanizer. He is a man who loves pleasuring women. He can show you a world you have only fantasied about.

So what happens when this sex-mad womanizer decides to finally find The One?

Starting off with a list of five women, Hayden sets out to learn the difference between lust and love. His adventures have him laughing, crying in pain, and begging on his knees as he battles to tame himself. Can Hayden really control himself around these five beautiful temptresses?

Taming Himself is the first in this five-book series which tells the story of Hayden's search for both love and pleasure.

Phantom Wolf

A book that is so dynamic and can pull my emotions free so easily is a 5 star novel.
★★★★★ *- Paranormal Trance Reviews*

Sia is a Phantom Wolf. Neither dead nor alive--and rotting from the inside--she is on the edge of her curse. Once a Phantom Wolf has been created, they hunt their blood pack and slaughter all their loved ones. Except for Sia, who woke years after her death to find herself rampaging through the land on a lonely path.

She continues to run from the rival pack that hunts her because she is a Phantom Wolf. Attracted to a scent, Sia finds her old best friend, who is now a grown woman. Having once saved Keeley, Sia takes the role of protector yet again, despite Keeley's involvement with the mysterious Alpha, Kiba, and his kin brother, Saith. An ambush separates the pack and the four of them blindly fight the new warriors that attack them: desperately needing to find out where the attacks are coming from, as Sia has vowed to protect Keeley. But at what cost?

Now being chased, Sia finds herself conflicted by the mortal and spirit world while trying to protect her kin. Sia must confront her fears, as well as the human lover who killed her many years before. It is not only survival Sia contends with, but her own façade that must be broken so that she may find peace within herself once more.

The Three Immortal Blades

Contains the entire Award Winning Collection. Karla Gray is an ordinary young woman that is taken from her mundane life into a world of blood lust as she begins to struggle with a unique ability. Karla is a Shielder; an exceptional fighter born with the rare ability to project a Shield for protection. However, Shielders are not the only kind that possesses such a talent. The Shielders battle a war that has been raging for centuries against Starkorfs, who harvest humans and Shielders alike to obtain a near immortality. Alongside the charming Lucas and selfless Paul, Karla must unravel the purpose of her curse and battle an unknown presence manipulating her thoughts; a mysterious woman who may be dormant for now, but has every intention of possessing Karla- mind, body, and soul. Within this new reality that Karla faces the search for the Three Immortal Blades begins.